The MetSche Message

by

Stephen A. Theberge

Best Wishes

stek

DLD Books

ISBN: 1523867477
ISBN-13: 978-1523867479

CHAPTER 1

The Emails from the Asylum Folk

To: Dr. D'Erable
From: Dr. Aguair
Date: 07–20–20xx, 3:59 p.m.
Subject: Dear Dr. D'Erable...I need your assistance.

Good morning, Doctor. I have been most anxious to discuss one of my patients with you. I took the liberty of mailing you a rather thick manila envelope with all the details. I must confess I was in a bit of a hurry, so I may or may not have included all the relevant identifying materials. But now you'll at least know that it was I who sent it.

I will only whet your appetite here. Although I was one of your best students, and even after five years of running my own clinic, I must confess that this patient has frankly stumped me and my staff for a diagnosis, and we could use your help. Let me know when you have received my package, and especially what you think after you have read its contents.
Sincerely,
Dr. Marilyn Aguair

To: Dr. Aguair
From: Dr. D'Erable
Date: 07–20–20xx, 6:01 p.m.
Subject: RE: Dear Dr. D'Erable...I need your assistance.

You have certainly piqued my curiosity. You are indeed one of the best students I ever had, so it troubles me that you are stumped regarding a diagnosis. At your young age, retirement is not an option. I will certainly be disappointed unless I *can* diagnose this patient, as I am not one to think that you'd be one to indulge in practical jokes. You must certainly remember that I was always very serious about my work.

I have enjoyed our brief contacts, notes, holiday cards, and so forth. I sincerely hope we will have more opportunities to talk soon.

Sincerely,

Dr. Stephen D'Erable

To: Dr. Aguair
From: Dr. D'Erable
Date: 07–25–20xx, 1:51 a.m.
Subject: RE: Dear Dr. D'Erable…I need your assistance.

Dear Marilyn,

I should certainly like to have your consent to meet with your patient, John Kline. I am of course as stumped as you are, but feel there must be some explanation for his assertions— beyond his love of science fiction, that is. Oh, by the way, you forgot to supply the "evidence" that John was speaking of. Please send it to me as soon as possible.

Sincerely,

Stephen

To: Dr. D'Erable
From: Dr. Aguair
Date: 07–25–20xx, 9:19 p.m.
Subject: RE: Dear Dr. D'Erable…I need your assistance.

Steve, I know that you are aware that I am not a good biochemist. In my opinion, Kline is obsessed with having this sample analyzed in a serious fashion. He wants genetic testing done on it.

I have arranged for you to meet with John any time during the first week of August. Thank you for phoning me yesterday. It was so good to talk to you in person for a change. I will be on vacation in Charlesbourg that week, but be assured that my staff will be fully cooperative with you, and they are expecting your visit.

Your suggestion to meet John alone was a fine one, as my presence would only skew your assessment of him. He is actually looking forward to a visitor. I am sure he suspects another professional is in the cards, but he never asked me, so I felt no need to tell him. He is highly intelligent and can read between the lines.

Later,
Marilyn

To: Dr. Aguair
From: Dr. D'Erable
Date: 07–26–20xx, 7:39 a.m.
Subject: RE: Dear Dr. D'Erable…I need your assistance.
Attachment: address.doc

Okay, Marilyn. I'll definitely meet with the patient the first week of August. Enjoy your week in Canada. The attached file is the address of a good friend of mine in France who can handle John's tests. Since my friend offered to do it for free, I couldn't pass up his offer. I think my friend was very curious as to why I wanted the tests done. I informed him that I was doing a favor for someone, and that neither of us was sure what to expect or look for. He certainly isn't too busy, but his eagerness and abilities were reassuring. I'll be in touch with you after your vacation.

Stephen

To: Dr. D'Erable
From: Dr. Aguair
Date: 07–26–20xx, 8:23 p.m.

Stephen, thanks for your kind wishes about visiting Québec and the surrounding area. I'll send the sample to France first thing in the morning. If we're lucky, we may be able to solve this mystery by my return. Take care.

Marilyn

Chapter 2

Chartreuse Hazes

i

It was so nice to visit my aunt and uncle this week in Canada. I also stopped in parts of Maine to visit some of my other aunts and uncles. Getting away from the big cities and seeing how the forests can darken the day and color the sky a deep green was such a refreshing feeling to have again.

It was also good to brush up on my French, especially in the suburbs of Québec, where my relatives live. Québec is not like any city I know stateside. True, they are bilingual and very polite in speaking English with me, sensing that my French doesn't brand me *une vraie canadienne.* At least my relatives were polite enough to discourse with me in the native tongue, although I suspect they'd also prefer to do it in English, a sad thing for me.

Even my relatives, raised in Québec, have all taken up English. This isn't the Canada I knew when I was young. English, although spoken, was much harder to find back then. I struck a deal with my relatives. They could speak to me in English, but I would speak to them in French. This way, we could compliment each other on how well we each spoke the other's language.

It is a luxury to have nothing to do. I confess that the Kline case has not quite faded from my consciousness. I always liked sci-fi to a degree, and have brought what John considers to be sci-fi classics along with me to read, in an attempt to understand more clearly his perceptions of aliens.

Well, Stephen, I will say 'bye for now.

ii

I am most impressed with the clinic. The grounds are very well kept. I feel sorry that you don't appreciate verdant New England. I haven't visited very often. I didn't think things could look any greener from John's room.

The trees pretty much blocked out the afternoon sun. He stated that the plants of this planet were a key to all he had to say. Before I could think or answer him, he stated that, although it was quite amazing that such diversities could evolve, they provide our oxygen—nothing compared to the plants on Metamo.

I asked him about the spindly plant that grew about two feet tall on his desk and what importance it had besides decoration.

He said, "My friend Stephen gave me some yellow-eyed bean seeds. He's liked them since he was a child. He knows that I grew up on a farm and like growing things. Stephen would have liked to do some gardening this summer, but as usual, things came up. He wants to come back in about a month, when they should have the pods on them. That will be kind of sad, as the bean is an annual, and it will be dead soon afterwards. I grow the plant not only for Stephen, but also in honor of Metamo. It is a very fundamental part of their culture and evolutionary process."

I did more listening than talking, which I'm sure John appreciated. At times, he seemed impatient about the things I didn't know, as though they should have been obvious to me. At least he did take the time to explain and to answer my questions. I wonder if being in your care for five weeks must have frustrated his imagination. I suppose he can come up with all kinds of coping mechanisms.

We both went outside late that night for a couple of cigarettes. I figured that being natural in such a restrained environment was the best thing. He pointed out all kinds of smells, insect noises, bird calls, and the like. I must confess that I felt an appreciation for nature that I hadn't in quite some time.

I engaged him in some discussion. I began, "So, John, how long have you been thinking of the aliens?"

He answered, "I was made aware of them on an alumni weekend a few years ago. The Schegnans were really the spokesmen for the Metans. They would make first contacts through human minds, and then, if one was receptive to the idea, he would meet a Metan.

"I met mine on a hot summer night two years ago. Oh, by the way, Doctor, the Schegnans have made it impossible for you to catch me in a trap. No matter how many different ways you rephrase a question to me, you will find it impossible to find fault with my story."

John was quite alert and aware at all times. I wonder if finding inconsistencies in his story would be of any use. I mean, I'm told that even a few good writers make errors. I couldn't resist calling to France to see how the progress on his sample was doing.

John was very consistent in not telling me anything about it. He would often say, "Oh, you'll find out in good time, and then you might even believe me. Besides, what are you so worried about?"

iii

I am grateful that this summer in Paris has been very rainy, or I would probably never have gotten around to your sample. I must say it was a pleasure doing this work for you. I regret that there is not much sample left to send back to you, as most of it deteriorated within a few hours after exposure to air.

You were not correct about the wax. The material that sealed the test tube was a very hard commercial plastic. I doubt that it was done by hand. The sample had a lot of spirals, with colors from plant shades to flesh tones, the beiges of many seashells, whites, blacks, violets, greens, blues, and numerous other colors.

Fortunately, I made a lot of computer records of the images from my scanning electron microscope and other instruments. As I said, the sample deteriorated long before I could finish studying it in real time. I took pieces from as many places as possible, slicing it up and examining them. By the time I got to the core of the material, most of it had evaporated. I have the core, which is about the size of a grain of sand, in a nitrogen freeze, and will await your instructions on it. What a shame! The sample was about the size of a large bean when I started. Luckily, I can study the photos and other data I recorded. I would have found out a lot more if it hadn't broken down.

When the sample dissolved, it turned into nothing. It smelled a bit like ammonia, gave off a light blue steam, and left no traces. I am hoping you can provide me with more samples, and do tell me where this came from. It certainly must have been a brilliant scientist who contrived this mass of flesh and plant, or a cross between the two.

I have never seen or heard of anything with so many chromosomes. I identified at least 709 of them. Again, please tell me what source this comes from. I can't find any colleague who could identify any plant or animal that it might be. My suspicions are that it was made by some brilliant genetic engineer. If so, he or she could certainly be famous. I don't think there has ever been anything approaching this type of sophistication.

iv

John and I had a nice breakfast in his room at my insistence. I want to thank and commend your staff for their gracious cooperation and accommodations. I had a good night's sleep and was very refreshed for talking with John before I went back to the West Coast this afternoon.

As you noted, his general knowledge is impressive. His knowledge of geography and other countries is commendable. I see you omitted the fact that he has a BA in psychology. This fact is very interesting as well. We talked quite a lot about this subject.

His understanding of general science and current events is also notable. He is very interested in the less fortunate people of the world and feels frustrated that he can't do something to help. He is, over all, a very stubborn person, but no more than you were when you were my student.

This innate inflexibility of John's is no defense mechanism or attempt to repress any unpleasant events in his life. He felt free to discuss the good and bad experiences he had in foster care when he was a child. If nothing else, his unchanging convictions are presented to show others that he is correct. He can be impatient when others don't see it his way, but can easily admit when he is mistaken, or that he is not all–knowing.

I instructed our Parisian colleague to copy and send back any and all data on the sample. I asked him to hold the remainder of the sample for the time being, until we meet in Boston for the convention next month. That sample is an enigma.

John insists that the information he possesses be shared with the people of the entire Earth, and that it would be a crime for any of us to hold these facts back. I think we have some interesting decisions to make. I commend you for not having given him any medications, for I suspect they would have only clouded his reasoning skills. I wonder what course to take. Have you any ideas? Are you going to release John on the 15th?

V

I see no reason why he should be held any longer. I must say I am professionally embarrassed not to have realized that John's ideas could be viewed as a religious belief system. His famed sample could be one of the mysteries of his religion. If you find that I shouldn't release him, please let me know. That is the schedule as far as my staff and I are concerned.

Chapter 3

Intake Report at Boston Convention,

Given 8–11–20XX

i

The patient was brought into our LA hospital ward after being found in a despondent state on a public street. She was quickly given the usual toxicity screens, and we found no evidence of any drugs whatsoever. Although she appeared asleep, her EEG was indicative of a coma state, while her vital signs were quite normal for an alert person. Her body also behaved as though she were asleep. This was odd, as she was standing, eyes wide open, at a crosswalk.

After about three hours in the hospital, she was "normal" again. She had no memory of events after she left a restaurant. Her behavior was indicative of severe panic attacks, most probably being brought on by her discovery of becoming conscious in the hospital. The ambulance drivers said she possessed no ID or even a purse. She looked like a professionally dressed lady, and we at the hospital didn't think it was likely that she was homeless. She was in fact quite well-groomed and clean.

We asked her the usual questions, but she was not very cooperative. She would only tell us that she had a very important message to deliver. We pressed her hard for details, but she was quite insistent that we were not the ones to whom she could entrust such an important "shennan" message.

You have all read the notes on the details of this patient. We will now open the floor for comments or questions on this case.

ii

After the man left the podium, Doctors D'Erable and Aguair looked at each other in amazement. Their expressions were indicative of a shared understanding.

Dr. D'Erable whispered to Dr. Aguair, "My word, Kline's religion seems to be catching on. What do you say we go for a drink?"

They left the convention early, as all the notes they needed had been handed out earlier. It wasn't arrogance that propelled them out of the hall, but the realization that they were the only two there who had a specific understanding of what had happened, and they were both used to (and bored with) the predictable observations of interns.

Neither doctor was in the mood to share his or her notes or experiences about John with the convention. They had never intended to. Both doctors had expected that attending the meeting would be an exercise in futility.

The course of action they both decided on was to personally contact the doctor in charge of this case and compare files. They were not too familiar with this man, but could only hope he saw the same thing that they did.

Disappointment came quickly. The doctor did meet with both of them, but he was not impressed with their notes on their patient, John Kline, nor could he grasp the importance of what D'Erable and Aguair possessed.

Before they left, Dr. D'Erable asked the patient, "So, who is your message for?"

The patient replied, "It is for one who can receive my Schegnan message."

Unfortunately, the other doctor had had enough and politely dismissed Aguair and D'Erable from the office. Dr. D'Erable was even beginning to doubt the whole thing himself. He was reassured by Aguair that whether this incident was a religious one, an alien one, or a lunatic's, Kline would certainly be expecting a message. They parted company, but needless to say, they both spent sleepless nights until the 15th. They would both meet John on that day, bid him farewell, and wish him luck.

Dr. D'Erable had assumed that Kline would be released on the 15th of August, but he received another thick yellow envelope the day before the patient was to be sent home. Stephen was a bit annoyed by Marilyn's "games" at this point, but then he realized that the envelope had no return address and foreign stamps on it.

Well, thought D'Erable, I suppose I'll take a look at this stuff and see what it's all about.

He opened the package to find a pile of unbound papers. It seemed to the doctor that the person who had sent this material could have been courteous enough to put it into a notebook, as the papers had the usual three holes down their left margins. The writing was in pencil, and it was printed rather than being in longhand.

Once he began to read the papers, the doctor was fascinated and read them all non–stop. Who was this Andre? Who had written about him? And what was more important, why had this unknown individual sent these papers to him?

Chapter 4

"Andre's Story, Part 1—His Evolution"

i

Andre's first memories of life, although he could not name them, would never have been believed. They began in a hospital, when he was two years old. He had many sensations and sights which were overwhelming to him, as he didn't have any words to put to them.

Out of the darkness came a piercing light from his right. He would later learn that others in his environment could control objects physically. At this particular point, he could not conceive that someone had made the light appear. Nor could he explain where he was.

In this darkness, there was a lot of space. He was lying on his back. It was as though the crying of the baby was what had brought consciousness to him. It was the first sound he had ever heard. He could not see much in the dark, but he knew that other forces were around him. This was especially true when the light appeared. The strangest thing was that the light made the crying sound to his right stop. He didn't know it was crying, nor even that it was another individual similar to him. These things would be taught to him later.

ii

Andre had no clear memories of the next few years, but surely he had been taught about his older brother, his sister, and his parents. He must have learned such things as their names, and indeed his own since the age of two. He was aware that he was five years old, but he certainly couldn't quite grasp exactly what a year was, except that it had something to do with a cake with candles on it. This cake, presents, and a party were very concrete to him. Andre loved candy, cocoa, and bright colors.

He had loved the bright colors of the Christmas tree his mother had put up. Mom had gone across the street for milk and had made a point of telling Andre not to go behind the tree. When she left, he wondered what could be so spectacular and bright in the back of the tree that he shouldn't see. Inevitably, he went behind the evergreen, knocking it over. Although his mother was upset, this incident did not gain Andre the punishment of his father's belt–strap.

He had once been so happy when his brother and sister had gotten the belt that he couldn't resist feeling proud of himself, and he giggled with joy. When his father discovered this after asking Andre what was so funny, Andre's pride was erased by the same punishment.

There were happy times as well. He had been fascinated by his dad's reel–to–reel tape recorder. His father was making a kind of family album and giving everyone a chance to speak. Andre was fascinated by the turning of the wheels and asked, "Can I talk to the record player?"

He recalled the fun of going to the amusement park with his siblings, and the family going to the peanut store. He loved the fudge and playing on the old Ferris wheel. It was confusing to Andre. There were so many good things, but he also recalled nightmares. He knew shortly after he awoke that they weren't real, and he wished that the pleasanter dreams were; furthermore, he wished that he hadn't awakened after pleasant reveries.

What were worse than the nightmares were the inconsistencies in the real world. Andre didn't understand how his father could be so nice, taking the family out and giving them treats, and then at other times using the belt on them. It was understood that this was a punishment for doing something wrong, but somehow it wasn't clear. Once, while Andre was lying on the couch, his brother jokingly poured pepper in Andre's left eye. Now Andre began to associate all pain with punishment, even though there was no direct connection between them.

It had been terrifying to awaken in the middle of the night after a strange nightmare. In it, he had turned on the faucets of the sink in the upstairs bathroom. Brushes appeared, making an eerie sound, kind of like dice rolling in a cup, twice in rapid succession, but more scratchy. He was relieved that the fear would subside after he had been awake for a while or had gone back to sleep and had a dream of cakes and candies and brightly colored, beautiful lights.

The idea of pain and discomfort worked its way into Andre's waking world. He didn't understand why, when he was at the barber shop one day, the man fastened the collar of the drape to keep the hair off his neck too tightly. Andre was confused; previously, he had associated the barber shop with the pleasure of getting gum balls from the machine. Later, Andre's mother was upset at the type of haircut his father had ordered for him. Andre liked his hair being short and feeling like a brush, but his mother didn't approve.

Yet, in all the discomfort, that summer brought the familiarity of Andre going to Canada to visit *grande moma, grand papa,* and his *oncles* and *tantes.* It was a joy to drive through the fields and woods and see cows and farms. He fondly recalled riding on the Saint Lawrence ferry. It was fascinating to watch things move slowly by as the car was brought across the water. It was as though things were moving to him, rather than Andre moving toward the destinations.

His understanding of his relatives' French was second nature to him. He loved the "pudding" his grandmother used to make. This dessert would be known to him later as "upside-down cake," but his *grande moma's* cake was much lighter and sweeter than the "upside-down" cakes he'd have later. He loved how she would make it with blueberries, strawberries, raspberries, and best of all, maple syrup. His mother and grandmother were concerned about his fussiness in eating, but they never denied him the *bons desserts*. He also liked breakfast with the home-made strawberry preserves on toast.

His Canadian relatives were always kind to him, although there were times when they were strict, especially when he and his brother and sister snapped the spring doorstops. They were fascinated by the sound it made when they played with the doorstops, and they actually found it amusing to hear their grandmother reprimanding them in French.

One day his aunt was preparing lunch. Andre couldn't resist the aroma of the pudding in the oven. His aunt answered the phone and was gone for a short time. The butter in the saucepan on top of the stove became a dark brown and began to smell funny. His aunt returned and asked Andre why he hadn't informed her that the butter was burning. Andre felt embarrassed and knew that his answer would not have been satisfactory. He thought, I thought that was the way butter cooked in Canada, but he could sense by his aunt's and mother's tone that they would not be interested in his explanation.

As that summer neared its end, Andre sensed good changes. Moving to a new house was an adventure. Having jelly sandwiches for supper the first night in the house was a treat. Andre also experienced heavy rainstorms and thunder, which were a great fascination for him. He loved the myriad colors of the lightning. Soon, however, rain would be another source of confusion. Andre didn't understand yet that the weather he liked wasn't connected to either good or bad events.

On this day when Andre was five, there were no bright colors to be found. There was a sense of emptiness all around him. The quietness of Mom and Dad, as well as his siblings, only added to the sense of something dreadful. The worst thing was that it couldn't be explained in terms of sweet tastes and beautiful butterflies with bright colors, or by the nice sounds of thunder and the beautiful effects of lightning.

The rain was very heavy as he walked with his parents into a huge brick building. They entered a large room with many sets of tables and chairs. It also seemed very dark. Wasn't nighttime for bed? Andre now realized what was going to happen and why he had felt so empty; he was expected to go into this large room alone, without his mother or father. Would he ever see them again?

At this point, he began to cry uncontrollably. Andre couldn't recall so many tears ever having run out of his eyes before. Maybe it was possible to stop them if he grabbed his mother's coat and buried his face in it. He must not lose her or let her leave. His mother exclaimed to his father in a slightly anxious voice, but saying the words in French, "It's time for supper."

Now his mother gently removed Andre's hands from her coat, and some lady gently took him by the arm and led him into the large, well-lit room as his parents departed. To Andre, the room appeared brighter on the inside than it had when he had viewed it from the outside. He was led to one of the tables and an empty chair. There were a lot more chairs and people ahead of him, and Andre at least felt safe that he was close to the place where he had entered; surely his mom and or dad would come and get him!

He didn't know what to expect next. Suddenly, he heard a

bell, a kind of *ding*, followed by all the voices speaking in unison. It sounded strange, as if they were all one person, but also like a whirring of wind. The voices seemed to be saying, "God is great, God is good. Let us thank him for our food. By His hands must dolls be fed. Give is this day our daily bread. Amen."

After the words, all the people, in synchronicity, pulled out their wooden chairs on the concrete floor. This din was not like any music Andre had ever heard. All of the others sat down together, and Andre instinctively knew to do the same.

Before him was a bowl of food. He knew it wasn't a nice dessert, nor was he hungry. Besides, this food wasn't given to him by Mom or Dad. He sensed that all the people around him were eating, and possibly enjoying this stuff. It didn't smell spoiled, but Andre's senses told him to reject eating this food. One small taste wasn't even a consideration.

The gamey meat smell must have hypnotized Andre, for he couldn't recall any other part of the meal. He next found himself in an upstairs room. There were two other boys in this chamber with him. One of them was listening to a radio; another was playing with some toy. They were both sitting on their beds, but Andre somehow preferred the floor. Perhaps he knew this wasn't where he was to sleep. Besides, neither of these boys was his brother.

After some time in the room, the boys tried to talk to Andre. He had never talked very much anyway, and new people, especially those not introduced to him by his mother or father, were none of his concern. The boy in the room who Andre had learned was Ralph began to laugh when a voice on the radio said, "The knuckleheads are out tonight." Andre found himself laughing along with Ralph. Andre didn't know why this was funny, but a strange new feeling came to him. Maybe this boy felt as lost as he did, and they could laugh together to share something.

Sometime later that night, Andre was in "his own room,"

except that the boy there named Stevie couldn't talk. He wasn't Andre's brother, either. There was a bed on Andre's left and a window in front of both of them. Luckily, Andre had a window to the right of his bed, so he could sit up and look out into the courtyard and see that it wasn't raining. He was tired and pretended that Stevie was not there at all. This was quite easy to do. Andre had never thought that there could be anyone quieter than himself.

iii

After a deep sleep, Andre awoke on his own to a chilly morning. The sky was a lovely deep blue, and now he could see all the beauty of the dark red bricks on the outsides of the other buildings. The sunshine helped him see all the lovely trees and grass around the grounds, as well. This helped him feel less alone and abandoned. Ralph certainly must have been a help in giving Andre a good night's sleep.

Among all these myriad scenes and warm feelings, there came something that made Andre realize that he might not be lost after all. He smelled such a lovely sweetness in the air. It was not familiar to him, but Andre knew that certain smells were associated with lovely things. The scent told him that at last he would be eating something sweet. After having eaten no supper, he was pleased that soon he would taste some lovely treat. Wherever he was, or for whatever reason, this new home was going to be fun indeed.

Now, once again, he was in the large room that the others had called the "dining room." He was led to his seat of the night before and told, "This is your seat, Andre. Always remember to sit at this table in this chair." Before he could sit down, the ding went off and all the others recited the words of the night before. Andre realized that he might do well to learn all those words.

Upon sitting down, he found a feast. He had his favorite cereal to eat, a boiled egg, and finally the lovely dessert, which he liked the most of any meal. The others called this dessert a "cinnamon roll." It smelled nice. Andre was fascinated by its spiral structure, but he couldn't resist taking a bite from it. The taste was luscious beyond anything in his experience. When he proceeded to take another bite, he couldn't help seeing that this dessert looked so different and fascinating compared to any he had experienced before. He couldn't resist unrolling the entire bun to its full length and placing it on his plate. Now that the spiral was gone, and he could see that inside was the stuff that made the bun sweet, he gobbled it up in sheer delight. He was curious whether it would have tasted even better if he hadn't taken it apart. I don't believe, he thought, that they can have any food for me that tastes better than this.

iv

The next few days passed in a blur. Andre wasn't sure what a Sunday or Monday really meant, but he knew that his parents would come to pick him up on Friday. Having breakfast was the highlight of his day. Why, even at some lunches and dinners, there had been tasty sweets.

The only problem was that there was a bad lady who insisted that Andre eat things he didn't like. She would threaten to withhold his dessert if he didn't finish the things he didn't want to eat. She should have been told how stubborn he was. He would sit for hours, chewing but not swallowing what had been put into his mouth. He'd sacrifice a dessert rather than be forced to eat something he found repulsive, especially tough meats.

The only routines he had taken from home were waking up, going to sleep, and of course meals. It would take him a few weeks to learn that swimming, arts and crafts, science, and all his other classes were on a schedule. The end of the week would be marked by a loud wailing at noontime on Fridays. The plaintive, high-pitched sound slowly rose to a screech, held for a second, then slowly went back down and was silent. Andre's teacher informed the class that the siren was tested on Fridays. In his later years, Andre would learn that the siren was at the arsenal, that the tests were the remnants of the days of World War II, and that the habit of testing hadn't faded even after so many years.

V

A month or so of routine had finally set itself upon Andre's mind. Now he could predict and anticipate his favorite classes ahead of time. He liked science the most and was very happy to assist in the many experiments which were performed. He'd had no idea that the world worked this way. It was mysterious, but Andre knew that if he was attentive, he'd learn all there was to know.

Mondays meant swimming class. He didn't like the way one of the teachers had thrown him roughly into the water to watch him surface. Andre thought the bad instructor must realize that she was scaring him. On one occasion, he had grabbed onto her, digging his nails into her skin. He hadn't meant to hurt her; he had only clung to her out of fear of being taken out into the deep water.

The periods before and after swimming class made his learning to get around in the water more tolerable. The nice swimming teacher brought the group to the pool and back through "the tunnel." For Andre, it was a pleasure to smell iron pipes, hear the steam, notice some puddles on the floor from the leaks, and make an adventure of getting to class. The darkness, pierced by dim light bulbs, was scary to some, but Andre enjoyed this nice teacher. She insisted on silence and made a game of it, and those who obeyed were given a sweet treat. She would say, "Chinese school has just begun. No more laughing. No more fun. If you show your teeth or tongue, you will pay a forfeit." Andre didn't really know what a "forfeit" was. He didn't know about "Chinese school," either, except that China was a place far away, maybe even farther away than Canada. He recalled hearing about "indoor China" and figured they must all get around in tunnels similar to those he'd been in. In any case, he knew that being quiet and not opening your mouth would guarantee a reward.

Soon the tunnel trips became part of the routine, and Andre found the wonder of it wearing off. He did appreciate the trips when they kept him out of the rain, snow, or cold. By now, he had fallen into his expected place by obeying the rules, but it seemed that outside forces always interrupted his plans to be a good boy.

This particular Monday would be a very eventful day for him. Swimming wasn't Andre's favorite class, but when he got through it, science class would be there to greet him. Wearing his trunks, he had been prepared to go to the pool. He had stopped in the bathroom and was moderately interested in the events that were to follow.

As he entered the stall, his foot slipped behind him on the wet floor. He couldn't catch his balance, and he went down swiftly. His chin hit very hard against the toilet seat, and he bit his tongue from the impact. He felt a searing pain; it was unlike anything he had ever experienced before. He knew he was bleeding, but he proceeded at a normal rate to tell his instructor, who was downstairs at the swimming pool, that he was hurt. His mind seemed to be in an odd, semi–awake state. Although the pain was severe, and the bleeding was profuse, he felt calm. A force that he could best describe as daydreaming came over him.

When the nice swimming teacher saw him, she exclaimed, "Oh, God! Andre, what happened?"

Due to his injured tongue, Andre answered in a lisp, "I banged my chin on the toilet and bit my tongue."

The teacher re–uttered the "Oh, God!" a half–dozen times or so, and the next thing Andre perceived was being walked to the school infirmary. He felt as though he was dreaming, but he did sense the cool drizzle on his head. A long wait to get to the infirmary didn't strike Andre as odd. It involved the tunnels, a cab ride, and then a large dark building.

So, thought Andre, this is what hospitals are for. He was vaguely familiar with the concept of such places. However, he didn't really grasp what was going to happen to him, even after hearing others exclaiming that his tongue was bitten and that a part of it was hanging out and would have to be sewn back.

He was placed on a gurney and secured with what he thought he heard a doctor say were "ghost sheets." He was sweating profusely, and the pain was quite severe again. He sensed that he had been given a shot in the tongue, and he couldn't understand why they were trying to hurt him even more. With all his strength, he tried to escape, but that only made him sweat and feel weaker.

Next, he saw orange thread that looked quite thick. The doctors were doing something with it inside his mouth. The pain was intense, radiating all over his body. As weak as Andre was, he felt as though he would vomit, and so kept up the struggle. He could only hope that the bands holding him would break, or that these bad people would realize that they were hurting him and stop at once.

None of these things happened. Andre spent a sleepless night in bed. The pain was bad, but different than before. His cheek on the side that he was lying on filled with blood, which overflowed onto his pillow. When he switched sides, the throbbing continued. He went back and forth in this fashion all night.

The next morning, Andre continued to wonder from whom this great punishment had come. He vomited some blood after swallowing it all night. He felt weak, and he couldn't see what kind of naughty thing he'd done to warrant such treatment.

vi

All in all, things went well in the next few weeks. In some ways, not being able to eat solid food without pain was a blessing, because Andre wasn't coaxed to eat the foods he didn't like. The problem was he didn't get much dessert, either.

He was used to the routine, now. His parents picked him up on Fridays and brought him back to school on Sundays. While injured, he missed the routine of stopping at a restaurant on Sunday afternoons after church. His father would joke, "Now the camel is filling up for the week."

It was Halloween. Andre must have been kept home for a week or so due to his bitten tongue. He recalled his brother and sister trying to make him say "Trick or treat," but he wasn't doing so well. His parents decided that he should stay home. Oh, well, at least he could look at his jack-o'-lantern. That wasn't long lived, as he was drooling a lot, and somehow the candle was put out by the spittle. Ah, so the punishment from the unknown source continued.

Time brought things back to normal. His mother's impatience with Andre was baffling to him. Why had she given him chocolate milk when she knew that he would dribble it all over the table? This caused her to snap at him, as if he had injured himself on purpose.

In a week or so, Andre was back in school, being brought there and then picked up on schedule. His eating habits were back to normal, and he was no longer dribbling. Someone commented upon his return, as if he couldn't hear them, "How can someone bite their tongue?" Andre felt hurt. He didn't understand why people said hurtful things, and he could almost wish his fate on that girl. But he didn't really want to hurt anyone.

This particular Monday morning, Andre awoke and noticed an itchy bubble on his stomach. He had been looking forward to science class, as the class had been taping many batteries together, and today they were going to light up a bulb. Mary, his favorite housemother, noticed the bump and exclaimed, "Oh, dear. You have chickenpox. You'll have to stay in bed and miss classes for a while."

Andre's first instinct was to protest. He was also afraid and said, "Will I turn into a chicken?"

Doing a good job holding back her laughter, Mary gave a slight chuckle and said, "Oh, no. You're sick and have to go to bed."

Andre said, "I promise I'll go to bed after lunch when science class is done. Please let me go, and I'll come back then."

Mary answered, "You won't even care about that by this afternoon. You're sick and have to go to bed."

Andre naturally obeyed his mentor. She was right. Well

before afternoon came, he was running a fever and felt weak. By afternoon, science class was the furthest thing from his mind. He didn't recall much of the next week except sleeping, having diarrhea in bed a few times, and Mary being attentive to his every need. The itchy bubbles had multiplied rapidly and had migrated to almost every point on his body. Soon Andre didn't even worry about why this sickness had such an odd name. He got better and went back to the routine.

He was informed that the light bulb experiment had gone well, but that the light was very dim. In all this, Andre had noticed the leaves' brilliant colors and had fun running through piles of them with the other kids. He had found the glory of discovering what a horse chestnut was. He loved the frosty mornings.

They learned about seeds in science class. One bright, clear morning after breakfast, Andre pocketed a raisin from a bun he had enjoyed eating. He dropped the raisin down the grating, which he knew had dirt in it, and he enjoyed seeing the light come in through the window. How wonderful, Andre thought, that there will be a raisin bun tree coming up in the spring.

He was fascinated by the dewdrops, which reflected the sunlight in a rainbow–like fashion on the cold mornings. The sky, the smell of the leaves—all the wonders of nature were so glorious and new to him. It seemed to be his secret, as nobody else mentioned how amazing these scenes were.

Andre very much enjoyed his routine, now. He looked forward to playtime with Ralph and David, his best friends. He marveled at the sunrises and sunsets and was fascinated by weather changes. However, he couldn't understand why his pleasures were so often thwarted by others, especially bad houseparents.

The wicked old lady who tried to make Andre eat the food he hated so much was reported to be sick, and everyone was gathered in the playroom to write her get-well cards. Andre's first instinct was to write something like, "I hope you die. I hope you never come back again." He knew he'd be punished, though, if he followed that instinct. His parents would be disappointed. They had been shocked enough when a friend of his, Joey, had come to his room and had introduced him to the lovely colors that resulted from peeing in the light sockets. They had done this for a couple of weeks before being found out. His parents and Andre's favorite housemother were very disappointed indeed.

Mary, Andre's favorite housemother, never made him eat what he didn't like. She was very caring and nice to him. She was almost as good as his real mother, perhaps even better. Mary was very concerned that Andre had followed Joey's bad example with the light sockets. She worried about his slipping and falling in the urine, and she wondered for two weeks why her lights had gone out. Andre hadn't realized that he had such power, but he wanted to keep in Mary's good graces and vowed to be as good a boy as he could.

Except he found it impossible to be the best boy that he could. There was a very popular television program that the older boys and girls watched. Andre was aware of TV as being something not quite real, but it evoked a sense of imagination and wonder. He was allowed to view programs which were educational, or, for his entertainment, shows which were age-appropriate.

The older kids' show stuck in his mind. There was talk of a vampire, whatever that was. This monster bit the necks of people. What a fun thing to do! It would be an adventure, but even Andre knew there was something about it that could get him punished.

Late one night, he could not resist the urge to play vampire. He could hear Ralph snoring loudly two rooms over. Ah, thought Andre, now I can have a little bit of fun. He slowly worked his way to Ralph's room. All this time, he knew that he'd be in trouble if anyone woke up, or if a houseparent discovered his nocturnal wanderings.

Finally, he was at Ralph's bedside, where he bent over Ralph and quite roughly bit the other boy's neck. He was aware that Ralph was stirring and knew that he was probably waking up. Andre quickly and quietly ran back to his own bed.

These episodes went on for a few weeks. It was entertaining for Andre to hear others talk about the character from the television show being on campus. Yet Andre had a few close calls. He had almost gotten caught by the staff one or two times, and besides, the novelty of being a creature of the night was wearing off.

There was a short period during which he awakened in the night, yelling from nightmares. All the people thought it was his roommate, Stevie. Andre had felt punished enough, both justly and otherwise. He didn't want to hurt Stevie, but he assumed that since he couldn't hear, Stevie would be none the wiser if Andre said, "Yes, he woke me up last night, too." All the time, Andre felt vindicated and safe from the unseen punishers.

vii

Now Thanksgiving had passed. Andre had met a friend, John, who was an older boy and sold such lovely goodies at the school store. All the boys were brought there on Mondays for a treat. His parents were wise enough to give Andre money to buy stuff, although it seemed that he always wanted to buy more.

John was a shrewd salesman, but to Andre, he was mainly a nice, older boy. John also had some interest in French. Andre's father said that he was like a radio station. "When we drop you off, you speak English. When we pick you up, it's back to the French station."

Andre taught John the French word for snow, *neige*, and other words relating to weather. They both loved snowstorms and thunderstorms, and they talked incessantly about the climate, science, aliens, and the like. Andre knew that John wasn't as qualified as a teacher, for he didn't know as much as the science instructor. Andre was sure, however, that John's imagination must make him better than any teacher he'd had up to that point. Alas, once a week was too little time to talk with John, so they arranged to meet in a clandestine fashion on the rare occasions when they could get away with it.

Yet, as much as Andre and John discussed nature, Andre couldn't help feeling that only he had a clandestine relationship with its wonders. He would be awestruck when he awoke on a frosty, clear morning. The shiny glaze on the grass was so new and fascinating, sparking his imagination. It was not surprising that he couldn't find the words to share his wonder with others.

When the week of the school Christmas party arrived, Andre developed a fever. Mondays were always exciting here. Lately, the Monday night Cub Scouts meetings had become more interesting, because the lights had been going brown almost every week in the middle of the meetings. A few times, they'd go completely out, and Andre would marvel at the bright emergency lights. He remembered one Monday in Scouts when the lights went out very slowly, growing browner and browner until there was no light left. Andre liked it most when they looked like diarrhea. He could think of radios going at slow speed, and even fancied that the water would trickle out of the pipes. He was a bit disappointed and surprised when he discovered that the water ran normally at such times and that the TVs and radios simply didn't work.

Andre felt quite weak this particular Monday. He knew that the Christmas party for the school was tonight, but that he wouldn't be attending, as he was confined to bed. However, rather than getting upset and thinking he was being punished, he felt very lucky. He'd get to see Santa on the roof, while all the others would be at the party awaiting his arrival. Oh, yes, he was the luckiest boy in the school!

Andre thought about the past few weeks and his friends Ralph, David, and John. Ralph and David were both unique, but he felt most akin to John. Andre had taken up the habit of wandering off when boredom struck and had stumbled on the "upper school." This was where the older boys and girls were, and it was the dream of all the youngsters to be there.

One day when his tongue was just about healed, Andre heard music from the great hall. This was the place where all the big events of the school took place. He heard a boy singing something like, "God bollow that star..." He was amazed at all the sounds of pianos and percussion instruments he'd never heard before. What shocked him was when the instructor, only known to Andre as a boss, kept interrupting the music and yelling, "No, no, retard! Again!" Andre didn't know why people had to be punished for no apparent reason. The music would start again, and the bad grown–up would interject with this "retard" again. Andre knew it wasn't nice to call people names, and he was no longer looking forward to going to the "upper school." He later learned that John was the one who was singing. Andre wondered if John felt hurt by this yelling. Soon their friendship grew.

Andre was still gazing out the window at the dusky sky, the snow, and those lovely lights which had been put on the trees. He would be the one to see Santa on the roof. He remembered the week before, when he was outside in front of those big Christmas lights. There was a boy near him who didn't speak. Andre overheard some talk which he didn't understand. "He was in Vietnam, threw a hand grenade. That made him deaf and blind, and he lost his right hand." Andre felt especially bad about someone losing a hand. It must have hurt many more times than his tongue had. He was curious and wanted to see what someone with no hand was like. Out of curiosity and empathy, Andre took the boy's arm in his hands. He gently rolled back the sleeve of the thick winter coat the boy was wearing. He noticed an arm which came to a smooth flat top where the hand should have been. Andre didn't know why, but his sense of pity caused him to lick the stump once and place it gently on a red Christmas bulb which was on the evergreen tree. The boy didn't protest. Luckily for Andre, nobody noticed his unusual act. He only felt that he was being kind to the boy in showing him caring and understanding.

Back to the reality of the blue snow and Christmas lights, Andre was getting impatient for Santa's arrival. From behind him came the voice of Miss M., one of the "bad" housemothers.

"Andre," she said, "do you want to see Santa Claus?" Before he could think of her as a bad person who was often curt and not usually given to good moods, Andre found himself following her downstairs to the playroom. When they entered, some lady was reading "'Twas the Night Before Christmas." When Andre got to the center of the room, the lines, "...and down the chimney he came with a bound" were uttered. The next thing he knew, Santa appeared in the fireplace with a loud thud and the sound of sleigh bells ringing.

He had never seen Santa come down a chimney before. It was hard for him to imagine Santa coming down the small oil-furnace pipe at home. He knew Santa was magic, but he did prefer the large fireplace entrance here to imagining Santa having to shrink to get into his house. Andre would never know how big a favor Miss M. had done for him that day by allowing him to see Santa landing in the fireplace.

Andre wasn't disappointed with his gift. He didn't know what it was, though, or what to do with it. He knew that some sad boys and girls would stay at school on the real Christmas, which was when they got the good gifts. Andre knew that Santa would come again when he was at home on Christmas Eve and was saving the good presents for then.

Christmas had come and gone. It was the dreary season of midwinter, but things were going well. One morning, after a good breakfast, Andre, Ralph, and Robert, a boy who wasn't particularly nice to Andre, were brought into a bedroom which wasn't Andre's. All day they had to lie in bed, doing nothing but listening to a radio. The boys didn't understand what was wrong. Andre didn't feel sick, nor did Ralph or Robert.

What seemed a long day became late night. Robert threw up, and Andre couldn't resist laughing at him. Robert had always been unkind, and Andre felt justified in laughing at the boy. Robert was removed from the room and sent home.

As for Ralph and Andre, things went back to normal as though nothing had gone wrong. Andre felt a bit guilty that Robert had almost been in tears when he had been made fun of for being sick, yet Andre didn't feel bad enough to apologize, and he felt that the boy's meanness was somehow deserving of his laughter.

viii

Now the snow was gone. Andre did so much like the sights, smells, and sounds of nature! He was very happy in his classes, talking with his three friends, also manipulating the housemothers to eat as little "good food" as he could and getting as much dessert as he desired. Gelatin was the one dessert he hated. There were a few times when his mouth was overflowing with a horrid artificial taste of grapes, and another time, he was given coffee gelatin.

All in all, Mary was his most beloved housemother, because she was so good to him. Andre's parents were now picking him up on Saturdays and bringing him back on Sundays. This was strange, but now his parents were taking him to stores, and his mother had taken to making him a chocolate cake every time he went home.

Mary was very kind to Andre. One Saturday morning, she was taking him for a walk when a pigeon flew by in front of them. Mary said, "Hello, birdie!" She was always thoughtful and kind. She had noted the foods he liked and never fussed over what he didn't like eating. Andre could remember only one time when Mary had disapproved of his behavior.

That was the time his best friend, David, was joyfully singing something he had learned at home. David repeated, "Mothers and the fuckers, mothers and the cuckas, mothers and the shitters." Andre thought this was a nice thing to learn and began to sing along with David. Mary overheard them. She was very upset and took the boys upstairs and washed their mouths out with soap. Andre heard David spitting, and when it was Andre's turn and Mary was scrubbing his mouth out with the washcloth, he didn't see the connection between what he'd said and Mary's strange behavior. In time, Andre would overlook Mary's idiosyncrasies, as otherwise, she was always nice.

He could look forward to Saturday mornings and Mary giving him nice treats for breakfast. He knew his parents would come soon to pick him up, and he could look forward to going to stores, treats, and his chocolate cake.

Once, his brother and sister told him privately that he should tell their mother he wanted a vanilla cake that week instead of the usual chocolate. His mother was too smart for them, though, and she made the chocolate that Andre preferred.

Now this night was different. Andre didn't know why, but he wasn't allowed to go to bed with the other kids. He had some kind of test to do. He recalled going to the *clinique*, as his mother called it, every week. This was a place of waiting. When the waiting was over, the doctors would treat him, with bright lights in his eyes. Sometimes even the colors would be different. He knew that he had to take drops in his eyes, but he didn't feel "sick in the eyes" the way he did when he had a cold or fever. His eyes did hurt sometimes, along with a headache, but he felt healthy. He thought it was actually fun to have his drops administered at mealtimes.

He recalled one week when Mary was with him after he'd visited the clinic and then vomited in the car. Mary let him have a jelly donut and a glass of milk for supper. He liked hamburgers, but he didn't feel up to one that night. Mary always understood that way, and never pressed him to eat if he didn't feel like doing so.

This was a strange evening. All the children had gone to bed. Mary was the only one with him. Andre could tell that she felt sad, but he didn't know why. He didn't know why he had to stay awake, and he was very tired. Mary would say, "Oh, poor dear..." The TV was on. The programs were not like any he'd seen before. He recalled hearing about "...flying police..." and "...the aliens are friendly..." The night blurred on with other memories of ladies screaming in terror and very bad men on TV. He must be a big boy to be up this late.

The next day, Andre was brought into a small room with no people in it. It was totally dark. Nobody was around, and Andre wanted to ask someone if he could use the bathroom. He was trying so hard to hold it in and was moving around a lot. Once in a while the door would open, and a lady would say, "Andre, stop moving!" This was odd; how could they see him? There weren't any windows there. And what had they taped all over his head? After Andre had made a few attempts to be still and hold it in, the lady came in and said to him, "Here, drink this." He was given thick, sweet, mint–flavored syrup which he reluctantly drank down. Soon he felt sleepy, and he wet the bed he was lying on.

He recalled a bright silver light, like the flashbulb of a camera. This one made a little snap noise, different from any camera he'd ever heard. It flashed faster and faster, until finally it was flashing very rapidly and sounded like moth wings beating. He recalled that it "galloped" at one point before it was at full speed.

He was later cleaned up and the tape was ripped off his head. He recalled Mary exclaiming, "Oh, you poor dear!" as she picked glue from his scalp. Andre was sent to bed early. It was dusk out. He couldn't recall it ever being this light when he went to bed. It didn't matter to him, for he couldn't recall ever having had such a deep and dream–filled sleep up to that point.

The end of Andre's first year at the school was approaching, and the school took on a festive atmosphere. The students had an afternoon off, and they made and flew kites. Andre very much enjoyed others' ability to make and fly them, but he didn't have much luck doing the same. His kite got tangled up in the trees. The silver reflective plastic that was used was more interesting to him.

This last week, they had ponies at the school one afternoon. He enjoyed the affair well enough, but he wondered if the animals were as hot as he was. At least there was the occasional thunderstorm, during which he could marvel at the lightning and anticipate loud booms of thunder.

Now all the students were on a bus. Soon they arrived on the waterfront by the sea. Andre smelled lovely sweet cotton candy and other delights. He very much enjoyed the small rollercoaster and Ferris wheel. Before they left, a walk on the beach found him searching for shells with the others. He found a mussel, which he learned was a live animal. He fancied the thought of having this blue beauty as a pet of his own.

When they returned to school, he placed the bivalve in his

bottom drawer. Nobody took the time to tell him that it should have been returned to the shore, or that it needed saltwater to live in. In fact, probably no one knew that he had pocketed the mussel.

Later that evening, Andre went to check on his pet. He discovered a lot of blue water around the shell in his drawer. He somehow knew that the creature was dead and that he had made a terrible mistake. He disposed of it in the trash and resolved to learn how to care for creatures in the future.

ix

During the summers at home, Andre was fascinated by all the sounds of insects and the small amphibians in his yard. Although he also enjoyed nature at his school, being mostly alone in the summer gave him the opportunity to observe still more wonders.

He recalled one particular summer which seemed very rainy and plagued with thunderstorms. As if this weren't enough to excite him, he observed, for the first time, how odd the sky looked before a storm, with a strange, yellowish, cloudy glow, later becoming an ominous lead gray and producing vivid yellow lightning and loud thunder. At first, Andre thought this phenomenon was a morning event, occurring shortly after sunrise. But one evening, he noticed the yellow sky before sunset. He was then treated to a marvelous downpour with its associated flashes and roars.

One sultry, sunny summer day, Andre was listening to the radio. He had always been fascinated by weather reports and felt that the forecasters understood his feelings. This day, it was mentioned that rare, tropical "swirl clouds" would be visible that afternoon. Andre hadn't yet figured out that the weather predictors could be wrong, for he hung on their every word. Their fallibility would become evident later.

That same afternoon, he was walking home and realized that a shower was developing, coming in behind him. He was elated, as it wasn't raining across the street where his house was, and he resolved to race home to beat the rain. Soon, however, the curtain of droplets caught up with him, finally overcoming him. Now the storm was typical of all others. He tried to explain to his mother how intriguing this had been to him, but she didn't share his enthusiasm.

As time passed, Andre grew more and more attuned to any odd colors of the sky; he began to associate them with snow, rain, and so forth. However, it was rare to hear anybody else mention these things. He learned that most people weren't as interested in such things, or perhaps they were simply less observant than he was.

Andre had heard the term "eclipse," but he didn't know exactly what one was. He was informed that it would get very dark. Most important, he was told not to look at the sun. It was fascinating to see a nearly dusky sky at noontime come and go. He was also informed that this wasn't a "total" eclipse, when it could get as dark as night. There was also going to be one the following summer, when he was going to Canada with his parents. Andre had expected to see the dark blue sky, but he was told it would be even darker than the last time. Unfortunately, it was cloudy and raining the day of the eclipse. He was pleased to see the gray sky get very dark for a short time, but he longed for a richer experience.

The next few years went well for him. A new building was erected at the school. They had many attractions there. Andre saw a glass-blower, Mickey Mouse, and a number of very interesting movies about volcanoes, the solar system, and other kinds of scientific wonderment.

Now the lights weren't going brown on Monday nights, but they had been showing a recreational movie on this particular night. Andre was fascinated by all sorts of gadgets. His friend John had only been there for one year, but Andre had impressed upon him his own playful curiosity, about bugs to frogs to phones.

This particular Monday night in Cub Scouts, Andre was busy playing with a phone in the hallway, a phone with no dial. When he picked up the receiver, he heard, "Good evening. Switchboard." He should have stopped, for the lady called back, alerting the scoutmaster and causing Andre to be reprimanded. He had done this at home, where he was able to dial various numbers. He was fascinated by the operator; the lady magically made the telephone ring without the usual spaces between the rings. This was quite mysterious to him. Now his parents entered, picking up the receiver. Naturally, they scolded him for this, but their anger was much greater when they got the bill the following month.

Once, on TV, Andre had heard someone on a show playfully telling the operator that they'd like to dial the number "one two three four five six seven eight." It was only natural for him to follow the lead. He also rang up many other numbers starting with the number one, not realizing that each time, he was reaching a long distance number. He always hung up after the expected "Hello," for he didn't know what to say. He was even more fascinated by automated messages and strange noises than by actually reaching a person.

The movies on Monday nights in the new building were very entertaining. Andre loved *The Court Jester* and many other magical movies. He wished there were more daytime movies about science. He loved learning about things in his world in science class. In addition, his friends were becoming closer to him.

He had classes in this new building with a different teacher than usual, Miss D. She was nice most of the time, but it was confusing to hear her comments about having "forgetful days," and Andre didn't understand her bad moods. She did make things interesting to learn, though.

Andre had never heard about dreidels or Chanukah or potato pancakes before. The entire class admired Miss D., and they often hid until she arrived. The children would come out exclaiming, "Happy birthday!" or as time went by, "Happy Friday!" Miss D. seemed patient and delighted with the accolades. But one day, the students were informed that Miss D. would be a little late. They were told to just read or do their homework until she came back. None of them realized that their next "happy" wish for her would be a mistake.

They all hid behind the desks or in the closet when they heard Miss D. arriving. When she entered, they exclaimed in unison, "Happy funeral!" Miss D., almost in tears, explained how such an event was a very sad thing and that they should not have wished her a "happy" one. Andre felt very bad about having said this thing, but as bad as he felt, he still didn't know what a funeral was, other than sad. However, he knew she was upset. He did not think to have Miss D. explain any further about it.

One Sunday night, Dave, Andre's roommate, vomited in his sleep. Dave was yelled at about it. Andre felt helpless about this situation. He recalled that once he himself had made just such a mess on the floor in that room before breakfast. He had not told anyone about it—not so much for fear of being punished, but because he didn't want to be harassed. Mary had found him out. She was very concerned that she could have slipped in the vomit and hurt herself. He should have told her, she said. Andre knew she was right, but he felt bad that he should be chastised for being ill. He felt even worse for Dave. People had always made fun of the other boy. He seemed to get sick every Sunday night, and once, it happened right at Andre's feet.

Andre had thought this all a silly game, and had laughed along with the others, until one Sunday, he had gotten sick on the ride to school. Andre was now taken to and from school by cab. His parents tried to get him on the big bus with all the other students, but there was some nonsense about him not being from the right state. His parents had explained that they could pick him up at the stop, as they lived only 15 minutes away, and the bus ride was preferable to their driving for an hour and 15 minutes each way. In any case, now people were being brought to and from the school via private car. Andre would ride with four or five others who lived relatively near him.

On the Sunday when Andre got sick, he was afraid to tell anyone. The others began to complain how it smelled of garbage. This made him feel more afraid to speak. When they arrived at the school, it was naturally discovered that he had thrown up. He was in the back seat alone. One child in the cab remarked, "Oh, my God! It smelled so bad, I felt like punching him in the mouth." Andre then realized many things at once. He shouldn't lie about anything, but even silence couldn't guarantee that he was safe. After a few days of being sick in bed at school, he realized that it was hurtful to others to make fun of them for being ill. What had been a silly game had turned into a sobering learning experience for him.

This summer was different. Andre knew that in September, when school started again, he would be going to a new cottage, one housing older children. Most of the pupils at the school considered this change a passage from childhood.

Andre's lust for science and more imaginative pursuits had been steadily growing, along with his body. He had always enjoyed the power of fire. It was the beauty of the varied colors and the power of the tongues of flame to put him into a sort of trance that attracted him to combustion. As a younger child, he'd been fascinated by light bulbs. Somehow, on his own, he had discovered that they grew brighter and brighter when he tapped them firmly in a certain fashion. Eventually the illuminated globe would be almost blue, and the bright flash of the bulb when it burned out was irresistible. Naturally, his parents would be upset by his burning out bulbs. Once, he'd burned his hand on a light and had gotten a large blister on his palm. That made this particular entertainment considerably less attractive in the future.

Another time, when Andre was about six and particularly intrigued by Christmas lights, he got the idea that he could illuminate a bright blue light in his mother's lamp. She had gone across the street for a bit to the neighbors' house. For what seemed an eternity, Andre tried to screw a small light bulb into a socket that was too big for it. After a while, he heard loud snaps and saw half a dozen bright blue flashes in the lamp's socket. He didn't know what to make of this situation, but a funny smell told him that something was not right. His mother discovered this shortly after her return home, and she was understandably upset that he had ruined her nice lamp. But he didn't really understand how this effect was possible.

His teachers were happy to stoke Andre's interest in science. He had one new teacher whom everyone liked, because she made class fun. She encouraged individual projects like freezing water outside. One particular morning, near lunchtime, she announced that today a solar eclipse of over 80 percent was coming. She made it more interesting by cutting a small pinhole in a piece of cardboard and placing it on the large picture window. The sunlight reflected onto the carpet, making it look like it was the size of a basketball. Everyone was fascinated by the shadow of the moon appearing and receding. The teacher's techniques were fun; at the same time, she illustrated very simply what an eclipse was really all about.

Later that year, Andre was told that a lunar eclipse was to occur. He knew that it would be safe to look at it, and that it would last much longer than one involving the sun. His patience was tested, but the strange colors of orange and red when the Earth's shadow covered the moon were exciting. A houseparent announced that air pollution particles made the colors, and that volcanoes could also trigger these bright colors. So now the sober issue of the environment came up, along with talk of many trees being dead by the 21st century. Andre felt helpless at not being able to save the environment. He was a bit scared, but his main impression was that nature was more powerful than man.

The houseparents, teachers, and staff at the school encouraged investigation of all types, from Bigfoot and UFOs to hypnotism. Andre was very intrigued by all the elements of science: belief, evidence, proof, and so on. But at this age, while he was entranced by all these ideas, he was not yet able to decide what was truth, myth, or speculation.

The issue with flames was stoked by some neighborhood boy this particular summer. The boy was using a very large magnifying glass to ignite tissue paper, boxes, and other things in a brick barbecue pit. Andre was determined to copy this behavior, as he found it scintillating.

Hampered by his not having a magnifying glass as powerful as the older boy's but with much patience, Andre learned how to use the sun and start flames. He always considered himself conscious of safety, but this hot summer day would teach him differently.

Andre had many long pieces of toilet paper, as it ignited most quickly and brilliantly. The flames promptly set the dry, mowed lawn alight. He was scared, but mostly, he was upset that he didn't know how to contain the spreading fire. He didn't have access to the garden hose, nor could he think right then where it was. He went to and from his house, a relatively short distance, with a small glass of water.

His brother discovered what was happening; he got the hose and extinguished the blaze. Naturally, his brother was upset by how Andre had dealt with the situation. He was most angry that Andre had used such a small container of water and hadn't used the hose or come to get him for help. The rage in his brother's voice made Andre cry. He was certain his parents would find out and punish him. To Andre's surprise, his brother, in rare fashion, held Andre in his arms. Thereafter, there was an understanding between them that had not existed before.

Later, Andre learned that his brother was indeed an ally. Certainly, his mother and father saw the black burn mark, quite large, in the lawn. To his amazement, nobody mentioned a word about the incident. This was shocking, as Andre's father, especially, had often scolded his older sister or brother concerning fire. Naturally, he was worried about the house burning down. This unusual behavior on his father's part was a relief to Andre, of course, but also instructive in showing him that his brother had some influence on their parents that he himself was unable to exert or understand.

Chapter 5

"Andre's Story, Part 2—Freedom under the Suppressors"

i

All in all, Andre was a happy enough child. He didn't dwell on the bad and tried to find hope in all the things in the future. Television had brought so many imaginative programs. He was fascinated by the Apollo landings, and the talk of a future probe to Mars was even more intriguing. The stories about the things that were possible but "not yet" were great treats. He had learned patience, to hold out. Once he'd been chastised for not eating and threatened that he would not get dessert or hear a great story, but he preferred to dream and be stubborn. Although all the children had heard "Peter Pan" and he hadn't, his imagination and optimism had prevailed.

The things that nature dished out were the most enjoyable of all. He liked thunderstorms and the unpredictability of snow making the ground white. It was people who spoiled Andre's fun, interfering the most with his plans.

During the last week of school, he was happy to go to the fair, where he could eat many treats and have fun with his friends. This year, when he was eight years old, he had imagined the school to be many things, from a giant helium balloon to a spaceship. If he couldn't have dessert, he'd imagine that he had an oven in his room and that he'd have a nice imaginary donut by morning.

When the fair was ending, all the children were headed back to their cottage. Andre, for the first time in his life, witnessed chain lightning, a bright purple color, over the pond. For the whole night, he and a few of his friends were in his room, gazing at the myriad colors and listening to crashes of thunder. Even when one of the bad housemothers insisted they go to bed, Andre mouthed back with profanity. That was a rare thing for him, but he felt that he must be allowed to see nature! He remarked how they could do nothing to him, seeing that it was the last week of school. The bad lady snapped that she'd remember to punish him the following school year, and Andre retorted that she wouldn't remember that far into the future. He got to watch the whole storm, finding it odd that some girls on the upper floor were frightened by the thunder and lightning and were screaming.

He was correct; there was no punishment the following fall. Not only did this woman forget the incident, but she wasn't there at the school anymore.

Andre was beginning to form alliances and different friendships. A girl named Lisa liked many of the same things that he did. They seemed to share the same minds. They were quite amazed that they didn't have to explain to each other what they meant when they spoke to one another. Others found their talk strange, even weird, but to the two of them, it was a playful time.

He was now nine. His largest concern was trying to understand why others were sad, how he could help them, and most of all, why people were so cruel to one another. He had met his friend John on a dreary winter night. John's neck was bleeding. He had impetigo and had been picking at it. A strange way to meet somebody developed into a close friendship—at least at first.

John and Andre did everything together. They made clubhouses in the trees. They went sledding on the big hill together. Much to Andre's liking, John and he started a log to see if they could predict the weather. They really didn't get it right very often, but they had fun, especially when one cold night they wrote, "Snowstorm will hit, with a white full moon." They never really worried, or even checked the accuracy of the book. They were diverted by too many other things.

One cold morning, they discovered a small, bright red rock. They both thought it looked like a stone from Mars. Ah, the pity of getting older, as they both decided that only the science teacher could tell them the truth about the rock. The science teacher turned out to be a big disappointment. Not only did she tell them that the rock was probably merely a piece from a broken brick, but she shattered the boys' dream of getting rich by discovering a Mars specimen at their school.

As time went by, Andre found that John was mocking him and Lisa being together. Yes, by the estimation of most of the class and others, she was a bit strange. But just because she and Andre liked Pink Floyd and Emerson Lake & Palmer and talked about science was no reason, as far as Andre could see, to make fun of her.

John was now playing with his new friend, Ricky. Andre didn't like Ricky's games, which were always about soldiers and being captured. John had also taken to roughing Andre up by making him do physical things that he didn't want to do and was not accustomed to performing. These activities were bad enough, but now Andre had been receiving physical blows from John. John had been so nice to him before. They had been roommates, and one time, they'd taken a pine branch from outside to make a Christmas tree for their room. They had had fun earlier that year with the "ghost walk" at Halloween. They had shared so much, but now, things were changing.

At Halloween, John made fun of Jimmy, a tall, skinny boy. Andre thought Jimmy was very nice. He was friendly and showed interest in talking to everyone. John jokingly called Jimmy a "bag of bones" as a Halloween joke, but Andre didn't laugh along with John. Another sickly boy named David W. was also nice to many people. Luckily, John didn't seem to have room in his repertoire to joke about him. Andre knew that David W. had something wrong with him, something to do with his brain.

Andre had enjoyed watching all the Christmas specials with John. Now, John was digressing into a stage of poking fun at the characters on TV. Andre wouldn't have minded this so much, but it seemed that John's humor was at their expense, and John didn't seem to make any distinction between the characters on TV or the people who shared their actual community with them. Andre found himself laughing less and less.

He tried to understand John's plight. John often spoke of his diabetic father being an alcoholic. He often related stories of his father being in the hospital due to his drinking, and how John had sometimes found him unconscious, lying in his own urine and feces.

Andre couldn't understand how drinking could do this. He recalled a time when his mom and uncle had been drinking and laughing together. His mother had said, "We're going to have a ball!" His uncle responded, "Whose ball?" Andre had assumed that drinking the "adult stuff" was for having fun. It was a concern when his uncle had trouble walking and almost fell down the steps, but all in all, Andre had assumed that drinking was associated with good times.

John went on about his sister, whom Andre had met once, during an open house, which the school held every year. Andre felt privileged to know John's family secrets and would never have guessed that John's parents were in the process of a divorce, whatever that meant. Why would someone hurt themselves? Andre wondered. He couldn't fathom how his own mother and father could split up.

This phase in Andre's life was supposed to be a step up; he had "graduated" to a new cottage. He now realized that this term wasn't entirely accurate, as the various three–story brick buildings were all connected, with a courtyard in the center. There was one building for the youngest children; the next one, which he was in, was for the older boys; there was one for girls; and another one was for "multi–handicapped" older children. John had joked that this last cottage was for the retards. Andre's best friends, David H. and Ralph F., were there. Andre often visited them—much to John's chagrin, as he had often called the two boys derogatory names. However, David H. was actually quite intelligent. Andre knew that there were other reasons people were in this cottage. David H. may have had some kind of emotional issues, but he was definitely not retarded, as he was in all the classes with John, Andre, John G., and the others.

John G. often spoke to Andre about naked girls, and they often talked about his parents' adult parties. They often went together to buy candy, and many times, they sneaked into the dining room to steal additional milk and cookies to get them through until supper. Andre often read the menu to John G., and they made tactical plans about candy and other ways of surviving the bad meals.

Andre's schoolwork was going well. The new teacher was kind, but her style was much stricter than expected, and studies were not as fun as they had been in the past. However, Andre liked school, probably more than most of the other students. He found it odd, though, that this teacher, Dianne, seemed to be very nice at times and very upset at others.

Dianne was good at stimulating Andre, but sometimes she was strange, in his view. Once, at her instigation, the students went to the local library to borrow books for schoolwork and pleasure. Andre wasn't very aware of time, procedures, deadlines, and the like, and he returned his library books late, incurring a fine. This upset Dianne. Andre was not sure why she was so unnerved. Borrowing the books had been her idea in the first place, and in Andre's view, she should have made everyone aware of the mandatory return date.

All the stresses of the year might have contributed to his not doing his required book report on time. He was always interested in doing his schoolwork, but for some reason, he hadn't gotten this assignment done. Dianne made him stay after school until he finished the task. Andre knew that reading a book and doing a paper on it would take a lot of time, probably more than the one day that she had given him. He picked a book out of her pile at random and began to read it. After an hour, he knew that he had made a mistake in picking such a book, one with so many pages.

After about an hour, Dianne inquired how Andre was doing. He lied, saying, "I finished reading it a little while ago." In fact, he'd barely started the assignment. She answered, "Good! Now you can start the book report." Andre's heart sank. He felt that he had no alternative but to wing it. He began to write, making up the story as he went along. There was always the fear in the back of his mind that the teacher would know he was faking it. Andre thought, What if she's read this book? The urgency of the tutor and Andre's feeling that he was committed drove him on.

After what seemed a long time, but was probably no more than three hours or so, he submitted his work. Luckily, Dianne hadn't read or remembered the particular book and gave him a grade of "C." Andre felt that was fine, especially since he hadn't done a real book report.

Andre boasted when he was 10 that he knew about "the birds and the bees." His parents, quite shocked, told him that he could talk to them about anything and ask them any questions. However, Andre sensed from his mother's alarmed and disgusted tone that this wasn't entirely true. He found books left around in his home, presumably by his parents, describing the details of sex. He also discussed this in some detail in his school classes, and the school library had information as well. When Andre was six, he had played doctor with a girl name Lynn in his neighborhood, and even with his cousins. Pictures in books also made this experience clear.

His cousins from Maine also filled Andre in on all these details. They had fun on summer vacations, going to fireworks, holding séances, and walking in the woods. Andre relished his summer vacations. For a few years, his cousins went through the séances and sex discussions with him. His uncle in Maine wasn't a favorite of Andre's mother. Not only did her toe get broken when he threw her in the pool, but she also thought that he drank too much and didn't know how to raise children properly. Andre's grandmother, who didn't get along very well with Andre's mother, shared this view.

Andre's father was very supportive. He taught him to respect nature, to respect all life, even to the level of insects. He wouldn't stand for killing a bug, but insisted they be let out of the house alive. Andre's uncle, the brother of Andre's father, was very tolerant, but also very strict with Andre's cousins.

Andre liked the Maine visits. It was an adventure to be taken to "R" movies. One summer, they had fun at the Fourth of July fireworks and were very interested in Andre's descriptions of what they looked like, from the way they spread out and faded. Andre would say, "That one had blue and red dots with a white flash." This describing went on for some time. When the finale came, nobody could stop for a description.

The most liberating part of the summer was when Andre's uncle brought him along with his father to see the movie *One Flew over the Cuckoo's Nest*. Andre sat through the previews of coming attractions. He felt like an adult when he heard the "bad language." His mother often cursed in French, and Andre knew what she was saying. His father swore in English and often talked about women's anatomies, so to Andre, there was nothing particularly new or special about the movie.

Now Andre was learning about very sick people. David W., the one with the brain trouble, died. John, Andre's roommate, had thrown up all night on their return from Christmas vacation. It was New Year's Day this year when they started school. Classes would start on the 2nd, but naturally they all came together the night before. Andre was surprised at his reaction to John's illness. He felt glad that at last John was receiving justice for his physical abuse of him. He felt somehow that God was punishing John for his cruel statements and negative attitudes towards others.

It seemed that every cottage had its bad houseparent or parents. The next morning, Mrs. D. yelled at John for not waking her up and telling her he was sick. She was obviously angry that the mess would have to be cleaned up. Andre thought that in spite of John's past bad behavior, he should be shown mercy during his time of sickness.

February brought new realities. David had died during the winter vacation. He was such a nice boy! What was wrong in his brain to cause this outcome? Even John was absent; they said he had pneumonia. Andre knew he would be free of John's tormenting for at least two or three weeks, but he couldn't revel in the fact that John was in the hospital.

John returned in mid–April. He recounted the episodes in the hospital. John and Andre resumed where they had left off. John occasionally vented his anger at Andre's physical ineptitude. He intimidated Andre by forcing him to do things that Andre preferred not to do.

Andre spoke with a slight lisp due to his previously hurt tongue. John jokingly mocked Andre's Christmas concert solo by repeatedly exaggerating how he had said "children" in the song. In his condescending tone, John had made it sound like "shildren." Andre became a bit self-conscious, but neither he nor anyone else heard "shildren." Only John had the mocking way about him.

Then, almost with joy, Andre recalled that Halloween, when their play had concerned ghosts. Andre had said, "...and it was as white as a sheet!" John had become very self-conscious and had accused Andre of making fun of his albinism. This was very hurtful to Andre. He felt sad and amazed that John could even think such things, especially after all the hurtful things John had said and done.

ii

It hurt Andre that nobody remembered his birthday in January. Apparently, somebody decided to throw a record across the room the night before his birthday. The bad houseparent, Mrs. D., asked everyone to "swear to God" that they hadn't done the deed. Andre had never heard this before, but he knew that swearing, especially to God, was wrong. All the children were amazed that he wouldn't swear with them, and so they thought he was guilty. The houseparents decided to punish the whole cottage until the guilty one confessed. Andre's birthday was spent with all the children being kept indoors under punishment. Finally, that evening, the guilty person was discovered and the houseparents apologized to all the students individually. Andre nervously accepted the apology, but he was still hurt that this was his 10th birthday present.

He shouldn't have been surprised. A few months earlier, he had gone with the Boy Scouts on their annual camping trip. Nobody had remembered to send his drops along. Andre wasn't a team player; he didn't enjoy the physical nature of the boasting boy games. He did like learning about the Civil War, but he sensed that most of the students were bored with this stuff. Sleeping in his winter coat when the nights went below freezing and sweating during the day, when the temperatures went into the 70s, was not fun for him either.

Even the bus trip down to Virginia didn't excite him. Nobody spoke with him during the trip, not even John. Richard, a boy who sat behind Andre, was always picking on smaller and younger kids. Nearly a half–dozen times during the trip, Richard grabbed Andre's head and pulled it backwards. Being a few years Richard's junior and not having any self–defense skills, Andre feebly struggled to break away, but he couldn't break the other boy's hold. Even when he cried out, nobody reprimanded Richard or intervened to stop the bullying. Andre knew that this trip was not going to be enjoyable, nor would anybody care about him or be of any assistance at all.

Toward the end of the trip, he was getting a headache and was glad they'd be home soon, so he could take his drops again. He knew the pain was due to his not taking his medicine and was angry that nobody cared about him. How could they serve black coffee with ice in it to children?

Back at school, the drops helped the moment he got them. Still, he was angry that he couldn't express to anyone what he thought. He wanted to yell at Mrs. D. for not remembering to send the drops along. That and the bad case of bronchitis he got a few days later caused him to decide he would never go with the Scouts on their trips again.

Andre loved playing with David; they had conversations about science and imaginative prospects concerning computers and all manner of things. David was very interested in obtaining his amateur radio license.

By mid–spring, Lisa was more in the picture. Although Andre didn't dislike her music, he soon tired of discussing it all the time. Yet he and Lisa shared many interests. They talked about how aliens might contact Earth, also about how certain music was actually about aliens and science fiction. Andre also left time to spend alone outside, or to read science books and fictional works in the library.

The oddest thing, in his opinion, was how John vacillated between moments of rage and friendship. One day he'd be forcing Andre to climb the backstop in the field, or some other such physical feat that was very difficult for him, and then on another day, he'd be sharing more of his grim family life. Andre's understanding of the issues was limited, but he sensed how bad things were for John. He found himself sympathizing with the other boy, but he couldn't forgive John for his abuse. He certainly didn't know how he could get even with John, and he didn't even really want to, but he celebrated the times when John was not bothering him.

By late April, John's behavior was better than it had been earlier, at least in comparison to the cold winter months and the days of February. That winter, John had drawn pictures of naked girls in the snow for Andre. These seemed strange, probably because the sketches required a lot of imagination and were nowhere near the pictures Andre had seen in books, nor anything like he remembered from his experiences with Lynn, the girl in his neighborhood, and with his cousins a couple of years before. Even *National Geographic* magazine could show Andre more than John had done. Also, Andre felt that John thought he was stupid.

He was taken aback when John announced, "Lisa said we could play around together. We did it on the back steps yesterday, and she wants to do it again with both of us."

That night, Lisa, John, and Andre were seated on the spiral staircase in their pajamas. It was a hard and fast rule that the boys and girls shouldn't visit each other indoors in private rooms. The big taboo was against boys visiting the third floor, where the girls slept. Since the boys were on the second floor, the girls' passage through to the first floor was tolerated, but it was clear that they weren't allowed to visit.

This rule didn't concern Andre or John. A couple of weeks before, Andre and Robert, a boy who was new at the school, had visited John's room. One day John G. and Robert were in the room. The boys were fascinated by hypnotism. They all tried to hypnotize each other and went on with the usual "Jump up and down!" or some such triviality to indicate that the hypnotism had worked. When it was Andre's turn to hypnotize Robert, Andre wanted to be sure that he had the power of hypnosis.

When he thought Robert was hypnotized, he said, "Now, take down your pants." To Andre's amazement, Robert obeyed. "Now your underwear," stated Andre, not believing that his powers were that good. Robert again obeyed, and Andre naturally felt he had earned his reward. John G. giggled once or twice, and then Andre stated in a clinical fashion, "Okay, pull them up and wake up." This incident took place with the bedroom door wide open. Andre didn't sense that he was doing anything wrong, and it was this same curiosity and logic he used on the stairs with Lisa. He had no sense that there was anything improper about what they were doing.

Lisa had one hand in John's pajama pants and the other in Andre's, while John and Andre took turns putting their hands in her pajama pants or had their hands there together. After a few minutes, John exclaimed to Lisa and Andre, "Why don't you both go in the closet of the corner room and I'll make sure nobody comes in." Andre and Lisa proceeded to that room.

Andre and Lisa were exploring each other, and by this time his pants were down. Sensing that Andre wasn't very interested in her that way, Lisa said, "You don't have to do it if you don't want to. I'll just play with yours." After a while, she became uninterested with her exploration and they both proceeded downstairs with the others, as if nothing unusual or important had occurred. Indeed, it was quite innocent and natural. They didn't discuss it again, nor did they find any need to explore any further in the future. They did become closer friends, though, sharing more of what John would call "weird stuff."

Over the next six weeks or so, the cold and snow of winter were replaced by a beautiful spring. Andre was more aware than usual of the plants, bird songs, and weather. He had never lost his enjoyment of snow in the winter and thunderstorms in the spring.

It was rare for him to awaken before dawn, but when he did, he was delighted to see the sky grow light and to hear birds of all kinds singing. There was one morning when he awoke to a brief but fabulous display of thunder and lightning, along with heavy rain. He admired the yellows and blues, the silver lightning, and the great crashes of thunder. The storm ended as rapidly as it had begun. He thought it was still late at night, but the clouds cleared to reveal a dark blue sky, indicating that the sun would be up very soon. The birds suddenly burst into song, as if to share Andre's wonderment at the storm and the beauty of the spring sky.

By May, Andre had taken up catching bees. He found a clever method of taking an empty soda bottle, turning it upside down, and placing it over a bee when it was pollinating a flower. He quickly learned that the bee always flew up, even when there was no cover on the bottom of the bottle. At least this was how it was supposed to work, and most of the time, it did, until he got stung a couple of times. Once, he had lost a bee on the ground and was scrounging along looking for it. His knee found the insect.

He started keeping the bees in the bottle overnight, until they ran out of air. He had a collection of about eight of them in a plastic bag, and his intention was to study them in a scientific manner. He honestly believed that he was following the work of great scientists.

One day he found a strange bee. A houseparent commented, "It doesn't have a thorax!" The bee was totally plant green in color, unlike anything seen before. The houseparent urged Andre to let it go, and he did. He would leave for summer vacation that year with a bee sting, and his quest for knowledge would continue.

The end of the school year was always exciting for Andre. This year, the students were taken to a new amusement park, where the rollercoaster was much larger and faster than the one he'd gone to by the seashore as a younger child. The festive mood seemed to affect all equally. It seemed to Andre that the spring weather further contributed to their happiness.

On this last night of school, neither Andre nor any of the house staff worried about bedtime or friends visiting and talking in their rooms. Ralph and Andre had regularly spent a great deal of time together. This night, Lenny was also visiting Ralph and Andre in their room. Andre liked Lenny well enough, but he didn't really know him that well. At least they all got along.

It was growing late, and it felt even later, but the boys' excitement due to the upcoming summer and the beautiful weather was keeping sleep at bay. As was often the case, they could hear the distant city traffic and sounds from the highway—and on this particular night, what seemed to be an unusual number of sirens, especially those of ambulances.

At one point, they could hear the loud blare of a very nearby rescue vehicle's distress signal. Lenny began crying, and he was visibly shaking with fear. Neither Ralph nor Andre could get an answer from the boy as to why he was so afraid, and Ralph was at a loss as to what to do about the situation.

Now Lenny was curled up on the floor, stiff and terrified, and they could all still hear the loud alarm of the ambulance. Andre felt hopeless as he touched the boy, trying to comfort him. Along with Ralph's supportive words, he tried to reassure

Lenny that everything was all right. He felt he should hold the poor boy, in an affectionate kind of way, but for some reason, he could not do it. Soon enough, Lenny calmed down, and the boys slept.

The next morning, Andre was still curious about the events of the previous night. He asked Lenny what the matter had been, why he had been so afraid of the sirens, but Lenny wouldn't answer. At this point, Andre felt a strange kind of pity and helplessness. He had discovered a previously unknown kind of human suffering, but also a novel awareness of how truly alone each person is, separate from all the other members of humanity. Andre's inability to console the boy was evidence enough of this, but all the other cruelties of the prior school year made him feel the sense of disconnection more acutely than he ever had before.

iii

His older brother and sister were nice enough to Andre. It was just that their friends didn't do much, if any, talking to him, let alone invite him to their parties or wish him well. He felt left out and alone, but he also realized that he could explore the world around him for the sake of science.

He caught many toads, bees, and other beasties that summer, letting most of them go after he observed them. His brother's and sister's friends had all successfully kept toads. Nobody bothered to tell Andre how to really take care of the things he caught, or even how long they lived. He felt bad that his toads never lived beyond two or three days.

All of the things that he felt and thought were intense, but he couldn't share them with anyone. Even his parents were often too busy to really have a talk. However, for a busy father, his dad was very understanding. He was concerned about how Andre treated his specimens. The boy did listen, for his father showed genuine understanding and patience. Andre felt the sadness expressed by his father at his mistreatment of the insects.

Andre's friend Mathew helped him and caught bees with him, but Mathew got stung quite often. One day Andre heard Mathew's father yelling at him from a window of the house. His father was upset that Mathew had caught so many bees. He told the boys how important bees were for pollination and that they died when they stung people. Andre had known this all along, but he had never before heard it expressed with such emotion. He was convinced that he must never catch another bee.

Then, a few days later, Andre saw a large bee in Mathew's pool. He knew that he had to rescue it. He gently lifted it out with a coffee can that was lying on the ground. He was a bit afraid, because it was a large bee, almost as large as a golf ball, but he opted to rescue it just the same. Once the bee's wings were out of the water, it flew away happily.

Andre's mother wouldn't approve of him having a pet, the way all their neighbors did. Even his father thought that feeding pets was an excessive expense, so Andre took to playing with all the neighbors' animals, especially when the neighbors weren't home. This way, he could learn for himself about the animals without others distracting him.

He had somehow frightened Mathew's rabbit. He let it out of its cage in the hopes of calming it down, but he soon realized that there would be big trouble if it were attacked by a dog. He wisely put the bunny back.

Andre's mother was quite concerned that he had nothing to do that summer, and she emphatically stated that he needed some activities to keep him busy. This opinion was vindicated whenever he would come home with cat scratches all over his arms and legs. He wanted to control more aspects of his life, and he was tired of things being beyond his power. It was a challenge to catch the cats. He used all his hearing to sneak up on them, just as he had done to catch toads and insects. He couldn't understand why they growled and rejected his affection when he grabbed them and held them in his arms. He would reiterate to them, thinking they could understand, "But kitty, I love you!" He would also sneak cans of tuna from home to feed them as a sign of affection.

One orange-colored cat, apparently older, was always lying around and was often sick, especially when it ate grass. The cat's gurgling and crying went to Andre's heart. He wanted to do something to ease its suffering. Although the cat enjoyed the tuna, it got very sick, and then Andre felt even worse. This reminded him of a summer when a neighbor's dog, which would often lie on a hot driveway in the sun, had been trying to eat some curly bits of Styrofoam that had been discarded on the ground. The black and brown dog was skinny, covered with sand, and very oily, probably from the cars that leaked in the driveway. Andre pushed the dog away hard and exclaimed "No!" many times. Inevitably, the mutt managed to eat the plastic when Andre's attention was turned away for a few seconds. For several days, Andre heard the dog on the hot, humid mornings, groaning loudly. Andre was sure the dog was sick from eating the Styrofoam, and he felt guilty and helpless about the situation.

Andre's mother warned him that his playing with animals and bugs would make him sick. He had been given antibiotics for a swollen knee caused by his episodes of playing with bees. He had ringworm on his arm. He thought it was clearing up, but his mother said it was going into his bloodstream, and that he would get sick if he didn't go to the doctor. He was given more antibiotics.

One night while catching toads, he stood up too quickly after a catch and hit his left eyebrow very hard on the corner of the neighbor's house. The result was a trip to the emergency room, where he got four stitches. He saved them when they were removed, admiring the way the knot looked in the black stitches.

In all this chaos, his mother became more worried. He would soon spend a week at camp, where he'd been two years before. This always lasted six days, from Sunday to Friday, but this year, they were doing a seven–day cycle, from Sunday to Sunday. There was also a three–week camp in Vermont, which he had never attended. His mother convinced him that four straight weeks at camp would be good for him.

Andre moderately enjoyed the week–long summer camping experience. He didn't mind the rickety wooden cabins, set up in military style with bunk beds and screen windows, over which shutters would be put down in rainstorms. Most people would bring sleeping bags, or put sheets and blankets on the beds. The food was vegetarian, and they had a very strange religious system. So long as they believed in Jesus and God, it wasn't a concern to Andre, and he never talked to his parents about it.

His parents had always given him extra snacks, anyway. He was used to supplementing diets with food from home. Surprisingly, the first year he had attended this camp, John from his boarding school had attended as well, and they had been cabin mates. At that point, John hadn't yet begun his tormenting of Andre or making fun of others. They both shared the horseback riding and swimming experiences, and they had a lot of fun watching the bug light zapping moths.

John and Andre vowed to escape to the island in the middle of the large lake to await their parents' return. This exodus never happened, as the camp activities continued and they both attempted the "Who's on First" routine at talent night. The idea of escaping to the island left their minds quickly enough.

John had never returned to the camp. This year, Andre was surprised to find that Allen would be his cabin mate. Allen was the one who had stated, years before, that he wanted to punch Andre in the mouth when he vomited in the cab. Andre was sure this was forgotten. Now there were pleasantries to share, such as when Allen asked, "Have you ever seen it get light in the middle of the night when it's cloudy, and then it gets dark again?" Andre had observed a phenomenon like that as well.

Allen would sometimes discuss the "end–times," and Andre respected the older boy's knowledge of science. Allen was concerned for the less fortunate, and Andre found something appealing in the idea of a God who would set things right in the end.

The week at camp went well, with Andre having fun horseback riding. This year would be the last year the horses obeyed instructions. In future years, they would learn the paths and not follow the steering instructions as they had always done before.

Pat, the head counselor of the cabin, was a treat. He was a tall and husky man of about 30. He also directed the music and campfire sessions for the entire program. Andre felt privileged. He saw Pat as a mentor and strong father figure.

Andre had also become aware of sparks of sexuality in himself, although they had not yet fully awakened. It was one thing to know about "the facts of life," but now he had begun to feel things and think about them.

A few weeks before camp, Andre had noticed fuzz on his body. He was so pleased, and he felt a childish sense of manhood come over him. He also felt that a man must shave this hair, and in addition, he wanted to have this important event of his life observed by someone else, preferably one who was going through a similar experience.

After Andre had finished his shaving in the bathroom, Timmy, a neighbor who was eight years old, two years Andre's junior, had been very interested in talking to Andre. Not only had Timmy found gold in the woods, but he was very happy to invite Andre over for swims and to have Andre alone with him in his home–made clubhouse. Both boys were interested in catching bugs and toads.

The day they met, Timmy had no trouble convincing Andre to play in his clubhouse, where they talked and explored. This went on for a few weeks, until one day Timmy announced, "Oh, my mother won't allow me to play with you anymore, because she found sand in my underwear." Andre didn't see why this playing was an issue, and he wondered if Timmy's mother had told his mother about the sand. He would never know, as his mother never mentioned it, but only said that he should play with boys his own age.

At camp, Pat was popular with all the campers. Andre was looking forward to hearing a horror story that Pat would tell. Andre had taken the stage on talent night, telling a typical horror story with its usual ghosts, squeaky doors, and scares around every corner. What made him a big success was that he added sound effects, using his throat, teeth, and more to imitate the squeaky doors and thunder. At last he felt accepted.

Pat began his tale of horror. It was basically about a man who didn't believe in the power of the devil. This foolish man dared the devil to appear to him and reveal his power while the man was in the bathroom. After a few hours, nobody had heard from the man, but they heard a dripping sound coming from the bathroom. When the man's friends entered, they found his burned flesh and blood smeared all over the walls, floor, and ceiling.

The next day, Allen asked his close friends whether or not they believed the story. All of them, along with Allen, laughed at how foolish this story was. Andre felt like interjecting and stating that he believed the story, but he didn't want to be the butt of laughter. At school, he had seen how others had been amused at Lisa's expense.

There were junior counselors in the cabin who were very nice. A younger boy named Jimmy habitually wet the bed. These counselors were very patient with him. Andre was sad when most of the roommates laughed and made a joke of these incidents. Andre wished he could comfort Jimmy and ease his suffering.

Andre felt very close to those few figures of authority who did try to comfort Jimmy. Andre also found it possible to elicit comfort from these young men, by using his body language and lying in bed in a certain fashion. These counselors would make their good–night rounds with only with the dim light from the porch. Their tone of voice told Andre that they understood his thirst for attention, and their friendliness to him increased.

Finally, the week was over. Andre's parents arrived and were preparing to take him on the six–hour drive into Vermont. He was not as excited as he'd expected to be, but figured that going to camp would be better than being lonely at home.

He felt upon his arrival that he already wanted to go home. These people seemed to be having too much fun, and he knew that he'd be lonely here. However, he also knew that his father would be angry at having spent all that money on gas if he said he didn't want to stay, and his mother would no doubt be angry that he hadn't said earlier that he didn't want to go. He was quite used to his feelings being questioned, not only by his friends, but also by his parents. In general, he felt that he had to hide how he felt, for others didn't understand him. In addition, people often criticized his likes, dislikes, wants, and needs.

Andre met the counselors and his cabin mates. He didn't dislike anyone, but he would have preferred to be playing with toads or bugs, or maybe a cat would be nice. He had no need to fear disapproval from animals. Then again, even the cats ran away from him. He found the supper boring. At least they had real meat, and he heard that the menu was really good. He figured that his lack of appetite was due to his feeling down.

Three weeks seemed a long way off, but he resolved to make the best of it. He was happy that they had a nature and science activity. They even had microscopes, which he'd always wanted to see. He was even happier to hear that they had science fiction story telling. These activities weren't available at the other camp. Oh, they had had raccoons and other animals at the previous place, but a real science teacher was a joy.

John W. and Mario were the campers Andre identified with the most in his cabin. John W. had been with Andre at the boarding school some six years before, but for some reason, he'd left. He didn't remember Andre very well. Andre felt akin to Mario, who was his own age. Andre looked up to John W. for advice, and he enjoyed learning about science and sci-fi. Andre wanted to know more about this realm. He'd not yet been allowed to watch *Star Trek*, so he could learn a lot from John W. Whenever Mario wanted to learn about sex from John W., Andre thought, Oh, good! John and Mario will want to talk to me. I can teach Mario about that! John won't ignore me so much now.

This wish of Andre's was short-lived. John W. asked Mario, "Do you know why you can't fuck all night?" Mario didn't know, but Andre answered, "Because your balls don't have enough sperm in them to do it." John stated that Andre was partly right, but retorted, "Most of all, it's because you don't have enough energy to do that all night, and the sperm isn't the big issue."

Andre also tried to talk to John W. about *Lost in Space*. John W. dismissively answered Andre that, "The Enterprise is more realistic as a flying ship than the Jupiter Two." Andre now sensed what was happening; John W. wanted to be Mario's friend. Andre felt that the older boy didn't want to bother with him and explain things to him. That privilege was clearly reserved for Mario. Now it went beyond Andre being called weird for talking about sci-fi, and he felt that he wasn't accepted even by those who shared his interests and imagination.

Jane Von was the name of the lady who taught the science and nature activity. It would be a while before Andre realized that her name wasn't James Bond. In any case, she made the time fun, and it passed quickly. Andre spent as much time as he was allowed to in the science room or going on nature hikes.

A few other campers and he were asked if they wanted to watch a fox being skinned and were told that it would be very interesting. Andre protested, "I don't think it's right that you killed an animal for us to study." Jane said, "Oh, no, we found a fox that had been hit by a car. It was still warm when we found it. We wouldn't kill animals to study. Besides, they'll have other nights with science fiction stories, but you'll probably never have a chance to see a fox get skinned ever again."

Andre was convinced, although he really did want to hear some sci–fi stories. It was interesting to see the surgical precision used to skin the poor animal and to listen to Jane explain its anatomy. Contrary to what he had expected, it wasn't a bloody affair at all. Some people left, feeling the whole thing was disgusting, but Andre was fascinated at how the skin was removed like a coat; it was also interesting that the inside was very pink and shiny. The smell of fresh flesh wasn't much to his liking, and he suspected that many left due to that odor, but Andre realized that this was simply the way things were.

A few days later, maggots had gotten into the fox's skin, which had been left behind. Andre liked watching the segmented larvae on the wall–projecting microscope, and he was happy to see eggs along with pupae for real, rather than just reading about them in a book.

That same morning, another counselor reported that someone had found an injured mouse somewhere. Jane sadly commented that it would be better to put it out of its misery, and she placed it in a jar of ether. Andre felt drawn to the powerful scent and went to where the anesthetic had been kept. He saw the lifeless mouse in a sealed jar with the milky–looking chemical that had put it to sleep.

He also observed the bottle from where the liquid had originated; he heard that someone had inhaled it once and passed out. He knew that the gas was used in hospitals, and he'd probably been given it as a child, for his nine operations that his parents often spoke of. He slowly began to sniff in the vapors. He felt a bit dizzy, but Jane intervened and removed the bottle, stating, "We don't want you to faint and hurt yourself when you hit the floor. Go outside and get some fresh air. You'll be fine in a minute." She was right, as the outdoor air felt very refreshing.

Even with all this activity, Andre still wanted to go home. The first week was coming to a close. He was in the director's office talking to his parents and was emphatic in telling them that he wanted to leave camp. They asked him why he'd want to do that when it was so much fun there. He couldn't find the words, and could only come up with, "I don't know. I just want to go home!" He didn't know how to express the fact that he felt isolated from the other people at camp, and he felt that revealing this fact would only net him criticism.

Joe, the gruff director, intervened and told his parents, "I think we'll keep him here another week. It'll be good for him." Joe hung up the phone after acting so polite to his parents and bidding them good–bye.

Andre's next week was miserable. He felt as though he'd been given a punishment for something he hadn't done. It was worse than the birthday when he'd been so unjustly punished, along with the other innocent kids in his class, for throwing a vinyl record. Back then, his birthday had been ruined, but now he had another whole week, or maybe even two, at this camp.

The activities became more rigorous. The kids were taken on five–mile hikes to pick blueberries. Andre liked that well enough, except for the blazing sun. He would always remember returning and drinking cold, fresh spring water.

Then they were taken into the mountains to spend the

night in small, two-man tents. Andre was looking forward to the campfire, where he'd been promised sci-fi stories. He was disappointed that there was only one told, and he thought it was a bit babyish, as well as not very imaginative. It was basically about how aliens had seen strange TV signals from Earth and were puzzled by how we lived. At the end it was revealed that the aliens had been viewing a cartoon. How stupid! he thought. If these beings were smart enough to know about our Earth, surely they'd be able to tell that they weren't seeing real humans.

Now he really wanted to be home. He had started to write a sci-fi story about a manned mission to Mercury. Surely, he thought, he could come up with something more interesting than extraterrestrials watching cartoons.

While on the bus back to the camp from the overnight camping trip, Andre felt fortunate to be sitting near Mario. John W. had apparently grown tired of talking with Mario about sex and sci-fi. Mario asked Andre if he'd watched *Star Trek*. Andre sadly replied that he wasn't allowed to watch it. Mario was understanding and told him, "Oh, that's okay, Andre. You know basically what it's about. I mean, they go to other planets and meet aliens, kind of like *Lost in Space*. So all we have to do is pretend that everyone on this bus is an alien." Mario took the lead, as he was most familiar with the *Star Trek* characters. Andre felt somewhat inept as he attempted to play along, but he felt proud that Mario had given him the privilege of being part of his game.

After Andre had struggled through the second week of camp, his parents were to pick him up the following day. He had felt that Dennis, a camp counselor, was trying to be friendly, but that the man didn't really understand. When Andre was in the nurse's office, where he was given an aspirin for a headache brought on by a crying session, Dennis had talked to him like a child.

Andre felt liberated when his parents and sister came to pick him up. His mother stated, "I don't know why you wanted to go home. It's such a beautiful place. It's nice country up here." His sister then said, "Besides, you only had one week left. I'd be happy to go camping for a month."

Andre feebly tried to state that he was just sick of camping, but his sister probed some more, trying to figure out why he didn't like it. More accurately, she indicated by her tone of voice that it wasn't right to not like camping.

After all the camping, and a week or so before school, while playing with Kevin and Scott's cat and one of his other neighbors, Andre was foolishly using a large rock while observing how the kitten was jumping and playing along with him. This game went on for a few minutes, until Andre, or the feline, miscalculated the stone's motion. The rock rolled over the kitten. Andre's heart sank as he rushed over to help the animal. He observed the creature on its back, kicking at an invisible force with its legs. Then the cat's eyes glazed over and it died.

Andre's heart was sickened. He dared not tell anyone. He felt so guilty when the neighbors got home, and Kevin, the youngest, was talking to his friends and saying that he didn't know why his cat had died.

iv

Back at school, John seemed to have forgotten how he had treated Andre the previous year and was talking with him again. Andre foolishly tried to explain the cat incident. John punched him several times and was furious that anyone could be so cruel. Andre was amazed that John could feel this way about the kitten and at the same time inflict pain on him, yet he also felt that his punishment was deserved.

They learned that Jimmy J. had died that summer from the heart trouble he'd been suffering. Andre didn't understand why John seemed unconcerned about the other boy's death. John had always made fun of Jimmy's skinniness, which was very disturbing to Andre. Once, Jimmy had been so upset by John's taunting that he had lain helplessly on the floor, as though he'd simply given up.

Andre now felt helpless as well. About a week after camp, he'd begun having horrible, vivid nightmares about the devil coming to destroy him. This happened almost every night. He would always have this dream just at the point when he would wake up, causing him to think that it was real. It would be about a year and a half before he realized that it was all a dream. This devil image never occurred during the day. Although Andre scared himself a lot about it, reason prevailed in the end. The power of Pat's story was strong, but Andre "dared" the devil in a way by challenging the terror of his nightmares to express itself when he was wide awake. Until the time that he figured out the depths of his fear, these dreams would become part of Andre's despair and feelings that he was powerless against bullies.

John's maltreatment of Andre continued in a similar pattern for the whole year. Most often, he forced him to perform physical feats. John rarely hit him, but rather used the macho tactic of intimidation. One day in the spring, John goaded him into jumping off a wall. Andre checked the wall later. It was true that it was only a few feet high, but the principle of it was that John had to have proof that Andre wasn't a chicken.

Andre would have been fine if he had known how to land. John's forcefulness didn't help, of course. Andre landed awkwardly, falling on all fours on the pavement. He hit his chin and bit his tongue when he hit the pavement. It wasn't bleeding, and it wasn't anywhere near as severe as the accident he had

had when he was five, but the pain lasted a few days, haunting him and reminding him of the past nightmares of his early childhood.

Andre recalled how he and John had been at the religious camp for a week a couple years earlier. They both hated the vegetarian food, and a real camaraderie had developed between them. The week had passed swiftly enough. All in all, it wasn't such a bad experience, so long as they both shared it. Had John forgotten all the past fun they'd had together? But Andre had finally learned not to provoke anger in others. He knew, perhaps better than most, the wisdom of the saying, "Bite your tongue."

Perhaps the real cementing of their friendship had come on the day at camp when they were swimming in the lake. They were both paddling far out from the dock, which had two vertical sections joined in the center by a horizontal one. The lifeguard blew his whistle, warning them to come back in, as neither John nor Andre realized that they were going out so deep. Inhaling for breath, Andre suddenly got a huge gulp of water from the wake of a passing motorboat.

He couldn't breathe in or out. He felt the water in his chest and tried to breathe. A sense of tingling and great urgency came over him. His actions were now controlled by what seemed to be an outside force. He tried to get air, and he couldn't sense that he was getting the water out of his lungs. He grabbed onto John as if the other boy were a raft. Naturally, John struggled, trying to get Andre off him. It seemed like an hour, with John continuously pushing Andre up and Andre mounting John. John's head kept going under the water, and his white hair looked cloudy and frantic as he tried to raise his head up for air.

All during the struggle, however, John had been paddling toward the dock. Finally they both emerged from the water. Andre's legs and arms ached from his long, panicked exertions. Everything was blurry, and he could barely stand up; he thought he might pass out. John accepted his explanation about the boat and said how frightened he had been, because everything had happened so quickly. This accident made them closer than they'd ever been before. But how quickly time had erased the tight bond they had formed that summer! Andre now feared that friendships weren't meant to last, yet he knew he couldn't simply give up the struggle and be lonely forever—although there were times when solitude seemed preferable.

John, Andre, and an older boy, Ray, had known one another for several years. Andre had always respected Ray, mostly due to his being several years older than either John or himself. Ray was very outspoken and seemed to wield a power over the staff that neither Andre nor John possessed.

This spring, Ray convinced the houseparents to let him form a band. He met with a lot of resistance at first, due to the fact that the music, hard rock, was viewed by many of the older caretakers as offensive. Ray won out, and the band was formed. He invited John and Andre to be in the band with him, along with a few other students.

Both boys were very excited at the prospect. Also, with John and Andre practicing, it gave John less time to harass Andre, and a new bond between them arose. However, the imagined fun of being in the singing group was short-lived for Andre, as Ray was a perfectionist, and going over a song again and again took away from the glamor of actually being a "star."

The night of the presentation went well, but both John and Andre, having a small backup singing part, sensed that their performance was imperfect, at the very least. But the celebration afterwards made all their effort worthwhile. Andre's stomach had never been so full. With prideful joy, he boasted to many other boys that he had eaten an entire pizza pie. The memory would always be inspiring, but reality had a way of ruining hopeful dreams.

Chapter 6

Breakfast at Ruby's

i

Doctors D'Erable and Aguair met early in the morning on the 15th of August, the day they would send John Kline home.

D'Erable couldn't help thinking that Marilyn Aguair must know something about the envelope he had been sent, the one containing information about Andre's life.

"Marilyn," he said, "I know that John is to be released today, but as I haven't talked to you in a while, I'd like to know if you can help explain this mail that was delivered to me yesterday."

Marilyn looked carefully at the outside of the envelope. She then took out the papers and leafed through them. Her expression was one of surprise. She put the papers back into the envelope. "Stephen, I'd like to borrow these pages, or at least get a copy of them, in order to study this matter. Who do you suppose sent them?"

"I don't know. John's mystery was a handful. My thought was that you had sent them, until I noticed the stamps."

"Hmm, I noticed. I don't know anyone in India. Do you?"

"I visited a hospital there some years ago, but I really can't think of anyone who would send this story to me."

"Yes, you would expect that Andre would write about himself, that the story wouldn't be in the third person. I wonder what the person who sent the papers is trying to do? He or she must want your help. Was there anything in the package to indicate how or where to contact anyone?"

"No. There were no last names or anything like that. My suspicions are that this party will try to contact me in the future. Andre's story only went to the point where he was 10 or 11 years old. The sense I got from reading it was that the story wasn't finished."

"Yes, Stephen, I agree. And by the way, I'm glad you suggested this place to eat. This feta cheese omelet is great, and the coffee is good, too. About John—no, he isn't harming anyone else or himself. I assume that his ideas about extraterrestrials are, as we both figured, a sort of religion."

"I concur. I'm mystified by the test tube, but I suspect that John is using that material in the same way that people use the Shroud of Turin, to add mystery to what he's saying. Of course there could be a different explanation for his behavior or stories."

ii

Stephen and Marilyn were with John Kline in his room. John had his suitcase packed and was ready to leave.

Marilyn spoke first. "John, I want to thank you very much for your cooperation. The fact that you admitted yourself to this facility indicates a lot to me. My thoughts are that you came here to convince me of a truth that you believe in. I wish you the best in your future and hope that you won't hesitate to call on me if you need to."

Stephen added, "It was a pleasure talking with you, John. I hope you will achieve your goals."

John said, "Dr. Aguair, it was my pleasure to bring you the words of wisdom, and I am satisfied that you saw fit to share them with Dr. D'Erable. The plan I tried to set in motion has failed miserably. It was my understanding that you would have been given a message by now! It would be so clear to all of you if you had been given this wisdom. Something has apparently gone wrong.

"There seems to be some reason beyond my control, or even beyond that of the Schegnans and Metans, as to why I haven't heard the words needed to set my final plan in motion. You've read my explanation of these aliens, and I've talked at great length to both of you. But unfortunately, someone or something has altered the grand plan. The details aren't all known to me, yet, but I'm fearful for the future. The message I've been awaiting hasn't arrived, and now I fear that it never will."

Dr. D'Erable recalled the convention. Why hadn't this other patient specifically asked to speak to John? The doctor had been right in that John would be expecting a message, but he didn't think that all of this unfolding "plan" would be sprung on the doctors a few moments before John was to be released.

Dr. Aguair said, "John, we would like to be of help." She also suspected that there was a connection with the patient at the convention, but she didn't know how to broach the topic without planting ideas in Kline's mind. She continued, "We very much want to share the message, but honestly, how can we know how to assist you if we don't have a clue concerning how to proceed? You're very vague about the whole thing. We only wish you could be more specific."

John said, "It's not easy to explain. I suspect that one or both of you have been given a clue, but unfortunately, the connection between the message and me hasn't been understood. I don't think that any aliens of higher intelligence would want to change the course of our evolution, even if we were on the path of self–destruction, as I am afraid the whole of humanity is.

"That is not to say that there couldn't be intervention if they desired it. Think! We, the human race, have a lot of potential. You have both read my explanations of the beings I speak of. You should know that these higher minds are not arrogant, and they want to give developing races a chance. I thought you realized that they want to assess the world, and if they deem us worthy of contact because of our potential, then we should be able to figure out the subtleties they use to talk with us. Perhaps I'm being too optimistic. Maybe we aren't worthy of their assistance. I find this idea hard to believe, though, or why would they have bothered to go this far?

"I suppose it was my mistake. Maybe this wasn't the time or place to find the message I've been anticipating. I was sure the time was right to learn about Andre, John, Lisa and all the others. Sorry for that. The mistake was all mine. I am not perfect, but I was sure that the awakening was now! I must have read Psel wrong. I did expect to hear about the suppressors and Andre's place in the puzzle!"

At this point, Aguair and D'Erable exchanged the same glance of recognition they had shared at the convention in Boston. They had both understood that the patient there couldn't possibly have come up with the word "Schegnan" on her own. Andre was not the most common name, but there seemed to be more than coincidence going on here. Neither doctor was going to accept an extraterrestrial explanation, but they both knew that some kind of cogitation was necessary at this point.

Dr. Aguair spoke. "Ah, John, I am rather embarrassed to tell you this, but I seem to have forgotten to clear some of the red tape regarding your release. Could you wait here for us while we clear this up? We'll only be about half an hour."

"Of course," said John. "What's a half hour in the grand scheme of things?"

Chapter 7

Frantic Discussion

i

Stephen D'Earable and Marilyn Aguair left John to wait in his room. They went to Marilyn's office.

"Sue," said Dr. Aguair, "please have some coffee and pastry sent up, and oh, have the nurses make sure that John Kline in room 913 is kept waiting for me to return."

"Yes, Doctor," replied the secretary.

"So, Marilyn, let's not beat around the bush. We've been working with each other for long enough to know more or less how we both view this development. You also know that I'm curious to hear how you see things. I'm sure you feel that we are equals, now, as I'm no longer your instructor. So, what do you think?"

"Steve, it's obvious. We can talk about John's religion all we want. We can take the risk and send him home without revealing the package you received. I'd like to read it, but I take your word for it that there's nothing there to help John out, although he'd no doubt rationalize the whole thing if we shared the story of Andre with him. If John's belief in beings from outer space is some kind of delusion, won't we be fueling it by sharing what we know? We can't make him stay here, and I doubt he'd agree to spend more time here, especially when he was so prepared to go home today."

"Yes, I totally agree. Why don't we just give in and take our chances? I'm curious as to how John will react to this seeming breakthrough. My fear is that we'll be making fools of ourselves in the end. I only wish we knew about that mystery patient from the conference. It's a shame that doctor was so rude and didn't see the connection between John and her, as we did. I'll make a note and do my best to try to find her. I suspect the doctor won't be any more cooperative than before, though. We have to find a way to talk to this patient on our own terms. Here, Marilyn, I've also jotted this note for you. I suspect we can get something done if we work together."

Marilyn picked up the phone on her desk, dialed it, and spoke. "Could you please have John Kline escorted to my office?"

ii

Soon after, John was brought in and seated with the doctors. His expression was one of relief, indicating that he already knew that his message was soon to be revealed.

"So, John," said Dr. Aguair, "Dr. D'Erable and I have, as a matter of fact, just been given some unusual information about a certain Andre. A girl named Lisa is also mentioned. The only thing is that Dr. D'Erable doesn't feel that there is any connection with your aliens in these papers. Isn't that right, Doctor?"

"That's correct," said Dr. D'Erable, "I don't. To tell you the truth, it's just a story about a boy growing up. It's true that there are many interesting things that happen to Andre, but as for your Metans or Schegnans—"

John interrupted. "The whole message wasn't to be delivered at once."

Marilyn had an idea. "John, I don't want to force you into anything, but surely, as you yourself have stated, if Dr. D'Erable and I are part of this message process, then your aliens must think us worthy of being part of the process. I think we should arrange to meet regularly. I can share the message with you, and with your help, we can decipher it."

John answered, "Of course. That plan works perfectly! I feel honored to be a part of the aliens' plan."

After John had been dismissed, told to go home, and asked to make an appointment to return in a few days, the doctors shook hands.

Dr. D'Erable said, "Well, that was easier than I thought it would be. Good work, Marilyn. I've never seen a better job of convincing a patient to come back for outpatient counseling."

Chapter 8

Untying Some Knots

i

Dr. Aguair was in her first meeting with John since she had agreed to share Dr. D'Erable's mail from the anonymous sender. She had no idea how to proceed with this session, but she was sure that John would help her find the right direction somehow.

"So, John," she began, "I've been curious about many things since we had Dr. D'Erable's mail read to you. I'm curious about the message that is hidden there. Dr. D'Erable and I have no way of deciphering it."

"There's nothing hidden there. You should take it all literally. You must both know that Andre's biography isn't complete, or weren't you aware of that?"

"I suspected as much, but if what you say is true, then why should anyone care about Andre? How does it tie into your aliens?"

"I know that you and D'Erable have taken notes. You've been taking down everything I've said. Surely you can see the connection."

"No, John, to be honest, I can't. Why don't you summarize it all for me?"

"Okay, Marilyn, I will. It was such a nice, crisp September morning today. It reminded me of those faraway worlds. Metamo and Schegna, as you know, are about 13 light years away. It is said that when we are wise enough, maybe when some astronomer sees a star wobbling, then we'll know where these beings are. I will read from the summary I wrote. See, I do listen to you, Doctor.

"My name is Mellamo. I am from the planet Metamo. The planet is about 120 million miles from its sun. Our sun is remarkably similar to the Earth's. The solar system we share with the Schegnans is remarkably similar to the humans'. We have 11 planets in our system.

"The first two planets are very similar in size and distance to your Mercury and Venus. Our Mercury is a reddish color. Our Venus is slightly larger than yours, but otherwise it is identical. The third planet from our sun is called Schegna. It is very similar to Earth. Schegna has nine distinct land masses that spiral outward from the poles toward the equator. The ratio of land to water is 70%.

"Metamo, my home planet, is the fourth planet from our sun. It is, like Schegna, about 8,000 miles in diameter. We have about 60% water compared to our land masses, which range in size from one–half mile to thousands of square miles in size. The land looks as though it was placed around our seas in a random fashion. They are scattered almost evenly around the planet. The shapes of the land masses are generally oval or oblong. We have some that look like splotches. Some land masses are long and thin.

"The oceans of Schegna and Metamo are similar to one another and not unlike Earth's. Schegna's sky is a magenta color, due primarily to microscopic volcanic dust trapped in its atmosphere for millennia. Our sky looks like the humans', except that it is darker, kind of like late afternoon in winter if you're in New England. The atmosphere of Schegna is almost identical to Earth's. Metamo's is as well, except that our general environment contains toxins from volcanoes and our evolution that would probably be deadly to humans, or at least make them ill. Schegna could support humans well, as its climate is nearly identical to Earth's.

"Metamo and Schegna have seasons similar to Earth's, as well. However, we are much colder than Earth, on an average of 20 degrees, due to our distance from the sun. Our temperatures range from –75 to 30 degrees Celsius, but we are usually about 20 degrees colder than you are.

"Schegnan and Metan evolutions are similar to yours, but we branched off in different directions about 125,000 years ago, since our sun is a quarter–million years older than yours. We have observed that the universe is not confined by age and size, as humans believe, but that it is an infinite entity.

"When Metamo's mammals arose, there was much more volcanic activity than Earth had at the same stage of its development. These conditions of toxins made life even more tenuous than was seen on the human planet at the same point in its evolution. We had a lot of plants and fewer warm-blooded creatures. Our dinosaurs were rare, and they didn't catch hold— due, we have observed over years of study, to higher rates of toxins in our soil, water, and atmosphere. When things did catch up, the life that survived was much more vigorous, as it had to adapt even more than it did in your solar system.

"The evolution of Metans took place at about the same point in our evolution as yours did, but with a strange twist. While creatures similar to shrews were developing on my home planet, our plants were going through amazing changes. They were almost wiped out by the poisonous conditions of Metamo, as was almost all life.

"Many annuals were in danger of death, but about 100,000 years of astounding changes took place. A plant which is very similar to your bean plant, specifically the yellow–eye variety, was in danger of extinction. The best way the threat could be described would be to call it a plant cancer. Many trees and other varieties of growth didn't survive.

"As the bean plants were nearly wiped out by toxicity and unusual lumps which were robbing the life from them, an astonishing evolutionary leap occurred. As the dying continued and they shriveled up, leaving few seeds, the cancers fell off them.

"One day, as we like to say in our legends, but which probably took tens of thousands of years, the cancers which fell off the plants adapted to live on independently when their hosts died. At first they were not much more than photosynthetic lumps, about the size of a marble. They could eke out a life from our sun's rays. Soon, the plants they came from became a bit more resistant and made a meek comeback, allowing the cancers more time to evolve.

"In time, the plants almost exclusively gave up seeding when they died and actually had a symbiosis to allow the lumps to evolve. They would drop off and by now were able to sense and achieve locomotion. They even had insect–like legs, ate like omnivores, and photosynthesized, as well. These beings were now on their way to an independent evolution from their plant hosts.

"In time, they had amassed a very large number of genes and chromosomes. They were able to change some of their own genetic instructions to deal with specific conditions in their harsh environment. In about 250,000 years, they evolved through many similar mammal stages like the Earth's and eventually became humanoid.

"We, the Metans, are the result of this process that I have described. We are able to reproduce the same way humans do, but those same plants are still on our planet and leaving behind what we call pure Metans. We call ourselves this name because we are able to consciously change our body structures—

whether we came from a set of biological, warm-blooded parents, as you do, or whether we fell from our ancient revered bean plant. I am, incidentally, born of a bean plant. At one time in our history, this became contentious, but now we're all able to coexist. There isn't any difference between a sexually originated Metan or a plant-originated one.

"Like most of our species, I can metamize. This means, if, say, in a week, you wanted me to appear as a cat, I could go into a sort of hibernation, shed or absorb all my human tissue, and reshape myself in a feline form. At the heart of all Metans is the true being. The specimen you had analyzed in your French laboratory was a dead relative of mine whose last wish was to be sent to Earth. I'll get to that later.

"No matter what form we choose to take, there is our essence somewhere in the body controlling all the action. So we can only metamize to something bigger than a bean and smaller than an elephant, although we prefer the humanoid form the most, as it is what we evolved into most naturally. If you were to do an autopsy on a dead Metan, the anatomy would be strikingly humanlike. You would find somewhere in the body that specimen most similar to the one we sent to Earth. It would most likely be in the brain or head, and with a good microscope, you'd observe that it had tendrils which went out into the humanlike brain, controlling all the functions.

"People on your planet would find our brains more developed than yours, especially in the cortex region. Upon further observation, the core of us, the controller which contains the hundreds of genes, alleles, and chromosomes, but is no larger than a few beans or large marble, is the actual essence of us.

"It was once a great form of entertainment to go away for a few weeks and come back as something else, say a bird or a dog. This process takes from a few days to a few weeks to complete. It also expends a lot of energy and requires a great deal of concentration. About 20 percent of our species is incapable of metamization of any kind. The rest of us who can do it risk a five percent chance of death if we choose to do so. We suspect that this gift is to be used in times of severe evolutionary crisis.

"The Schegnans, in comparison, had an evolution virtually identical to humanity's. Both Metans and Schegnans went through periods of wars and famines. In time, we discovered each other when we began to explore our own planetary system. At first, we could observe through our telescopes that our nearest neighbors had buildings and cities. In comparison to what happened on Earth, this cut short the periods we wondered if we weren't alone in the universe.

"In time, we began to send out probes, landing them on one another's planets. Our other planets are quite similar in composition and distance to your Jupiter, Saturn, Uranus, Neptune, and Pluto. The other two planets in our system orbit our sun at about 10 million miles farther out than Pluto is from your sun. These outer two ice balls are about twice the size of your moon. They are almost identical.

"Our dual partnership greatly enhanced both our cultures' knowledge. The Schegnans are what you'd call psychic, but their abilities are much more complex than that simple human concept. They have a keen sense of intuition, as well as the ability to sense things like microexpressions and minute temperature changes, and are able to determine chemical changes associated with different emotions. They are also able to judge magnetic and electrical changes associated primarily with living beings, even plants.

"The ability of our nearest neighbor to appear to read minds was indeed impressive and of great scientific interest. The Schegnan humanoid would not appear to have any extra organs or sensory appendages, but they have become so fine tuned that it is second nature to them to be able to anticipate and understand those with whom they come in contact. It has even been alleged that they can bridge the stars with their powers and communicate with other races with a power they call telelinking. This has probably grown out of their great legends, as Schegnans are known for their literature and music, but their scientific accomplishments are also noteworthy.

"We have some empirical evidence that the rare Schegnan, say one in a thousand, can accomplish many mental feats. We have been able to demonstrate telelinking between our two planets, which are about 35 million miles apart, and there is no reason why this ability couldn't go farther out into the cosmos, but there isn't a Metan scientist, Schegnan poet, or anyone else we've known who can explain this extra ability.

"So it came to pass that we combined our abilities in many creative ways. We partnered in deep space explorations. We explored nearby stars. We had quite a relationship until we embarked on a journey to your solar system.

"The MetSche, our cooperative dual-species alliance to study the stars together, agreed on many strict ethics. We didn't want to interfere with the evolution of any worlds, especially ones that were developing, or ones we felt had great potential to become advanced. When we embarked on the journey, it was revealed that in our ancient times, neither of us would suspect that the other's planet had life. A Metan didn't think a purple-skied world could support life, and a Schegnan didn't think a dark blue-skied planet could support intelligent life, either. Luckily we had telescopes to see that we were wrong. Truly, our alliance was a rare one. Not only did we have one planet with life in our system, but two of them. We haven't found any other systems that could boast such good fortune, nor do we believe that it is even very likely.

"We came upon Earth at the time that your ancient Egyptian culture was blossoming. This discovery was the first world outside of our system that had life. Oh, we found microbes on another star system, which was a great discovery, but a culture of humanoid life was truly amazing. The sky was immediately remarked upon. It was brighter than our dark–blue sky and also that of Schegna. The climate was great for the Schegnans, and even we Metans liked your colder climates.

"We both realized the potential of humanity. It was distressing to see how very warlike your race was, but we weren't surprised, as Metans and Schegnans had passed through a similar state of mutual destruction. We waited and watched for millennia, and by the time you had discovered the power of the nuclear bomb, we had to make some decisions.

"The Schegnans seriously considered some kind of intervention to bring your species into a peaceful state of existence. Both of our races had long ago adopted a policy of not interfering with alien races, but they felt so strongly about the way humankind was going that the alliance was in danger.

"Metans and Schegnans had never before found themselves at odds about such an ideal as not interfering in evolution. It was now time for serious decisions to be made. The Schegnans were willing to break the age–old alliance. The Metans were quite concerned. How could they stop the Schegnans from doing the unthinkable? If the Metans tried to arrest the actions of the Schegnans, they might themselves affect the evolution of a planet.

"This is our hope for humanity, that co–existence will flourish. One thing we note is the natural skepticism of your kind. This trait can be of great use in science or it can be a stultifying force. I don't want you to take this evidence on faith, but realize that only recently has your kind found many oddities. You never thought life could exist near volcanic vents or use noxious chemicals as its basis. While you marvel at cracking genetic codes, you are still awestruck at how life can adapt in ways you had never imagined or even found in theory. Let me say this to humanity: Life, when it is fortunate enough to evolve on a planet, has great adaptability, or that existence will perish. We believe that, with all your technology and your underestimated physique, you will not die out any time soon. Our races are much more concerned that you will use your science to destroy one another. Yet we are also optimistic.

"We have the technology to lay waste to your planet, but this idea is quite repellant to us. One Metan ship could do the job in a mere few hours. A fleet of them could do it in five minutes. So, since we are nonviolent, why would we bring this fact up? It is only that human beings think that their technology is quite advanced, when in fact, it is very primitive. No, we would never resort to this primordial way of thinking, one rooted in violence. After all, you humans are not able to survive a simple hurricane or a rogue terrorist attack. The whole of your kind is quite inept at dealing with virtually anything that is not in the routine.

"So you needn't fear waking up and having the Metans and/or Schegnans vaporizing your cities with blue lights coming down from the sky. Peace, although it has been espoused by many leaders but truly understood by only a very few, seems to us at times elusive. We grant that your species has made some headway in this area, but your great military power belies your words.

"Yours isn't the only race that has gone this route. Indeed, our own planets evolved from such barbarity. If we hadn't, we might feel differently about Earth. That fact is the only reason we hold out hope for humankind. When your leaders become truly interested in their duty to the average citizen, then tranquility may grace your world at last. Metans and Schegnans are aware that they are not perfect; they are neither omniscient nor omnipotent. We do, however, have an eon of evolution over you, so it's logical that you should heed our advice. We don't desire conquest, but universal coexistence.

"The word 'alliance' is a good example of how your language is not sufficient to explain ideas like the MetSche. The alliance was much more than saving the remaining populations of our planets. Your Darwin's ideas touch the surface, but the principles of survival and growth go much further.

"The time that I am talking about is now 50,000 years in the past. The few leaders who waged the holocaust on both of our worlds were viewed as having a recessive gene that was probably once valuable for hunting or survival. Many of your human conditions, murder and so forth, can be explained in this way, but then again, one can't blame all behavior on inheritance.

"Even at that long-ago time, we were considerably more advanced than Earth is today, but we had falsely assumed that the negative traits of violence were already diluted. Our leading scientists proposed a revolutionary experiment. This work was to be done for much more than the elimination of negative conduct. We had theorized that there could be unforeseen mutations that could, in a natural way, eliminate the Schegnans and/or Metans. It was only in the last few millennia that we actually proved our idea by observing a small handful of planets much more advanced than ours go through what might be called devolution.

"The Schegnans sent 50 representatives to Metamo and the Metans sent 50 of theirs to Schegna. The words, again, are inaccurate. These 50 exchange scientists were to undergo a great pioneering effort. Half of the 50 on each world were male, and the other half were female. We will go into this later, but 15 of the 25 Metan males and 15 of the females were considered to be pure Metans, while the other Metans were from sexual roots.

"These representatives were to become totally immersed in each other's societies, much more so than in the past. The final goal was to have interspecies breeding. We felt that it would be arrogant to think that either of our cultures or its genetic traits could or would survive by themselves. This undertaking was a contingency plan for the future.

"After about 50 years, we saw the practicality of the grand study. Most Metans conceived and gave birth with no problems.

This outcome was expected, as well as the fact that only 52% of Schegnan's mating resulted in a conception, and of these, only 48% resulted in normal births. The other non–productive joining of sperm and egg resulted in miscarriages, which usually occurred within a few days of the mating. The occurrence of bad mutations on both planets was almost negligible, with the Schegnans having a slightly higher rate.

"It will be obvious later, but the MetSche decided not to have two Metan mates for each Schegnan female. The decision was seen as equitable or equally inconvenient to both the Metan male and Schegnan female. The anatomical issues will become obvious at a future time.

"The offspring of the experiments on both worlds also mingled their genes with the general population to further enhance genetic diversity. Some Schegnans, although rare, could metamize, but many more Metans found they had obtained the Schegnan's ability to link minds.

"There have been no official studies on humans' ability to mate with Schegnans and/or Metans, but there have been a lot of legends, and good science states that a human would no doubt be enhanced intellectually. Due to the relative youth of the race, it is doubtful that humans would acquire the ability to metamize or develop the Schegnan mind abilities, but then again, a rare birth would also be a possibility. This notion is not thinkable to the MetSche at this time, but there have been unsubstantiated stories that 'rogue' members of our alliance have interbred with humans.

"The experiments above were viewed by our cultures as a great success story. This is the reason why we continue the work today. Every millennium or so, Metans and Schegnans find 50 representatives from their planets to keep the mixing of the gene pool going.

"Well, Doctor," John concluded, "I don't have much else right now. You may be able to piece the rest of the puzzle together until I gather more material for you. I don't know the whole of what Andre has to do with all of this puzzle, but the Schegnan representative I am in contact with assures me that everything will be made clear when all Andre's details have been received by us. I am most anxious to find out myself, but I do have some ideas. Oh, Doctor, I want to thank you for giving my friend Stephen the bean plant. He was most anxious to see it. It will no doubt please him to see how many pods are on it and how healthy it is."

Dr. Aguair said, "John, I'm at a loss. If you're in contact with an alien, why can't they just fill in the blanks for us? I don't understand why this must be presented in such a mysterious way."

John answered, "We can't presume to tell them how to do things, given their advancement in evolution as compared to ours. Besides, why do you presume that they are all knowing? What more do you want?"

ii

Dr. Aguair was deep in thought after she had dismissed John from her office. The whole methodology of John's unwinding a mystery was fascinating and annoying to her at the same time. She would have dismissed his entire story if it weren't for the test tube that they had analyzed.

Marilyn didn't want to believe Kline's story, but she did want to understand what he was trying to tell her. Neither she nor Dr. D'Erable had ever had a patient that was so dynamic. They couldn't find anything wrong with John, but they were both interested in unraveling what he was saying, or trying to tell them.

Neither doctor could accept that John's words were merely to promote a self-made religion. Most people didn't go through such an elaborate process to explain a belief system, let alone one that dealt with extraterrestrials. Maybe the story about Andre was a way for John to share his childhood with the doctors, yet John had seemingly had no trouble explaining his past before.

Dr. Aguair returned from a luncheon with Dr. D'Erable, which they both left as baffled as they were when they had started. Dr. Aguair was preparing to finish her day with more predictable patients and duties, when she was surprised to see a large envelope in her mail. The foreign stamps and lack of return address instantly flashed recognition and curiosity in her mind.

Surely, she thought, my patients can be postponed for the afternoon while I try to figure all this out.

Chapter 9

"Andre's Story, Part 3—Germination"

i

Now Andre was excited. He had whetted his appetite with the wonder of science. The Apollo missions and Skylab were most inspiring. He longed to read science fiction stories. The speculations of the future were fascinating.

For some unknown reason, his mother was not inspired by these things. Andre's father was more understanding and had allowed him to watch *The Andromeda Strain*, as well as other movies forbidden by his mother. This only sparked his interest more. Andre was an avid reader of all kinds of science books in the school library. Even on summer vacations, he looked forward to the bookmobile, so he could learn as much as possible about his world. Now he was ready for science fiction.

Being around 11 years of age was one of the most wondrous times of his life. He was so excited to get a transistor radio at Christmas, as it represented a world of freedom for him. He was fascinated by *Mystery Theater*, which aired just around bedtime. After a couple of weeks of school, Mrs. D. had discovered that many of the children were listening to radios, and she forbade this practice. Andre only had to use his imagination to get around this prohibition. He just plugged in the earphone and lay on that side until Mrs. D. made her rounds. Apparently the others had given in to her, for when in March, Andre exclaimed, "Oh, 'The Snow Blizzard' was on *Mystery Theater* again last night," the reaction of "That's good" showed him that nobody was interested, nor were they talking about late night radio exploits.

John and Andre's relationship calmed down. At least John was no longer physically abusive. It was a bit annoying to hear him poking fun at just about everyone on TV, but Andre would laugh along with John, even though he felt it wasn't justifiable to do so. When John poked fun at Ralph, David, and Lisa, Andre's best friends, Andre would not laugh with him. He couldn't find words to defend his friends and felt that he'd probably be wasting his time if he tried.

The feeling of futility had developed into Andre not reporting any of his illnesses. When he had gone to camp for those weeks when he was 10, he had somehow thought he had contracted lead poisoning from a drop of paint he had gotten in his mouth from working on ceramics. Rather than tell anyone, he merely asked what was in the paint, and when he was informed there was lead in it, he suffered in silence. He was probably unaware that Pat's devil story was influencing him subconsciously. It was odd that he felt relatively peaceful until he got home, but the first night back, the nightmares of paralyzing fear and helplessness came upon him. By contrast, he slept quite peacefully the night Pat told the story.

This pattern repeated itself once in metal shop. Andre got a very small splinter in his finger from working on something, but he told nobody. Even when a large boil developed some weeks later and it began to hurt, he spoke to no one. Only his piano teacher discovered it one day when she grabbed his finger to show him the correct position to play. His cry of pain and her discovery of the boil ended that. The pain of having it scraped was bad, even with the numbing spray the nurse used.

John and Andre were now to embark on a sort of adventure. They were now called "Pioneers," and they were to leave the school to walk across town to go to a regular school for the day. This was exciting until they discovered how unpleasant it was to walk to the school earlier than the others started class and in all kinds of inclement weather. They were also disappointed that their day ended earlier than for the children at the boarding school.

Andre's spirits were always uplifted by the crossing guard named Mac. He was always in a good mood and cheered Andre up. John and Andre didn't understand why they had to bring their white canes, as they both felt they could see well enough, even the walk light. John said of Mac, "We don't need him to help us. We can both cross streets by ourselves." Andre agreed, but he was glad that the guard was there, if only as a friend.

The school away from school was a disappointment to Andre. John seemed to feel the same, but he reported himself happier than Andre. Nobody acknowledged Andre. John was separated into another class, and they rarely saw each other there during the day. They only met to go to and leave the property.

Andre felt he wasn't learning anything there compared to his real school. Nobody talked to him, and he could understand that a total stranger was not welcome. Yet at his real school, all his friends had been total strangers at first. Perhaps it was his knowledge that the program was only for a year that helped him resign himself and not try to reach out.

He was never invited to play sports with the others. He would probably have regretted the invitation, as he had never cared much for athletics, feeling that he was simply wasting his time there. He could easily disappear backstage in the gym or go around a corner outside, and nobody was the wiser. Or maybe they simply didn't care. At least nobody poked fun at him the way John was doing to others.

ii

In February, Andre received the bad news that he needed an eye operation. He'd been told many times by his mom and dad that he had had nine of them by the time he was two years old. By this time, Andre had heard people discussing certain drugs and how good they made one feel. He had heard some talk of this on TV, about how bad such drugs were; he had the impression of criminals and bad people dealing in these substances. Lisa had stated that having an operation was fun, and that the gas made her see pretty colors. Once, though, she had felt as though she was having a nightmare.

Trying to be the optimist that he felt he had to be, Andre decided that it would be fun to be put under. The day came, and he felt silly being told to lie down in bed in the afternoon in his pajamas. A burly black doctor had come to give him a physical, but he only took Andre's pulse. Andre was disappointed that he didn't complete his job.

At midnight, Andre was given apple juice and told by a nurse, "Don't be nervous. They'll give you Pentothal. It's good stuff." An orderly had mentioned earlier to him, "You'll be singing in the operating room."

When morning came, Andre was told to bathe and make sure he didn't leave any water in his ears. He was then given a shot in each buttock, which felt kind of like being punched. Soon he felt himself floating on a stretcher and awoke before he realized the operation had begun. Now he felt quite lousy, a bit sick. Time seemed to drag by, and with a patch over his eye, he couldn't tell if it was night or day. The nurses giggled when he asked what time it was and they told him "It's eight o'clock." Andre queried, "In the morning?"

After this, he felt that at this rate, the night would drag on forever. He began to cry because he had no visitors, and the pain of the surgery along with his tears got him worrying that he'd lose the sight he had.

In the morning, his patch was removed and he was released. While waiting for his parents, he noticed that the sun shining on his face with his eyes closed felt like a knife. Soon all of this passed. Andre wasn't too keen on having any more operations, as they told him that they were only to remove cataracts, and that he shouldn't expect to gain any more sight. For a few weeks, he did have some improvement, and he fancied that he'd be driving a car someday. Alas, his doctor was correct. The effects wore off, and Andre's vision was back to where it had always been.

Later in the year, Andre was uplifted by *Free to Be You and Me*. He fancied a world like the one the songs portrayed. Andre could accept others' likes and dislikes, but he didn't understand why these people who gave the lessons didn't live up to them. The hypocrisy of it all was disheartening to him, but he held onto the hope of it and cherished the friends that he did have.

By now, Ralph and Andre had spent a lot of time together. One day, Andre, in his usual fashion, conducted a "science" experiment. They had gotten into Batman quite a lot and very fervently believed that the arch-villains from TV had been prowling the grounds of the school at night. Ralph was also convinced that a "bad guy wrestler," which Andre didn't follow, was also lurking around.

One day, as they stood by a black car, Andre asked, "Oh, Ralph, what color is the wrestler's car?" Andre knew Ralph couldn't see a thing, as he had witnessed Ralph cleaning his glass eyes many times. Andre was shocked when Ralph guessed the color.

Okay, thought Andre, I'll test him on the car's size and license plate number.

To his amazement, Ralph got that right as well. Andre found it difficult to believe this was coincidence, especially when, one

Wednesday, he bet that he knew what one boy was thinking about. Andre guessed, "You're thinking of going home on Friday." The boy stated that he was correct, and that was enough to set Andre's mind going into all sorts of fanciful directions.

June came, and Andre and John had finished their duty to the school by participating in their assigned program. They had both thought they would get to go to the upper school, where the older junior high school boys and girls went. They were shocked to learn that they were being held back, and both stated that they had been ripped off. One more year as lower school boys felt like such an injustice! At the same time, Andre sensed that somehow he must have missed something at that other school and hadn't learned a thing. Summer would ease their feelings and memories, and the next year would be relatively normal. The upcoming season would bring Andre many new lessons and experiences.

iii

Andre must have had some sort of hangover from the previous year. He enjoyed listening when his mom's friends visited, and he felt himself as much an adult as they were. One day he gulped down a drink and exclaimed, "I drank Janet's screwdriver!" His mother informed him that it was plain orange juice.

Andre's only older brother had given him the smaller of his two paper routes. Andre could deliver his dozen or so papers quickly and have a little pocket money. It made him feel more equal to his brothers, as he had no other way to match wits with them socially or intellectually. He always felt belittled in their presence, especially when they talked about sex and drugs.

Shirley, one of his mother's friends, visited regularly. She was always happy to cheer Andre up and even insisted that he be allowed to talk and listen when she talked with his mother. His mother would ask him to go out and play, but Shirley could always override her wishes.

They would discuss religion on various levels. She being a Protestant and Andre being brought up a Catholic made for very interesting discussions. Perhaps his mother feared that Shirley would be a bad influence on him, but Shirley's ideas about papal infallibility and the individual's heart, rather than the idea of confession, weren't subversive to him. Indeed, Andre's father had often voiced these ideas to Andre in private, but not with such eloquence and vigor as Shirley did.

Shirley had a very vivacious personality, and she gave both Andre and his mother an interesting alternative to a Catholic upbringing. He found it stimulating to discuss God and such from different viewpoints. Andre's mother was not so easily swayed, and still insisted that they go to church every week. Andre didn't really mind this activity, but he was not so taken in as he used to be, due to Shirley's new insights.

Shirley's lust for God and life had a negative side. She seemed very sure that Andre could be granted a miracle and that he could be a great musician. He was somewhat familiar with the stereotype that all blind people are musically gifted. The truth was that he had become disenchanted with piano lessons. He was quite aware that he wasn't gifted and might not even be average.

Andre's mother continued to go out with Shirley. Shirley took her friend to a fortuneteller, who had many things to say, good and bad. Andre's mother was shocked that the woman "knew" that Andre was getting a big gift, but also that there would be a robbery in the neighborhood. The theft never occurred, but yes, Andre got his piano.

He knew better than to say he didn't want a piano. Indeed, he was actually quite caught up in all the excitement. Besides, Shirley's immutable faith in him did a lot to boost his spirits, even though he knew deep down that he wanted to be a scientist of some kind when he grew up, not a pianist. Yet it was exhilarating that others seemed to gawk at his puny abilities. It was very easy for him to get an audience and then great approval from Shirley and the neighbors, even though his "concerts" were not much more than they'd been in school when he'd practiced.

He was now aware of how easily so many others were taken in by magicians, fortunetellers, priests, and so forth. Even at this young age, he had some sense of the scientific method, and he was amazed to realize how much people accepted on mere emotion, even if the facts to the contrary were right in front of them. The biggest mistake he would make was to assume that others would share his enthusiasm for science and all that it implied.

Consequently, the honeymoon with the piano quickly wore off. His parents didn't push him too hard, yet they would often persuade him to practice even when it was not what he desired. Perhaps it was the sense of the monetary value of the piano and the great expense on his father's part that caused the boy to capitulate. Inevitably, though, any guilt or second thoughts were not enough to make Andre an accomplished pianist. In the end, he was not even a good amateur performer for the neighbors.

He wished he could go back in time and fix it so that his parents had never purchased the piano. He was sad that they saw only music in his future. Now, with his body and mind entering a new phase, he definitely had a flare for and great interest in math and science. He was especially interested in automation, robots, the future in space, and science fiction. He knew very well the difference between a fictional future of possibilities and the realities of current science. He was enthralled by the hopefulness of tomorrow, but he was also aware of the dark possibilities, especially when it came to mankind's ability to be cruel, selfish, or generally chaotic.

Things that Shirley, Andre, and his mother shared were strong faith and belief. Shirley had been very interested in taking Andre to see a healer, but this time, Andre's mother had won. That hot, humid night, he spent a few hours alone in his room upstairs in tears. He didn't want to attend the service to spite his mother, but rather to ask for a miracle for an unfortunate boy at school. This boy had no sight at all and was obviously what some people called retarded. This label was not only offensive because most people used it incorrectly, but it was also a cruel dagger. Andre cried, half–praying that he hadn't meant to be selfish in wanting to go to the service; he was pleading with God to heal this boy instead of himself. This tearful wishing was imposed upon a background of increasing bodily awareness.

It was a joy to deliver the papers and have a jump on the news. The headlines seemed to be full of hope. At last, the Vietnam War was over. The Apollo–Soyuz mission was a definite sign of hope. The Viking mission to Mars was a pleasure and maybe could answer some questions, although Andre found it hard to believe that there was life there. Watching TV was a joy. To see the U.S. and Russia cooperating on the screen gave him a sense of ease. It was a nice change from the history and atmosphere in which he had been brought up.

In all this optimism, Andre felt that he had nobody to share it with. He wondered if his being away at a boarding school had something to do with that. The efforts he made seemed fruitless. His best allies were Mathew and Jimmy. He'd known them for years, but they'd been spending less time with him in the past year or so. A clique seemed to be developing in the neighborhood that he was not part of. At times he was glad of this, as he sensed that some of the members were bullies, to judge by what they said and did. Andre didn't relish physical fights, which were more common in the neighborhood than they ever were at school.

iv

That fall, school began uneventfully. Andre had no great fears. The cab rides were more interesting than before. Tim was an older boy who liked *Star Trek* and all sorts of scientific things. He readily engaged Andre in discussions about things from life on Mars to thunderstorms. These were not popular topics of conversation among most of the kids at their school, so to find someone willing to talk about them was a treat.

Andre had grown numb to the bad aspects of people around him. He continued to enjoy his classes and to improve in his subjects. At this point, he was still optimistic about the possibility of a better future being on the way for all of humanity.

The highlight of the year was election day in November. Andre had stayed home for the week because he had a cold. By Tuesday, he already felt much better. It was a cold, crisp day. Andre was as excited as his father about the presidential race. If only he could have voted, the day would have been perfect. It was an exciting week, nonetheless, and he enjoyed being out of school for the week.

With the arrival of his 13th birthday, he felt he had reached an important milestone. He knew he wasn't grown up, yet, but he felt that he was just as intelligent as any adult. Indeed, the year at school was going quickly. He knew that soon he would be liberated to junior high school. He was sure the upcoming summer would be fun.

That summer, Andre's relationship with his favorite aunt solidified still more. For a couple of years, now, she had made it plain that she was very fond of him. Andre had always spent his summers in Maine and Québec. In Maine, he would see his paternal grandparents, aunts, uncles, and cousins. This was always a fun journey. His maternal relatives lived in Québec.

His aunt was in her mid–40s and lived with her parents, Andre's grandparents, in Maine. She had been a nurse and was willing to talk to him about many aspects of medicine. She even empathized with his enthusiasm for science fiction, although she herself was not a fan. She took him to the bookstore and treated him to a dozen books about poltergeists, UFOs, and psychic abilities.

Previously, when his mother made her frequent trips to Janet's house for coffee, Andre had been able to watch *Star Trek* and many other types of things his mother disallowed. She'd often state she'd be gone for 15 minutes to an hour, but he soon learned that she could be gone for two or three hours. Even when she would catch him, he would look forward to the next time, and she didn't do much in the way of disciplining him.

Yet this summer, his mother surprised him. She took all the books that his aunt had bought him away from him. Even his aunt couldn't convince her to give them back. Not only did Andre feel that this was a blow to his rights, but he also felt it as a personal slight, and he became disillusioned.

It was a hot summer. Andre spent time with Mathew, a neighbor. They had once caught bees together. Now, things seemed different. Although they got along well, Andre wanted to be closer to him, somehow. He often lay awake late at night, thinking of how he could be closer to Mathew. They didn't seem to have as much fun together as they had in the past. They were heading in different directions, and Andre could do nothing to change this fact.

He didn't fare much better during his usual stint at the religious summer camp. It seemed unusually hot, humid, and buggy this year, and there also seemed to be a lot more people than usual. Every year, Andre had entertained the idea that that particular year was the last he would attend, but he always found himself returning to the camp every summer. He was much less interested in the daily worship ceremonies than he'd been in the past. Also, Pat, the man in charge of all the singalongs, the one who had terrified Andre with his graphic tale of the devil, seemed more spiteful than in the past. His aunt was the only person with whom Andre shared this. She was very helpful in empowering Andre to, as she would say, "Fight the devil and tell him to go to hell!" This idea turned out to be very useful.

Andre was quite interested in controlling his dreams. At school, a roommate had instructed him that he could dream of Russell if he thought about him enough. Andre realized that he didn't know this Russell, and that was why he couldn't dream about him. Yet he seemed to be able to dream about going to the moon or into space if he thought of it hard before sleep. This same method helped him overcome and eliminate the satanic dreams and fear that had stalked him.

Being at camp, however, somehow felt like a loss of control. Since it was 1976, the year of the American Bicentennial, Andre had expected a great fireworks display over the camp lake on the Fourth of July. He was almost in tears that night when they didn't happen. It hadn't even occurred to him to inquire about whether or not there would be a celebration; he had just assumed that everyone at camp would be as excited as he was about the festivities. But that day, there was no mention of any Fourth of July festivities, and nothing was done any differently. It was just another day.

Chapter 10

"Andre's Story, Part 4—Through the Blinding Snow"

i

Andre was very excited as he entered his new room in the upper school. This change represented new hope for him. His roommates were at least familiar to him from earlier years. The two Michaels and John, his old nemesis, weren't going to dampen his spirits.

The new houseparents were all very nice—for a change. Andre especially liked Erma. The food seemed better than before, and he even liked all his new teachers. He was especially fond of learning algebra, was thrilled with the science program, and even liked Spanish. He would have preferred to learn French, but it wasn't offered. Spanish was the only foreign language course available, and it was a requirement.

He liked gymnastics the least. However, it was impressive to have one's own locker and a giant changing room for all the guys, with a large walk–in shower, which was new. This setting made the whole episode tolerable, as he could get himself weighed every week, although it wasn't necessary. Andre liked the attention of the teacher. Bill was not a mule driver, and he made the class almost enjoyable. However, running was a bit taxing, and it seemed fruitless to Andre.

All in all, the year went well. Andre had grown numb to the jesting of Michael and John, although he hated the fact that they poked fun at everyone, including him. The other roommate was much more appealing to Andre, as he didn't seem so willing to poke fun.

Chorus was another joy. Most of the boys used this class to bandy back and forth, irritate the instructor, and throw their jabs at almost everyone. Andre was attentive and enjoyed the class very much. It seemed that most of the others weren't as impressed, or maybe they just went along with the senior leader. Cornell was older than Andre and much taller. Andre had always been the tallest in the past, but now John, his nemesis, was catching up to him.

Andre felt intimidated by Cornell. It was Cornell's attitude that really did it. He was quite the clown, but always at the expense of others. Andre was attracted to him as an older guy to look up to, yet he felt belittled at the same time. Soon Andre mimicked him and the others to draw attention away from himself, or maybe to be accepted by the group.

Andre was glad to be more independent, now. He was allowed to go off campus, and he and David often went to the diner for coffee, to talk alone. Andre had also gone to other places off campus, places where he wasn't cleared for yet. He didn't feel that the teachers could accurately judge his abilities.

Ken had become one of Andre's favorite staff members. Erma was a good substitute mother figure, but Ken was much nicer than Andre's father. Ken's strictness, sternness, tall stature, and booming low voice all attracted Andre, but most appealing of all were the man's fairness and the sense of brotherliness that he projected. Many other students felt intimidated by Ken's style, but Andre knew the rules and how to keep in line. He couldn't help his strong emotional and physical bonding with Ken.

What really solidified Andre's feelings toward Ken was the school Christmas party. Every year, Andre had loved the real pine trees, the many decorations, and the authentic wreaths hung on the main doorways outside. The food and festivities, choral concerts, and all the other trappings almost overshadowed the festivities at home. This year, as in other years, gifts were exchanged via the Secret Santa method. Names were picked by students and staff, and only at the party did the recipients find out who'd gotten them their gift.

It was a lovely surprise when Andre received a large, exquisite tin of butter cookies and an equally impressive dark chocolate bar filled with hazelnuts. He hadn't specifically asked for these items, but was very happy that Ken had been aware that he was so fond of sweets and desserts. Anjali said that someone must have told Ken about Andre's likes and dislikes, but Andre was sure he'd never mentioned these items in particular. He knew that Ken was simply very caring. From that point on, Andre's respect and admiration for Ken grew exponentially. Although Andre knew that Ken would never be able to fulfill his fantasies, from then on, if anyone asked Andre what was on his Christmas wish list, he would tell them that it included butter cookies and a chocolate hazelnut bar. Forever after, Christmas would be incomplete without those trappings.

Christmas was a joy that year. Andre got up when it was starting to get light. The snow had begun to fall. It was the first white Christmas he'd had. He was overjoyed to get a calculator, which seemed to be all the rage that year. He loved any kind of gadgets, especially since he'd seen the computer and reading machine for the blind at school. The snow stopped by late afternoon, and he visited with his relatives. Everything looked and felt right to make it an outstanding and memorable Christmas.

Given that he was now entering maturity, it was becoming more difficult for Andre to concentrate, especially in the dull classes like woodshop. There he daydreamed, enjoying sexual fantasies. He was often late for these classes, and only stated that he'd been in the bathroom. This excuse wasn't taken very well by the teachers, yet it wasn't really a lie. Soon, he would learn to temper his urges, at least to a point.

ii

This summer, Andre's mother had convinced him to go on daytrips with a neighborhood recreational group. He agreed, figuring it would be the best way for him to meet new people.

It was now in his mind that he must be more adult. He didn't really enjoy going to the park pool. The people in the group had obviously been schoolmates for years. Andre got along with them okay, but he was still an outsider. He was finding that he was gravitating toward his older brother's and sister's older friends. Naturally, the few years in age difference made it difficult for him to really feel welcome, so he decided to strike out on his own.

His father went occasionally to the local bar, and a lot of the older people had mentioned that they sold cigarettes there in a machine and didn't care who entered. Once, Andre stole a cigarette from Janet, his mother's regular visitor. He went behind Jackie's house and sat on the footbridge to smoke it. It was about two feet above the water, but the ditch ran dry in the summer, and this was a good hiding place with all the tree cover. He found it interesting that he got very dizzy and even a little nauseated from smoking the cigarette. He figured that being a big boy, he should be able to put up with the discomfort.

One day, he was able to put two quarters into the machine and buy his first pack of cigarettes. He wore out the novelty of it all in a week or so, sneaking into the dried-out riverbed in the afternoon and feeling very smug about getting away with such a no-no.

Still, he had felt proud of himself for venturing into the adult world, a bar, where he could purchase his smokes from the machine. The annual camp ritual was approaching, and he wanted to have some cigarettes to smoke in case the opportunity arose.

By some fluke, Andre's parents were to pick up Ray and drive him along to the camp with Andre. This prospect was exciting, as Ray had left the school some years ago, after they'd had the band, and Andre hadn't seen or heard from the other boy for some years.

The ride was very interesting, to say the least. Ray was bragging about his adult knowledge, and he quizzed Andre on various aspects of being a grownup. Andre knew most of what Ray was talking about, so he simply faked a "yes" answer when Ray asked him if he knew about so-and-so. Ray was also singing various sexually explicit lyrics to songs that he considered cool. Other songs concerned the use of various drugs. To Andre's amazement, his parents were totally silent while all this was going on, and they never asked him later about Ray.

At camp, Ray was quite vocal in telling his friend Robert that he'd brought marijuana and PCP to the camp. Andre was practically begging Ray to let him try some pot, but Ray was concerned about getting caught, and even when Andre told him that he'd brought his own cigarettes, Ray was still not moved by Andre's pleas.

In the middle of the week, coincidentally, the camp had prepared a demonstration of the dangers of cigarette smoking. Later that night, Andre was alone, smoking a butt, and was caught by a camp counselor. Naturally, they took his cigarettes away. When Andre learned that Ray had been caught smoking pot, he was actually relieved that Ray hadn't let him go along.

When Andre's parents came to pick him up, they asked, as usual, "So, how did Andre behave this week?" The junior counselor in attendance nearly gave Andre away. But a swift look from Andre and his insistence that nothing unusual had happened were enough to silence the counselor, and his parents were none the wiser. He returned home without cigarettes but relieved that he had gotten away with something. He would continue his experimentation.

Then it came time for his paternal grandparents' wedding anniversary. With all the relatives there, his cousin Sue was able to smuggle him some beer, which he drank behind a bush. After the fourth one, he was feeling quite giddy. His older cousin Jean asked, "Andre, are you drunk?" He naturally denied it, but it was obvious he was staggering a bit.

Actually, his own mother didn't know what was going on. She was just wondering why he was so vocal, singing and laughing. Andre simply answered that he was overjoyed for his grandparents, to which she replied, "That's fine, but you don't have to act like a little kid about it!" The husband of one of his cousins, a man Andre respected mostly because he'd given him a ride in his Corvette and was always interested in Andre's conversations, remarked later that night that he knew Andre had drunk beer, and also that Sue was his "pumping station." Andre didn't sense any disapproval in the man's tone of voice, and he felt that this was an unspoken endorsement of his drunken exploit.

When Andre told an older girl in the recreation group about his drunken time at his grandparents' anniversary celebration, she stated that she didn't believe him. Andre sat there on the bus, shocked. What about it was so hard to believe? Her reaction only reinforced his feelings that he had nobody to share with, and it made him feel even more alone.

iii

Andre was very happy to be starting eighth grade. He had become proficient at running the small snack bar and relished the idea of earning a bit of extra money to spend on food, coffee, and other treats. He wasn't a big fan of the school's food, although it was better than it had been when he was a child. But he did feel a need to supplement his diet with frappés, donuts, and other goodies.

David was really the only friend with whom Andre could discuss science and math and speculate on the bigger issues of the world and universe. Andre had taken Ralph out with him on various occasions. Andre enjoyed Ralph's company, but for some reason, Ralph had been put in another cottage with the "retards." Soon, Andre realized that Ralph had some emotional problems, but Andre always considered him a good friend. Even David had been segregated when Andre was younger, and they had to meet secretly, as the staff didn't approve of their friendship—or, more likely, they didn't want to be responsible for David being out of their sight or Andre not being accounted for.

The year was going well. The best part of it was that David was Andre's roommate. They could share a lot late into the night. They were both growing up. Once, they smoked cigars, and of course others noticed the odor. Erma, whom Andre had always respected, was more concerned with the fire hazard than with the fact that they were smoking. She sent both of them to detention after school for a few days. Andre hardly considered this a punishment. He very much admired his gymnastics teacher, who oversaw this ritual. All he insisted on was quiet, and he'd say, "If you have homework, do it. If not, find something to read. Just don't bother me, or you'll be back tomorrow."

Andre had been sent to his gymnastics coach most often from cooking class. Andre liked the cooking teacher, but he felt that she was treating the class too delicately. He didn't want to hear that frying was too advanced at this stage. She wasn't impressed with the fact that he had done things at home that were far more advanced. She insisted that one must prove oneself in her class and complete the prescribed course. Andre wasn't really mouthy, but just the fact that he talked back some and insisted on being stubborn had him sent to detention. He would often get himself punished just as an excuse to visit his coach. Andre found the quiet he imposed more conducive to study than the designated study hall.

By early February, he learned that it wasn't going to look too good on his school record to be punished so often, especially considering that he was on the college prep track. Furthermore, Sally, his advisor, who was also his algebra and biology teacher, found this juvenile behavior beneath his abilities and potential. "I'm surprised at this, Andre," she said. "You're such a good student otherwise."

Andre was very excited about all his classes at school. He also sensed that his oncoming adulthood was somehow in conflict with his goals of being a good student. He felt great hope for the future, one that would see him going to college and being a contributor to science. But he also wanted to be able to enjoy the finer things in life.

This Monday morning in February was cold and gray, with light snow falling. In the past, John and he would anxiously wait to hear on the radio, "No school today. All schools in..." They could both relish the fact that they wouldn't have to trudge off to class. Yet here, even with snow, there were no days off, so they always had classes. At least it was preferable to be in a boarding school than to have to walk in the cold and snow to their school away from school.

This day was different. By noon there were a few inches of

snow on the ground. Such a winter treat had always been a nice aesthetic touch to the usual day-to-day activities. But today, school was dismissed early, and teachers who commuted daily were concerned about a great storm. This day would usher in the first series of snow days at the boarding school that Andre had experienced.

Monday night brought the usual excitement on television. Outside, the wind picked up, and the snow was very heavy. Large snowdrifts were beginning to form, and there was the sense that the teachers who weren't on campus would really not be able to make it. Andre actually looked forward to and liked most of his classes, but he was delighted by the novelty of a mini-vacation.

This hope was realized in the morning. The only teachers close enough to school to make it were his gymnastics teacher and the teacher who was in charge of the student store. Andre had persuaded his coach not to push him too hard. In addition, the man put up with his slight tardiness and general lack of interest. The teacher did, however, insist on *some* effort on Andre's part. This way, he wouldn't get a really bad grade for the class, and he had the satisfaction of knowing that he was good enough to meet the high standards that were set for him.

With the snow, along with the semi-vacation atmosphere at school, Andre was happy to put on his gym shorts and do a little running for his coach. He was happy enough just to be in the man's presence, for he was one of the few people who didn't make fun of Andre and who was understanding of his physical shortcomings. Andre was impressed with the fact that his gymnastics teacher was so muscular and had a good sense of discipline. He appreciated this ethic and applied it in his own way when it came to his math, science, and literature studies.

It was a fun week. Andre spent a lot of time in the student store, drinking coffee and eating chocolate and muffins, in addition to listening to the jukebox. He and David did a lot of talking there, as well. Andre liked working behind the counter and making sales. It was a joy to know that every order he filled meant a little more money at the end of two weeks.

The happiness of that week was short lived. Arrangements were made to have teachers brought back to school. By Thursday, the school was back to its normal daily routine, while on the outside, the other schools and surrounding city were in a quiet mode. By Friday, restaurants and other venues were back to normal, but the staff and teachers at school had insisted that nobody venture off campus, as it was too dangerous. Andre felt that if things were back to normal outside, he had the right to sneak away from school with David to enjoy it. The snowbanks gave him some second thoughts, but they both forged ahead anyway.

iv

Spring brought stronger emotions and heightened awareness to Andre. He had ventured all around the campus in his usual wanderings. This particular day, he was in a bathroom stall, thinking of how he needed to connect physically and emotionally with someone. Not only did he want understanding, but he also felt that he could give peace and comfort to another person. There was another boy in the bathroom who was much younger than Andre. After a few minutes, Andre felt a sense of disgust and shock that he could be thinking this way. He left and found himself in tears on the grass, wondering and crying out, "What's wrong with me?" He was in a general haze of loneliness and sorrow for a couple of days after that.

By now, he had been able to boast to John that he had tried

smoking marijuana with his older brother, and that it didn't seem to have any effect on him. Andre didn't understand what the fuss was all about, and he found it strange that John had brought the subject up the very day Andre had returned to school after trying pot with his brother. A couple of weeks later, he went with his brother again. This time, he became well aware of how the drug could change his moods.

On occasion, John brought some pot back to school, and they both found places near the gymnasium or in a closet to indulge. Andre's brother would take him out with his friends to do the same. Andre enjoyed this escape. He also enjoyed feeling more "normal," one among his brother's friends and more of an equal to John.

To Andre, the best thing about his independence was that he could drink as much coffee as he liked. His mother often worried about his blood pressure and general health, in addition to forbidding him to use caffeine. His father was not concerned, nor were the people at the school, so Andre enjoyed coffee both on and off campus.

In April, on a Friday morning, when he was getting ready for breakfast, he stood up and his heart seemed to feel funny, beating very fast, and he felt a slight pressure. When breakfast was over, he felt these strange and scary sensations again. One good thing was that he could be late for ceramics class with an excuse. However, he was very frightened.

The nurse told him to come in on Monday morning, as the doctor wasn't able to examine him right away. The nurse did a preliminary examination, looking for collapsed veins, as she emphasized when she placed the stethoscope on his crotch. She noted that his heartbeat seemed a bit slow, but couldn't tell him much more.

The afternoon came, with Andre very worried. He was about to get in the cab for the ride home when the sensations struck with more intensity than before. He felt weak, and thought he might faint. This experience was terrifying to him, as he seriously wondered whether he'd live through the weekend and even get to see the doctor. He didn't feel that he could confide in anyone about his worries. His mother was very prone to worry, especially when it came to medical issues. She would even stoke his worries by adding her own.

Monday afternoon came in its own time. Andre's heart seemed fine most of the time, and he hadn't experienced too many more palpitations over the weekend. He very much liked this doctor, an older gentleman. Andre knew that his examinations were for evaluation purposes, but he felt glad that the doctor paid attention to him and didn't seem judgmental. Andre felt the warmth of trusting someone who had his interest at heart.

This exam was a bit of a surprise for Andre. He didn't have to disrobe, but only had his pulse and blood pressure taken, along with the doctor listening to his heart. The doctor said, "It sounds like a perfectly healthy heart to me."

Andre was amazed when the doctor asked him yes/no questions that seemed to target exactly what he'd felt, especially when the physician described it as a fluttering. He was also able to deduce that Andre's pulse was never over 160. He even knew how long the episodes had lasted.

In the end, the doctor got Andre to tell him how much coffee he'd been consuming. The advice he then gave, in a very warm and understanding manner, was to not indulge in that second, third, or fourth cup of coffee quite as often, and not at every meal. There was also the fact that Andre took coffee breaks between meals. With these excesses in mind, the doctor advised Andre merely to use discretion and cut his coffee consumption.

Following that sound advice, Andre was amazed at how quickly his bad symptoms disappeared. This cure only enhanced his respect for the medical man. He'd certainly not wasted the good doctor's time by visiting unnecessarily, but Andre was always glad for an opportunity to see him. Usually the annual physical was it, but the occasional cold or rash was inevitable.

Andre's relief that his heart wasn't giving out was a welcome prelude to the upcoming summer vacation. He was still able to enjoy his coffee, and he did so regardless of comments made by some of the staff. The remarks were usually to the effect that he'd be late for class, and that "This isn't a coffee klatsch." He had learned how to enjoy the taste and lift of coffee, which he felt he had a right to, but also how not to overindulge.

By the end of the year, Andre almost fancied himself an adult. He had decided to skip the junior class fair and go with Ralph to the commons. There they chatted, caught up on old times, had coffee, and ate. Skipping the fair might have gotten them both in serious trouble. However, Andre was correct when he convinced Ralph to go by saying, "Oh, nobody will even miss us! They'll be too busy having fun."

Andre had entertained the idea of going off again and skipping the final assembly, but there were no takers. Surprisingly, even David didn't want to skip it. There, to Andre's total amazement, he received the top prize for scholarship, a certificate, and a $50 savings bond. He was totally shocked. What would he have used as an excuse if he hadn't been present for such an honor?

V

That summer, every week or so, Andre's brother would drive him around to the park or drive-in theater, where they and his brother's friends partook and generally had a carefree attitude. But the excursions were no longer that enjoyable for Andre. He only went along in the misplaced hope of finding a new friend or companion. He became more and more disheartened with his brother's friends. He saw the same types of people he'd seen everywhere else. They made fun of others and of each other, and he was starting to find the marijuana smoking tedious.

He was finding that the drug was making him nervous and paranoid, yet his deep desire for acceptance overrode his common sense, and he simply went along with the crowd. The cycle continued all summer, and even after he entered ninth grade. He felt more and more isolated as he continued with the same repetitive behavior, but his desire for acceptance would not let him break free.

In July that summer, Andre and his family moved to a new house. He was mildly excited and found the new house acceptable. Although his brother and he had always shared a room, and it was no different in the new house, Andre now felt that this was a violation of his privacy, and he longed to have more time alone.

Moving into a new house and neighborhood didn't bring him much in the way of new friends, and he was glad that he was often home alone with his younger sister, Karyn. Although she was eight years his junior, they had gained a great rapport. This summer, Andre introduced "Tea Time in Jolly London" to her. This game was a great way to sneak coffee or tea past his mother. Karyn knew, though, that their mother disapproved of caffeinated beverages, and sometimes when Andre made tea for them, she said, "I'm telling!"

But forbidden fruit is always the sweetest, and Andre had succeeded in planting a desire for tea in Karyn. By her playing waitress, or house, or some husband and wife scenario, and with their mother not always paying close attention to them, it was easy for them to have their beverages without much incident.

While Karyn preferred tea, Andre was able to enjoy mocha, hot chocolate mixed with instant coffee.

Years before, when Karyn had been born on a Saturday night, Andre's mother's water had broken before she was taken to the hospital. It was during all that tension that Andre learned of his mother's worries. He knew, of course, that childbirth was serious, and she had had other crises, like her thyroid operation. Andre had learned of and maybe even picked up the anxiety in his mother's personality. He didn't think she was a hypochondriac, yet he sensed that she often worried beyond what was reasonable.

Karyn had naturally made her own friends, but she and Andre were often left to entertain themselves when the older siblings went out. Now that he was older, and she was no longer a baby or toddler, he assumed some of the responsibility of being with her. Even when Karyn woke him up earlier than he would have liked, he was able to put up with the annoyance. He was happy that he had a more natural relationship with her than he could remember ever having had with his other brother and sister. Also, she looked up to him because he was older. Being her senior, he could watch what he wanted to on TV, and he could spark in her at least some interest in science fiction. Given her young age and her corresponding intellectual capacity, she didn't always understand spoofs, such as one on TV detectives that they watched together, but Andre was able to calm her and explain adult humor and satire to her.

As Karyn grew, their closeness would fade, yet she would always be the most understanding sibling Andre had. The differences in their maturity lent much to the relationship. What was most important was that he could be himself and teach her before others' judgments and prejudices could take hold.

That summer, a new family moved into the neighborhood. They had a young daughter who was about Karyn's age. Andre was happy that his sister would now have a more age-appropriate playmate and maybe even a close friend. It was very unfortunate that other neighbors—and even Andre's father at one point, which was shocking to Andre—made note of the fact that the neighbors were people of color. It was good that the slang terminology of his youth wasn't used to describe the new family, but despite Andre's hopes that race relations were improving, the attitudes of the past seemed to prevail.

Andre didn't know how to disarm these inconsiderate people, and he knew he was outnumbered. Prejudice was too prevalent. Karyn's relationship with her new playmate didn't blossom in a natural way, as it would have if there had been no interference from prejudiced parents. They might have become close if the words of others had not spoiled the budding friendship. The new neighbors soon moved back out of the neighborhood, and Andre thought he knew why.

Incidents like this one were disheartening. Why color and race were such an issue had troubled Andre since he was very young. He'd met people of many different ethnicities at school. There, they taught tolerance and acceptance, as well as the attitude that one should simply not bring unnecessary attention to such things as race and ethnicity. Karyn might not be a bigot or racist, but now her exposure to bigotry and racism had tainted her previous innocence. She was basically a good–hearted individual, but as she got older, she too would at times joke about race. Yet no one is perfect, and Andre could recall jokes that he himself had uttered as a child. Sometimes he had even gone along with John at school. So perhaps he was no better than anyone else.

When he was about eight, Andre had learned a racial ditty at school, complete with stereotypical accents and rhythm. His father found this cute, and he told Andre to recite this to all the relatives, who also found it entertaining and often asked for an encore. Andre recalled that his mother and one aunt had found this goading very distasteful and wrong. Now Andre, being older, couldn't excuse his past bad behavior. He was deeply sorry that he'd ever acted like a bigot, and he was thankful that his school taught awareness of these issues. Sadly, such instruction was not universal.

vi

The prestige of being a high schooler was a source of great hope and joy for him. Andre knew that he could find acceptance from his teachers by continuing to be a good student. Unlike most of his peers, he enjoyed most of what he learned. David and Andre could share in the joy of learning, but they were both being excluded, ridiculed, and socially isolated by the others for having these views.

Even with David as his closest friend, Andre couldn't express a deeper desire to be accepted. He felt alienated among all the people he should have been close to. Even David had an unpleasant new attitude; he had become more combative in terms of schoolwork. Especially in algebra and geometry class, he had become most interested in being right, and he even seemed to take pleasure in Andre's occasional mistakes. In short, David had become boastful and arrogant. He exhibited this attitude in other classes, as well, and then even outside the classroom.

Andre knew that he was generally sharper than David. He hated his own frustration with David and was angry at having to prove himself. He would have preferred the simple joy of learning and pride in showing his abilities. He had no wish to take joy in mistakes that other people made. However, he found himself accepted only by the teachers and houseparents. There was the further frustration of knowing that he was probably never going to have the kind of acceptance and physical contact he desired. But he could not stop his desires. They were all he had.

Andre felt this yearning most in gym classes. He knew he wasn't the strongest or best athlete in the class, nor did he really want to be. He didn't understand why he felt that his gymnastics teacher was the one he most wanted acceptance from, nor did he really want to know why this was so. All he knew was that perhaps the older teachers, especially the men who were stronger than he and much more self-assured, were the only hope of human contact he had, even though most of the time, such hopes seemed to be an exercise in futility.

Andre had never seen himself as a thief. By contrast, Joey, his wayward classmate, but still a friend, had the reputation of being a delinquent. Somehow, Andre had gotten the idea, perhaps with the help of David and/or Ralph, to peruse the cloakrooms in search of elusive change. Andre had developed rich tastes. He increasingly enjoyed going off campus to have good meals, coffee, frappés, and other things that took his fancy but cost a fair amount of money.

In any case, he managed to convince himself that anyone stupid enough to leave money in the coatroom would learn a lesson not to do so in the future. David egged him on in this thinking and behavior. On one or two occasions, Andre would be lucky to come back with a dollar or so, and he would treat David to coffee.

One day, Andre couldn't believe his luck. He had worked up enough courage to go through a pocketbook. To his utter amazement, he found a crisp $10 bill. A twinge of guilt came over him, but he quickly squelched it by reminding himself that he was teaching someone a valuable lesson not to leave their currency so exposed to thievery. He quickly pocketed the money and made his exit.

Pride and arrogance, emotions that had been mainly alien to Andre up to this point, played into his treating David and Ralph to the local restaurant. David was in on the secret, but they both thought it better to not fill Ralph in on the details of how the booty had been obtained.

The school principal called Andre into the office to ask him about recent thefts in the coatroom. Andre felt very nervous, but of course felt he had to lie. He exclaimed, "Oh, I don't know anything about that." Luckily, his good reputation and his ability to look the lady straight in the face and lie about it were enough to have suspicion drawn away from him.

He should have counted his blessings and forgotten all about the escapades, but now he was hooked. It was the sense of entitlement and the belief that he'd never get caught that kept him returning to the room in search of treasure. His boldness and attitude were probably what did him in. Now going through pockets became a ritual.

To his astonishment one day, the lady in charge of the students on that side of the school, not Andre's principal, interrupted him and demanded, "What do you think you're doing in here?"

Andre was speechless. He was so terrified that he thought he might lose control of his bowels.

The lady told Andre that his principal would be informed. "I'd better not see you in here again for any reason!" she said.

The principal was very upset, to say the least—not merely because he was a thief, but because, she said, "I believed you, and you looked at me straight in the eye and lied to me! You had us all fooled. You'll have to take this note home to your parents, and you'll have to write an apology note to Molly. I'll want to see that before you send it. And of course you'll have to pay her back the $10. I'll call your parents on Monday, so I suggest very strongly that you give them this paper. There will be more trouble for you if you don't."

Andre didn't want to face suspension, or whatever trouble his principal had in mind if he didn't give the note to his parents. He was torn and very anxious. In the end, he gave in to reason and gave the note to his father.

His father was more upset than he'd been in many years. "I won't have a common thief as a son!" he yelled.

His father then used the belt on Andre's bare bottom, something that he hadn't done in many years. Andre didn't think his crime warranted this kind of punishment, now that he was 16, but he knew some punishment was necessary. He knew that he'd done something very wrong and totally unacceptable.

He wrote the letter to Molly. At first he thought, I'll just get this over with and go through the motions of writing an apology letter. But as he wrote, he began to feel deep remorse for what he'd done. He wanted to put this episode behind him, and he felt that paying her back would be a huge relief. Later, he felt even guiltier when he found that Molly was not angry at him at all. She accepted his apology wholeheartedly. It was true, of course, that Andre had not wanted her anger, but he had expected it, figuring he had it coming to him. So to be met with none was very surprising.

This incident was very important in Andre's formative years. Earlier that year, even while knowing that what he was doing was very wrong, Andre had told a totally blind and mentally challenged boy that he would give him change for a $10 bill. He'd given the boy 10 pieces of paper which felt much like dollar bills and were about the same size. Andre felt quite smug about this incident until the boy tried to buy some items at the student store and was informed that his "money" was not real. The boy was understandably upset, but Andre knew he had gotten away with the subterfuge.

Now he was glad that he had not gotten away with his theft of Molly's money, glad that he had been caught early in his life. He didn't want to be a common thief, or any other kind of crook.

He felt very bad that he had managed before to rationalize his activities, even while he was relieved that neither his principal nor any other staff member at the school had found out about his counterfeiting scheme. If they had known about this additional act of delinquency, he'd certainly have been suspended and sent for counseling. Now it was easy enough for Andre to find his own way back to reform, as his intelligence and feelings of shame were sufficient to accomplish this change. He didn't want to see himself as anything like Joey, who had earned the reputation of being one of the worst juvenile delinquents on campus.

Chapter 11

"Andre's Story: Part 5—The New Sunrise"

i

Once again, it was a time for Andre to simply harden himself to the grim aspects of school life. The major difference, now, besides having a bit more independence and being responsible for some of his own decisions, was that he had a more vivid sense of how things could be. When he was a child, he could use his imagination. With the added aspect of physical maturity, Andre could now add new fantasies.

He had expected this school year to be a dreary repetition of the previous one and was pleased to find that he would have much more to do, schoolwise. He relished being very busy. He looked forward to singing a more major role in the upcoming Christmas concert, and he would be expected to do more than simply sing backup chorus at the spring show. He'd have a role in the play.

He was now staying on campus more often on the weekends. He was tired of cab drivers who got lost and of rides that took six hours to get him home when it should have taken only one hour. This also gave him more freedom and time to spend with friends. The staff was also involving students in activities such as movies and going to the mall or a local coffee house. When Andre did go home for the weekend, his siblings and parents were always busy with their own lives, and he'd be alone at home most of the time, except for church—which he could, and often did, attend with people at school.

One Saturday night, Andre was sitting near Anjali. He and she were having a good time giggling at the entertainers. They also shared the interest of chorus. Many boys joked about them being an item. Andre liked her well enough, but he couldn't really consider her a romantic interest. However, he felt relieved that he could show he wasn't a "fag" if he had a girlfriend—at least of sorts.

He liked Anjali, who was a few years younger than he was. He relished the idea of bragging to others about their hot and heavy romance. He suspected that the other guys weren't really having hot sex with their girls, either. But it didn't seem to matter, and Andre played along with the others, even though Anjali and he never breached that barrier. There was one occasion when she felt him up, but it was short–lived and never occurred again.

One night in winter, Andre went to visit David, as he often did. Robbie, David's roommate, was also there, and they talked and listened to music. Andre lay on the vacant bed, wondering why he couldn't just be the third roommate.

Andre had gotten a bit carried away in his reveries when Robbie asked, "Are you thinking of Anjali?"

Andre automatically answered shyly, "Yeah," but he really wanted to express something else. His fear of ridicule prevented him from breaking the limits he so desired to push past. Years later, he would regret not having voiced his true thoughts that night. But he never got any positive support in that direction, so the pattern of always hiding his true self and his desires would cause him to become even more introspective and shy.

Previously, John had habitually made fun of everything and

everyone, calling people "faggot" and making it a point to use a feminine voice and deliberate lisp to further illustrate his insensitivity and immaturity. But even he was much more serious this year. The chorus would be singing in New York, at Saint Patrick's Cathedral, also performing in front of the United Nations and singing at Rockefeller Center. In addition, David, John, and Andre were all considering college, and therefore were on the college prep track. They had all adopted a more serious attitude towards their studies. This was most evident with John, as he'd been more of a partier and had previously been in minor disciplinary trouble more often than the other two.

It was well worth all the after–school hours of hard work when Andre performed in the Christmas concert. There were three performances, with two days between each of them. Andre was swept up in the whole spirit of the season. He enjoyed each number and was so excited to perform the trio with John and Robbie. It was especially nice to sing a quartet with Anjali. All things seemed so hopeful and good.

Now when David and Andre went out to eat or for coffee, they felt that they had really earned the privilege, as they were putting long hours and lots of hard work into their studies. On the rare occasions when John and Andre went to smoke some weed, that was another treat. Yet Andre was finding that he was disliking it more every time. A counselor had impressed upon Andre that his true friends wouldn't care whether he smoked or not; he did not have to do that. Indeed, John didn't make any fuss when Andre said he didn't want to smoke.

There was no rest after the holidays were over. The schoolwork continued and preparations began early for the May performance of *Oklahoma*. John would play Curly, and Andre would be Judd. They both enjoyed practicing after school until supper nearly every day for the few months it took to get ready. In the meantime, the chorus was soon to go to New York.

ii

Mid–term exams were fast approaching. Andre had turned 17, not really thinking this birthday any more special than the others. It was his 18th year that he was anxiously awaiting.

One night, during the week of mid–term exams, Andre was brushing his teeth late at night, as he usually did. He sensed that there was someone else in the bathroom with him. This was obviously a mistake, but the feeling persisted.

Andre continued with his dental duties, and now he swore he could see a greenish glow in the large horizontal mirror in front of him, which reflected the shower stalls behind him, the three sinks, and the bathroom lights. It provided a full view of everything in the room. The light wasn't really a haze, nor was it very bright, but it was there nevertheless. It seemed to be the yellowish green of chlorine, but somehow it looked crisper and cleaner than expected.

As Andre rinsed his toothbrush in the hot water, the last part of the ritual, he thought he could hear a very faint chorus of voices that called his name three or four times. The voices were very low, obviously male, but they also sounded as though they were mixed with white noise, or perhaps rushing water. At times they seemed to fade in and out, like the effect of tuning in a radio station, but there was no static sound accompanying it. What was perhaps most remarkable was that along with seeing and hearing these very strange phenomena, Andre felt a sense of calm that he had never experienced before. That seemed to draw his attention even more.

Moments later, Andre distinctly heard the same voices saying, "We will help you; we will help you." Then he again heard his name called a few times, this time more clearly, but with the same apparent difficulty of a faint station signal. They said again, "We will help you; we will help you." All this time, the greenish glow in the mirror seemed to grow brighter, and his sense of peace and happiness was also magnified.

Then, as suddenly as it had begun, the episode ended abruptly. Andre was very happy that he had heard these spirits, but at the same time, he wondered if he shouldn't have some doubts about the reality of this communication. However, if the apparent occurrences were not real, then he must be going insane.

He told David and Anjali about it. They said they believed his story, but he attributed this to friendship and a kind of patronizing courtesy.

Later, Anjali and Andre were seated in the dining room of the girls' cottage when they decided on the spur of the moment to try to listen for these spirits. Anjali said that she felt a presence, but Andre was sure she was merely trying to be nice to him. He was determined to prove or disprove the spirits scientifically. He sensed a vibration coming from the table. It was definitely there, like a bee buzzing, but the sound was higher, like the hum of a fluorescent light. Anjali reacted with awe at the same time as Andre. There were only incandescent lights in this room.

Now it was clear to Andre what to do. He asked Anjali, "What do you think just happened?"

She answered, "I feel the table vibrating. Don't you?"

"Yes. I just wanted to make sure I wasn't crazy and wanted you to tell me."

At this point, their sense of the presence of a certain strength of mind and the vibrations all stopped.

A couple of days later, David, Andre, and Jerome, a boy from Jamaica who was new at the school that year and had expressed an interest in the spiritual realm, were gathered in Jerome's room. There, they opened their senses up and waited for a message to come through. Andre was again going to be as scientific as he could. All at once, a sense of dread overcame him.

Jerome began to utter repeatedly, "Jesus! Jesus! Jesus!" and David's breathing was very indicative of stress, which Andre attributed to Jerome's urgent voice. About 30 seconds later, things seemed to calm down and go back to normal. Andre asked the boys what they thought had just happened. Nobody had an answer, but Jerome said that he had sensed an evil presence there. Later, David used the term "weird" to describe the experience. He also said that he had felt fear in the room.

Anjali had agreed to go out to eat with Andre at a local fast-food restaurant. The truth was that Andre was fearful of going out alone after the experience in Jerome's room. They were both walking in the street. It had been dark for nearly an hour, and Andre kept thinking about the fearful force he'd experienced earlier. Suddenly he sensed, like a wave going over the trees above, undulations of terror worming their paths overhead. Andre's voice indicated to Anjali that he was terrified and that he was being pursued by some kind of evil.

Anjali said, "It's okay! Nothing is going to happen, and you shouldn't listen for spirits anymore. They'll contact you on their own if they feel a need to." This was very calming.

David and Andre had Spanish class together. The teacher was easily distracted by conversations unrelated to the lesson, and both boys had often gotten away with missing an entire lesson by bringing up religious subjects, especially relating to Biblical events and Christ. By Andre's and David's standards, the teacher's religious views were rather radical, but they all considered themselves Christians. Andre thought her opinion might be helpful. She thought all these events were due to stress related to mid-terms. Andre couldn't accept this explanation. He didn't feel stressed about the tests at all, and on the contrary, was quite prepared and was even looking forward to more of the good-to-excellent grades he'd achieved on examinations in the past.

To Andre, it seemed risky, but he needed a sense of closure

regarding the supernatural events he'd experienced. When he brought it up to the psychological counselor, he was surprised that she believed what he was narrating. He asked her why, and she responded that she could tell he was truthful, as she stated, "I could see in your eyes that you're afraid, so I know you're telling the truth." He felt a sense of relief, and he supposed that she would be the catalyst for his being committed to a hospital, or at least being given some kind of treatment, if she had any doubts. There never was any intervention by the school staff, so Andre felt he must be right about the spirits, or at least not crazy.

As the next two months passed, so did his sense of being contacted by an otherworldly being. He didn't pursue contact, given the bad experiences in the past.

Then there was one weekend day, cold and clear, when he was near the student store, alone. He sensed a sort of beckoning in the winter air. He went behind the store, near the rear exit, where there would be less chance of encountering people; there he awaited contact with the spirits. He couldn't quite make out the voices, but he was sure they called his name, as they'd done in the bathroom. He was also certain they repeated their promise to help him. Yet, in contrast to the first time he'd experienced them, Andre didn't feel the same calm that he had originally. There was no sense of dread and fear, thankfully, but he felt that he must cease this type of action. Never again did he seek spirits during his high-school years, and neither did they try to seek him out.

With his studies piling up, and with preparations for the chorus trip to New York City coming up, it became easy for Andre to almost forget about the spirits. He still wondered, however, what all of this had meant, and also, more seriously, what kind of help the spirits might possibly be able to give him. He concluded that he would discover the truth someday if it was the will of God. He also believed that evil was real, especially if one sought out things that weren't meant to be pursued.

iii

In New York, the chorus was split up into groups of two or three. They stayed with families at night, while they attended to their busy schedules and toured the city during the day. Andre roomed with John G. The family was very nice and offered them both large breakfasts for the few days they were there. Andre loved the eggs, bacon, coffee, juice, and pastries.

It was a shame that the Statue of Liberty was being maintained at the time, as he very much wanted to climb the torch. Seeing and singing at Saint Patrick's Cathedral was thrilling. The acoustics and size of the place were awe inspiring. His parents and the man who had married Andre's older sister, Denyse, attended and said how much they admired the performance.

The chorus went on a boat tour of the city, but the fog made it difficult to get a good view of the city. Andre made the most of it and was looking forward to the events to come. For some unknown reason, he was nervous when they were to sing in the lobby of the U.N. Perhaps it was mainly the waiting around which made him worry in a way he never had before. They sang "Let There Be Peace on Earth," and Andre soon felt better and forgot about how nervous he'd been.

The last night in the city, the chorus went to a fancy French restaurant. Everyone else took the chef's recommendation of *tranche noire*, a beef dish, but Andre figured that since he'd probably not get the chance again, he'd order frog's legs. This was naturally a matter of laughter for some, as Andre's nickname of Frog had been given to him in the seventh grade. It wasn't due to his French heritage, but to someone having said in gym class that he ran like a frog. By now, it had become a kind of affectionate nickname. Andre enjoyed the menu choice, though he thought it was a lot of trouble getting the meat off the boney legs. He enjoyed the espresso and cheesecake as well.

Back at school, the opening night of *Oklahoma* was soon upon them. Andre's mother and sister were attending that night and would take him home afterwards. His sister and her husband pulled him aside and asked him what he thought of his life the way it was and what he felt about his yet–to–be–born niece or nephew. Andre stated quite emphatically that he was happy to be alive and that they shouldn't worry about their future child having a disability. This opinion seemed to bring peace to his sister.

The performance went off perfectly. Andre easily improvised around a few mistakes with the stage props. He felt so much in his role that the audience was very impressed with his singing and the death scene.

After the play, John faced Andre and gave him a hearty, full–body hug, allowing Andre to feel John's body pressed firmly against his own. John said with joy, "Great job, Frog!" Andre was very pleased that he had some positive reassurance and a physical expression of approval, which he had always longed for.

With the school year coming to a close, Sally, the biology and mathematics teacher, informed David and Andre that, since they were among the top students in the school, they could participate in a six–week marine science program. The program was sponsored by the university and was mainly designed to test the students' preparedness for college–level courses.

iv

David's parents had agreed to drive Andre down to Virginia with them and bring him back. They were very nice, and they paid for Andre's meals on the 12–hour road trip in the van. Andre had never talked to David's parents for long stretches before, and he was pleased that they took some interest in his future plans. They were very supportive and understanding.

When they arrived, Andre was surprised that he couldn't see the beach. He asked how far it was, and was informed that even though the town's name had "island" in it, it was really on the mainland, and the real island was eight miles away.

David and Andre spent most of their time together. Many of the other students there obviously knew each other from before. Everyone was kept busy most of the day. Andre was glad to finally see the island and see the natural scenery. He was glad that David and he were rooming together. There was a third boy who shared the room with them; he was deaf. Andre felt sorry that he had never taken more time to learn sign language. But at the same time, he was glad that David and he could talk as late into the night as they wanted to without disturbing the other boy's sleep.

Most of the time was spent taking samples, and everyone had to do a paper on some marine topic. Andre was interested in comparing crab densities on two islands. He was also planning to throw out a message in a bottle to see where it ended up and who would answer it.

The time went swiftly. Andre learned what poison ivy looked like and that if he took a cold shower, he'd avoid getting itchy from contact with the plant. He was relieved to find that this advice was sound, and that he had no lasting ill effects.

During the last week, Andre and David were up unusually late one night talking. The summer weather had been oppressive and humid every day. A thunderstorm struck with vivid lightning, grand booms of thunder, and downpours of rain, which reminded Andre of the storms he'd enjoyed as a child. Unfortunately, this tempest brought no relief from the heat; if anything, it made it muggier.

The pizza party on the last night came and went, and then Andre was with David's parents, driving home. It was great to have some morning coffee. They dropped Andre off some time after midnight. Now he was looking forward to his upcoming year at school.

V

It was supposed to be a big deal to be a junior. All Andre could see was that homework and extracurricular activities kept him busier than before. He liked this very much, so long as he had some time to get out with David and do a few things on weekends.

This year brought a taste of independence to the juniors. They would all be given the chance, under supervision, to show that they could take care of an apartment and live on their own. It was okay to have his own place, even though he shared it with Billy and Joey. Andre would have preferred his own room, but he didn't mind Joey, as he was rarely there anyway. Nobody minded Andre's company, so things worked out rather well. Joey shared some interest in science fiction and music with him, so their time together was enjoyable.

The feeling of being older and more responsible than he actually was took root in Andre. He couldn't quite grasp that he still had a lot to learn about adult life. He was 17, after all, and in a few months, it would be official that he was a man. He was doing the things an adult did. So as far as he was concerned, it was already official.

He was now looking to prove his new manhood. He didn't just have to be aware of his new-found freedom; it was necessary that others approve of him, as well.

The idea that he was a man was reinforced by his teachers and the increased volume of schoolwork. He had decided to go the college-prep route in his courses and was looking forward to this new chapter in his life. He had always wanted to be some kind of scientist. His trip to Virginia had convinced him that he was equal to this kind of work. He wasn't too keen on being a marine biologist, but he did relish the scientific principles and the process of achieving goals. He had done well in geometry and algebra, but he didn't see himself doing this type of work in college. He was seriously thinking of computer science, and by midwinter, he had set his mind on this goal.

His parents approved of his going to college; he would be the first in his family to do so. Even though his father approved of this decision, Andre knew that he really wanted him to be a lawyer. What was certain was that Andre didn't want to work preparing pizza the rest of his life. He had not enjoyed the supervision of teachers for such a simple job. Moreover, the idea of having to wear a white shirt and dress pants was absolutely ridiculous. Andre had never hated any class job so much and had even bunked it one day. Naturally, his teachers expected much more of him than such juvenile behavior, especially since he was a college-bound student and was doing so well otherwise.

This didn't faze Andre too much. He had also resented the teacher who was in charge of teaching him daily skills, especially cooking and regular survival skills. Andre felt belittled and insulted by this intervention in his life. After all, he knew how to cook for himself and really wanted to do more advanced projects. Andre often talked back so he could get detention with his gymnastics coach, whom he liked and respected. Besides, detention was quiet and a good place for doing homework. The coach even accepted normal blowing off of steam and wasn't as critical as the other teachers.

Andre and David had been close friends since kindergarten. They seemed to be on the same page when it came to their interest in science, math, computers and a host of philosophical as well as theoretical discussions. They often went out to eat together and spent many hours together. Andre often felt David's company as a refuge from the peer pressure of most of his classmates.

They had both become interested in the Bible, especially because of current events, such as the pope getting shot and the president as well. They both felt they could crack Revelations and skipped a class one morning, when Andre read it aloud to David in the school chapel. They felt justified in this, as they often got the Spanish teacher diverted from the normal lesson plan by discussing Armageddon and spiritual issues. By the midpoint of the year, she had become more aware of their diversionary tactics and much stricter about the lessons. This switch was fine. Andre liked Spanish lessons and was good at speaking the language. He could practice at a restaurant a couple of times a year.

Now, after the Christmas holidays, this winter was very cold. All Andre really had to keep him going was his schoolwork, living in his own apartment, and David. Pam was still trying to convince Andre that David was a bad person. However, Andre could easily control her, now. She depended on him to be her lookout when they went to sneak a tobacco break. She loved her cigarettes. Andre and David were keen on trying various types of cigars. Andre made it clear to Pam that she would no longer be welcome if she didn't accept David as his friend. She reluctantly accepted, but made it a point to bad mouth David when she could. Andre and David were legal even as far as the school was concerned when it came to smoking, and Andre impressed upon Pam that he was doing her a big favor in finding a place for her to smoke. Both boys would have been severely reprimanded if anyone had ever learned that they were covering for Pam's smoking.

John had become less interested in Andre, and much more concerned with members of the opposite sex. He'd often tell Andre of his activities with various girls at the school. Andre was hardly interested, but put up with John's stories. The two of them had forged a close friendship over the years, and it seemed that lately, a lot of it went beyond words.

One cold clear night in midwinter, John asked Andre to join him and his latest girlfriend, Cindy, in the woodshop for a party. It was no secret that some of the students had procured some master keys and were able to gain entry to previously forbidden spots on campus. Even in the eighth grade, John and Andre had sneaked into a locked storage room near the gymnasium to smoke some marijuana.

This night was different only in its novelty. Andre now preferred alcohol, and even John didn't smoke much pot anymore. Cindy, John, and Andre were seated on stools at the large workbenches used for other pursuits during the daytime hours. The only light they had came from the Exit signs at the doors, and naturally, being discovered in this room, let alone indulging, would surely have been very serious.

Their classmate Joey had taken his girlfriend Linda into the bomb shelter on a few occasions to drink, and they had also discovered some barbiturate pills, presumably for medical use if a fallout situation really occurred. In any event, on two occasions, after drinking alcohol and taking the pills, Linda had to have an ambulance take her to the hospital. Andre could understand the girl making the mistake once, but the second time, he was in shock and very frustrated that she could have been so stupid.

Needless to say, Joey's reputation was very tainted. Not only did he have forbidden keys, but he was able to pick locks, and he had gotten into the bad habit of stealing things from the school, something that John, Andre, and Cindy didn't approve of. Andre didn't like to think of himself as a stool pigeon, but he had reported Joey to the staff before he was able to pilfer a large amount of property: tape recorders, phones, and more. Joey had never learned of Andre's betrayal, and was still letting Andre in on his secrets.

So John, Cindy, and Andre quietly sipped dark rum, straight up. Being noisy was never an issue for them when they celebrated. John had drawn a naked woman on the blackboard, and Andre made the motions of feeling her up and feigned a sexual moaning sound. The novelty and atmosphere wore off, and they'd all consumed a fair amount of liquor, so the party ended as quietly as it had started. Also, John had always been attentive to their surroundings; that fact probably explained why Andre and he had never been discovered. The boys also handled their alcohol well and gave no external clues to others as to their activities. Andre wanted to be independent with drinking, and so was looking for a way to make alcohol himself, rather than procure it at a store or bar.

He was very interested in biology, now. This new enthusiasm was probably due to the fact that the teacher was giving them more challenges and independent papers. Andre admired this teacher. She had kept him interested in mathematics and science, as well as being very positive in her thinking. She had also given Andre and David the chance to go to Virginia. After his paper on plants, Andre was now going to do a paper on yeast and fermentation. Ah, he thought, now I can kill two birds with one stone.

He had decided not to venture into the realm of fruits, as he was convinced that there was too much risk involved. This idea was also reinforced by his memory of his failed seventh–grade experiment. Now, armed with approval from his biology teacher and new book knowledge, David and Andre went to the mall for coffee. They were both excited to see if their experiment would work out in about a week's time. Andre felt almost like a child at Christmas when he was walking home with David with his packages of brown sugar and yeast.

After a week, Andre's concoction was ready. He was so proud of his ability, especially since his biology teacher endorsed his project; after all, she had let him do a paper on yeast and fermentation, so Andre figured he would use this knowledge for a more practical purpose than merely impressing his teacher.

He poured a drink for David and himself. The color was a cloudy brown, but the smell and taste were reminiscent of champagne. After the one drink, Andre decided not to risk getting sick, but since David was enjoying it so much, he let him finish the last four or five drinks. He was pleased and proud that David was drunk and not sick. Andre was a little upset that he himself had not drunk more, but he was still wondering if David would be sick in the morning.

Andre and David were now closer than they had ever been. Andre wondered later if David ever would have expressed himself in the way he had that night if he hadn't had Andre's homemade brew in him. Perhaps it would have happened in time.

Andre regretted that he had ever helped Pam by being her lookout when they went to smoke. He was upset that he had told her his confidential business. A day later, the principal called him into her office and asked him if he had made alcohol. She said she was certain he had the ability and knowledge to do so. Andre merely stated that this was not true, that he had been doing a paper on fermentation. Luckily, he had time to get rid of the evidence. He now knew that he could never trust Pam again, and he was also wondering why she was becoming so hateful toward David.

The rest of the year went on pretty uneventfully. The next highlight would be the class Junior Fair to help raise money for next year's senior trip. Andre spent most of his time studying and most of his free time with David. He was happy to be busy, but was now relishing his free time much more than he had before.

By spring, Andre had finished the apartment project and was back with everyone else. He was very happy to have his own room, and being alone gave him the ability to enjoy the evenings listening to music. Having his own room also afforded some appreciated privacy when David was there.

The Junior Fair came and went. It was fun selling balloons, cotton candy, and the usual items, but Andre was glad when it was over. He recalled the fair when he was a child and how magical it had once been. It was good to keep the tradition going and spread the magic to others, but he had never realized before how much work went into providing others with fun.

vi

At last it was senior year, the year everyone had raved about. There was the big trip, and if Andre had felt he was an adult in his earlier years, he knew that now he had earned the privileges of adulthood. He was now of legal age, so it wasn't a big deal to drink, although the school wouldn't tolerate it on its grounds. Andre felt more important going off campus.

The days were speeding by, and he was thinking about his collegiate future. By early October, he was very enthusiastic about the future. His enthusiasm was so great as to make him impatient with the present. He longed for graduation day, and he was thinking about celebrating his successes at having gotten as far as he had rather than about finishing the school year.

When Andre suggested a French song for the Christmas concert, the choral instructor seemed interested in this suggestion. But he announced that, by this point in the year, there wouldn't be time to fit the song into the concert. Andre had decided that he'd rather watch the concert this year than be in it, as he had been since seventh grade. His instructor was very disappointed and didn't seem to share his feelings. Andre tried to bribe the teacher by saying that he'd stay in chorus, at least through the Christmas concert, if the French song were kept in the repertoire. Unfortunately, there was nothing Andre could do to make that happen, so he went through with his intentions and dropped out of chorus.

He was more cooperative in his other classes. The school had come a long way in its experiments since he was a child. For a couple of years, the students had been mainstreamed to the public high school. Andre and David went every morning for an introductory psychology and computer science course. They had both decided to major in computer science in college, and Andre found this very exciting. He was interested in psychology, but he didn't like the way this instructor organized the course; it was mostly rote memorization of terms.

It was nearing Christmas, now, and Andre was very happy to finish the school year. He had been celebrating his future by going out with David on nearly a daily basis, to toast the new prospects awaiting them. It was now in his mind that all the things he was doing at school were lasts, and thus should be cherished. That was probably why he especially enjoyed the Christmas concert, as he knew he would not be there again to take part in it.

By February, Andre and David had become used to the

routine of the school day. They were also very particular about where they would go out to eat and drink, to continue the feasts of their younger years. Unfortunately, Pam was very interested in Andre, as always, but her insistence was greater than it had been before. In addition, she was much more forceful in her active hatred of David, and she made this very clear.

This particular weekend, Pam, David, and Andre were alone in the dining room after supper. Pam was going on with her insults about David. Before Andre could think of what he was doing, he grew enraged at her, especially since she didn't stop these rants when he asked her to. Besides, David was more than Andre's best friend. In an instant, Andre clenched his fist and struck her quite hard against the cheek. Fortunately for him, Pam couldn't see, and when she cried out how horrible it was that David had hit her, Andre left the room and hoped for the best.

Unfortunately, Pam got help. By that time, David was the only one there with her, and it looked as though he was going to take the fall. Andre couldn't allow this to happen. Before he knew it, he found himself entering the room again, defending David and confessing to having struck Pam. One thing he couldn't do was explain to the housefather his reasons for having done so, beyond a simple, "I was angry with her and don't want to talk about it."

Andre was no better at explaining his reasons to the school principal. As he sat in her office, he suspected that there was no reason he could give that would get him out of the impending suspension from school. The principal called his mother, and Andre was shocked to learn that his mother had told her, "These feelings he's having are a good thing." But the principal wouldn't budge on suspending him. She tried to reassure him that being suspended wouldn't affect his college record in any way. Andre hadn't thought about that before, and he was more upset by her stubbornness.

So his mother would come some 30 miles to pick him up, take him home, and then drive him back, all for a one-day suspension. Naturally, this was very distressing to both of his parents—not only because it was his first suspension ever from school, and not only because he was a senior in high school, soon to go to college, but especially because he had struck a female. Andre agreed with them, but he felt he should be excused, as he had acted in haste, and he wasn't normally a violent person at all. He accepted his punishment, but it was a long day. Andre longed for the whole thing to end and go away, as he knew it would eventually.

When he returned to school the next day, things were back to normal. The houseparents acted as though nothing had ever happened, and even others didn't mention the incident. Most of them probably didn't even know about it, as he hadn't told anyone except David. Luckily there hadn't been any witnesses. Andre was glad to learn a valuable lesson and move on with his life.

He would never understand the whims of the houseparents, even after his 14 years at the school. It seemed that room assignments would be changed twice a year. This ritual of theirs was especially disturbing this year. Andre had been sharing a room with David, a seventh-grader named Stephen, and Lucio. They had all gotten along very well, and when the change came in the second semester, Andre was placed in a room at the other end of the hall with a seventh-grader named Jimmy. It wasn't that he didn't like this kid, but Andre felt worlds apart from him. Stephen shared many interests with Andre and David. Andre simply couldn't connect with Jimmy and was resentful of the houseparents, especially when he came in at night. They rarely spoke to each other, except for an occasional "Good morning," "Good night," or "Lousy weather, isn't it?"

When Andre expressed his feelings to the housemother in charge, he was thwarted again. She said she understood his feelings, but she wouldn't give him his own room, or even put the rooms back to the old assignments. Andre got used to the arrangement, as David visited often, and Jimmy didn't spend much time there. Life went on pretty normally until Senior Prom season came along in May.

The upcoming prom and the class trip to Washington, D.C. were, it seemed to Andre, just rewards for all the hard work and other tribulations he'd endured all those years at the school. He looked forward to all the bustling activities. It would be his first visit to the nation's capitol. He happily anticipated enjoying the spirit of democracy, and he knew that for just short of a week, the atmosphere would be festive.

The class had chartered a bus for the trip. Chuck, the driver, was very friendly, talking to everyone and befriending all. Andre saw Chuck as being on par with a houseparent, but his amiability and genuine interest made the trip very enjoyable. Chuck, along with Ken, Andre's favorite housefather, knew a great deal about the D.C. area. The two men had relatives there and had lived there for some years in the past, so their native knowledge of the city would make the excursion more than a mere sightseeing tour.

Andre, David, and John G. were put in the same room. There were two or three to a room at the inn, which was an older but well kept place, akin to a military barracks or college dormitory. It was drab but reasonably comfortable for sleep. Besides, very little time would be spent there at all.

Andre found the breakfasts mediocre; the class budget would not allow every meal to be extravagant. Lunches were often skipped, but the dinners made up for everything else. Ken and Chuck would often confer and suggest places to dine, depending on the mood of the majority of the class and what type of food they desired. Seafood and Italian dishes were probably what Andre liked the most, and he'd have his fill, along with cheesecake and the rich desserts he prized. It was also a strange feeling to be of legal age and be able to enjoy alcohol in the presence of the school staff. Only six months earlier, this behavior would have been cause for disciplinary action. Everyone in charge gave their all to make the senior class's final trip one that would always be remembered fondly.

Andre was not going to let his memory be unaided. He took pictures of all the major landmarks, the Lincoln Memorial, the Capitol, and especially the Smithsonian Museum. He felt awed at photographing the Wright Brothers' first plane, a piece of Skylab, and so many of the other exhibits.

Ken invited the class to the home of one of his relatives for a short time. It was a large, luxurious dwelling where the class gathered in the lower level entertainment room, where there was an open bar. Andre did enjoy drinks, but this particular evening, he didn't really feel in the mood for indulging. His schoolmates reveled in the experience, as though they'd never had such an opportunity before. Andre was glad that his buddies were having a good time, but he was surprised that Ken and the others in charge simply allowed the funfest of freedom and drunkenness to go on. It wasn't that Andre didn't want them to be happy, but a slight depression seemed to be coming on.

This sad mood would annoy Andre on and off for the rest of the trip. He couldn't quite put his finger on its cause, but he assumed it had something to do with his feeling alienated from the others. It seemed that although he was respected by his peers for his academic abilities, he was never quite able to click with them. This feeling was not new, of course, but it was strange that it should rear its head now. Chuck's thoughtfulness this evening did help lift Andre's spirits. Chuck had written a short poem for each student, which he read aloud. The humor was very good, and the insight he possessed in understanding each individual was uncanny.

For example, Andre found it very astute that Chuck was able to understand how much he had enjoyed the play at Ford's

Theater, what a highlight it had been for him. Being in such a historic place and seeing a play in the tradition of that time had done a lot to lift his mood. Even David had seemed distanced from Andre during the trip, but at the theater, they both enjoyed the drama together.

The only real problem on the trip occurred when they went to view George Washington's tomb. They had arranged a private tour and had received a letter confirming this understanding. When they arrived, it appeared that the people in charge were taken aback by the arrangement. They were adamant that there was no way this tour could go on. Andre had to satisfy himself regarding the issue. He found that a letter had indeed been sent, and everything had been organized earlier.

Finally, the pleas of the teachers paid off, and the excursion commenced. Andre was amazed by the house and property at Mount Vernon. Seeing a piece of history was probably what made the whole experience so positive. It was unfortunate that the tour guides didn't share his enthusiasm. It seemed to Andre that they resented doing their jobs.

The last night of the trip had come. Andre and David had sat together for the whole trip, and Andre sensed David's distance. Maybe it was that David drank too much, something that had become more and more of an issue, lately, when they were out alone together. David was usually more vocal, depressed, or simply rude to others when he overindulged. Andre would not have long to wait for him to show his hand again.

Ken was seated in front of Andre and David, directly in front of David. David began to move his hands in Ken's direction. Now Andre knew that David must be in a drunken heat, as he'd seen many times in the past. Andre understood David's attraction toward Ken, and even shared it, but he knew discretion where David didn't. David's hands caressed and rubbed Ken's shoulders for nearly five minutes before he realized that Ken was not going to respond to his attentions.

That night, Andre, David, and John G. were in their room, unwinding. Ken entered and said to David, "David, if you don't stop with your dirty mistreating, I'll pound on you till your heart stops beating! Understand?" It must have been a moment of major embarrassment for David, and he answered, barely audibly, "Yes." Ken left the room. To Andre's surprise, John G., never shy, didn't say anything.

Andre spent the rest of the night outside. He felt lonely and depressed, almost to the point of tears. This feeling also persisted on the way home. He didn't understand why he should feel this way. Certainly the trip coming to an end was a letdown, but this sour mood was much more. Why was it so hard to understand one's own feelings?

The hoopla over the prom began. Andre didn't share the enthusiasm of his classmates, probably because he didn't have a special girl to bring along. He was determined to take a girl to the dance in any case.

Angie was thought by nearly everyone, including Andre, to be very moody and hard to get along with. Despite this fact, he had set his mind on taking her to the dance. She had never given him, specifically, a hard time. He also knew that Angie would be appreciative of being invited, as he suspected that nobody else would be interested in taking her.

It had been an unusually rainy spring. Nice sunny days were to be cherished, especially when prom season was approaching. Getting ready for the event was not as exciting as Andre had thought it would be. Going out to get the tuxedos and flower arrangements seemed more of a chore than anything else. It all struck him as time taken away from his leisure schedule, rather than fun.

Prom night came and went. Andre felt that he had done his duty by giving Angie a good night. She was shocked and excited when he gave her a good night kiss at the end of the dance. He hadn't wanted her to have bad memories of not being invited to the prom; he'd been concerned that this could scar her memories of her school years forever. After all the emotional baggage he would take away with him in a few weeks, he didn't want to be a part of anyone else's suffering.

The interim period from the prom to graduation was largely uneventful, save that Andre was exhilarated by thoughts of the future he'd have in college and beyond as a computer programmer. He and David spent a lot of time listening to music, going out for coffee, and fantasizing about the future.

It was strange how the prospects of days that had not yet arrived made people change. Most members of Andre's class, including John, were very busy with celebrating excessively. Andre could understand that to a point, but he felt that some control was in order. In any case, regardless of whether the others admitted it or not, and the fact that some people were acting ecstatic at being free of the school, Andre could sense a general sense of loss.

John's reaction was the most surprising to Andre.

One beautiful afternoon in late May, John approached Andre in front of the school store. Andre expected that John would ask him to join him in his nightly revels or the usual chitchat. To Andre's surprise, John's expression and attitude were quite serious.

John seemed very contrite, and he expressed his amazement at, but total acceptance of, Andre's relationship with David. Furthermore, he seemed all the more serious and driven by feelings of guilt when he admitted to Andre what was obvious. It was the fact that Andre had had a rough time at the school due to various individuals and circumstances. John seemed nearly at the point of tears. He said he was very sorry that he hadn't fully comprehended Andre's plight. It was true that Andre was given to few words, even under normal circumstances, but now he was taken aback and truly couldn't even think of words to comfort John.

After a couple of minutes, John reemphasized how truly bad he felt, and how much he regretted his own bad treatment, both physical and psychological, of Andre when they were younger. What struck Andre was that he didn't feel angry at John, nor did he have any desire to either not forgive him or to answer with a verbal spar. The genuineness of John's plea elicited only mercy in Andre. He was sorry that he couldn't really understand, even after all these years, what exactly had motivated John's cruelty, but even with this lack of knowledge, he calmly reassured John that the incidents were past, that they'd become much closer as friends since then, and that he knew John had grown out of all that. He forcefully emphasized to John that nothing John had done in the past was responsible for how he, Andre, had turned out.

This short conversation between them had come and gone as quickly as the puffy white clouds in the bright blue sky of that beautiful day. Andre was very heartened that they were able to reconcile. He felt especially glad that John could move forward, now, without feeling an undue sense of guilt. In turn, Andre was surprised at his own ability to so quickly and calmly exonerate John, without feeling anger. It was one graduation gift he hadn't counted on.

The yearly trip to the amusement park that the school took wasn't normally offered to those in the upper school; perhaps they felt the students were too old for this type of excursion. But when, for some unknown reason, the staff inquired if anyone was interested in returning, most of the older students were very excited. Andre was also happy to go back.

However, the large rollercoaster wasn't as much fun as it had been in years past. In fact, he felt dizzy for a while after he got off the ride. At least it wasn't raining that day, as it had been most of the spring. Andre mused that maybe the disillusionment he was feeling this time was merely part of getting older.

vii

The day before graduation was much more emotional for Andre than he had expected it to be. He had resolved to make this last day, as he had marked many of the lasts all year, to be one of the most special of them all. What could be done to remember this day? He resolved to spend it in reflection, alone if he had to, to give the event some special meaning.

His classmates, predictably, went off campus to revel in drink. Andre understood this feeling well. He almost succumbed to the temptation, but in the back of his mind, he realized that going off to drink would only be remembered as one more day in a string of days of revelry that had been going on all year.

Sitting in the courtyard was a joy. Andre knew this would be the last night he'd be doing this. It was such a nice, crisp evening, with a deep blue sky. Ah, this was something worth remembering! He felt a sense of loss, and yet he was very relaxed, as well. He felt calm and was even feeling ready for bed much earlier than he had been all year.

In his bed, Andre was in a haze of sexual fantasy. This was certainly one habit he had not gotten a handle on. In Andre's mind, he tried to make this fantasy more special than any others. However, his reverie was cut short, as the giggling of his roommate Jimmy ended any hopes of satisfying this hunger. The tone and way that Jimmy laughed convinced Andre that there was no point in continuing. He recalled that when he had been in seventh grade, a senior roommate had seemed to be lost in his own reveries, and Andre hadn't found that funny at all. Perhaps it was because this older student and he had talked about common things, and all that had made him feel more of a connection. Andre longed for his old room arrangement. Jimmy was just too immature for him.

A surprisingly good night's sleep and a good breakfast in

the morning both passed quickly. Afterwards, Andre would never be able to recall what transpired between breakfast and lunch, and before he knew it, the graduation ceremony was beginning.

There were all the predictable speeches. The words were intended to rally everyone toward a bright future, to exhort them to remember fondly the accomplishments of the past. The class sat in solemn silence as they listened to the message that they were now responsible for their own actions. Andre was swept up in the emotions, and he was sure that everyone else in his class was, as well, despite their bravado. David seemed the most affected of all. He was visibly upset, crying and sniffling a great deal.

John surprised Andre yet again when, in sharp contrast to the past, he tried to comfort David. His persistence and genuine understanding of David's plight did eventually work. David soon calmed down and things went back to their previous quiescence.

The highlight for Andre was being in line, shaking the hands of the members of the board of directors, and being given his diploma. He gave them a hearty "Thank you!" and went back to his seat, feeling a great sense of pride and accomplishment.

This sense of joyfulness was climaxed by the final gathering in the quad. It was a ritualistic gathering, with lots of picture taking and punch and cookies. All the families were there. Most of the goodbyes were solemn and quiet. Nobody made a scene, and even the troublemakers were unusually quiet. Could they be feeling the same as he was?

Then came the drive home with his mother and father. Andre didn't feel an urge to cry, but a genuine sense of loss overtook him. Despite his late decision on a college, based more on financial restrictions than real choice, the prospect of starting in September didn't seem so marvelous now. Surely, he thought, this feeling will pass. It will be a real challenge, one worthy of my best efforts. It will be great!

But lurking in the back of his mind were fears that he wasn't so special after all, not even particularly bright. During high school, fantasies of being accepted at Harvard or MIT had been motivators, but David, John, and Andre had all been rejected by a highly acclaimed scientific/technical college in the western part of the state. At first, they all cried discrimination, but later, Andre was almost relieved, as the cost of tuition alone was out of reach. He had been accepted by both Boston University and Northeastern, but being so wrapped up in celebrating the whole year made it almost impossible to accept either offer, as the money was simply not available.

The college situation was not the main reason for his low mood, however. It occurred to him that although the prospect of the future was a very good thing overall, its motivational quality seemed to diminish as an uncontrollable fear regarding many uncertainties, a fear that had been looming in his subconscious, cruelly forced itself into the forefront of his thoughts.

Andre chose not to drink that summer. The thought of celebrating, especially alone, didn't appeal to him anymore. There was also the sense that, even though his family had never been cruel to him, his time at the boarding school had made them strangers to him. True, he knew his parents and siblings well, and their behavior could be easily predicted, but a sense of having missed something special with them was another factor that made Andre feel low.

He didn't regret that his parents didn't have any special graduation party for him when he got home. Indeed, the thought had never crossed his mind. Even his father's positive words and obvious pride weren't enough to allay his mood. Andre knew deep down that his father was only half proud of him, that he had wanted him to go to law school, not pursue a degree in computer science.

The summer would see his mood and his ideas concerning

all he had believed be challenged in ways that Andre could not have dreamed of.

Chapter 12

"Andre's Story, Part 6—Interlude"

i

Hot and humid weather, the most repulsive of all to Andre, had reared its ugliness upon his world the very day he had graduated. It was in sharp contrast to the previous cool, rainy days of spring interspersed with occasional clear, crisp days.

Andre had bought a computer and figured he'd get some practice before college. He enjoyed the video games, especially the ones that talked. He felt he was the only one who could imagine that in a decade the computer would be a common household item. He also enjoyed science magazines and felt awe at having joined a science–fiction book club. All in all, he was able to suppress his sense of loss and fear. The computer helped him to escape the feelings he had about the unknown. He missed the joys of his old school, but the fact that he could use his imagination and his budding computer skills was enough to keep his dread at bay. This worked fairly well—that is, until the inevitability of the fall came crashing in upon him in mid–July.

There were two events that were coming up fast. Andre had agreed to take a one–week summer course, and a month later, there'd be an overnight orientation for the students at the college.

ii

By rights, this day should have been exciting for Andre. He was at the new college, at the student life office, where the details of the upcoming one–week course were to be laid out. For him, however, it was a very bad time. He had never before felt what he was now feeling, and he had no idea how to deal with it. He was terrified.

He hadn't chosen any of his actions, but he found himself sitting as far away as possible from everyone else. He would have preferred to leave. He couldn't find any signs of hope. Every word spoken by the professors brought him terror. He didn't understand why he felt this way. It seemed ridiculous to be so fearful of a simple routine. After all, John, one of the professors, was merely telling everyone about when they'd leave on the ferry, the time they'd return, and so on. Andre was surprised that John seemed to sense his feelings. For example, when certain words made him feel uneasy, John would use different ones. John would be a focal point for Andre due to his attentiveness to his feelings. Andre also liked the man's Australian accent and voice intonations.

When they were all on the bus going to the boat, Andre again found himself separated from everyone. Only when they were on the boat did John make it a point to speak to him. Andre felt pleased that he was asked about his former school and that this professor was interested in him. The thought of being totally alone all week with nobody to talk to was dreadful.

There were doubts in Andre's mind as to why he had taken

this course. It was a peer counseling program, which wasn't even a requirement for his upcoming computer science classes. He was interested in the specifics of the course and figured it would earn him three elective credits early on. He was a bit disappointed that everyone there was markedly older than he was—by 10 years and more. This partly explained why it was so difficult for him to connect with the others, but that didn't make him feel any better.

His thoughts that had started with the course introduction were more than just bad feelings; they had made Andre physically ill. The first day on the island, he couldn't eat his lunch and only managed coffee, which probably didn't help his already frazzled nerves.

He knew he was wise in taking a one-week course to get three credits, and when he found that the classes would take up no more than four hours a day, he felt a little better. He also felt much relief when the group was walking on the beach and John was with him, engaging him in conversation. This action caused Andre to feel a special connection with John, and he was glad to have these good feelings to cling to.

Earlier that afternoon, Mike, who was the peer counselor for the disabled in the student life office, had expressed undue concern (at least undue in Andre's view) about him wandering around alone, as there were drop-offs and all kinds of dangerous situations which could get him hurt. Andre, now angry with Mike, answered him in an irritated voice, "I had plenty of mobility training and have traveled independently in Boston. I don't think there's anything here that I can't deal with." Mike's lack of support and the fact that he had stated openly that he didn't think Andre could cope with a college environment didn't help Andre's confidence.

At least John interacted with him daily. He was interested when Andre was playing a space video game and asked all kinds of questions about it. What was even nicer for Andre was John's excited tone of voice, which made Andre realize that John wasn't just casually interested in him. Andre made it a point to latch onto John's every word when he instructed the group.

The classes were very simple. They were informed that there would be no paper to write; they would merely be questioned and tested on the techniques discussed. Oh, Andre thought, this will be simple memorization and mimicry. It was really only a five-day course, so he felt a little better that he wouldn't have to suffer for two extra days.

One older student named Paul occasionally talked to Andre. That him a bit more hope, but for some reason, he still felt the terror, especially at meals and social gatherings. He thought it was silly to have these feelings, but he could think of no remedy.

On the last night, the group was all gathered. John was going around the room asking individuals how they had enjoyed the week. He said he wasn't sure how people were feeling about it. Andre instantly recognized this as a pop quiz. He was amazed that many people were trying to allay John's fears and emotionally reassuring him.

Andre's turn came, and John asked, "Andre, please respond to my statement." Instantly, Andre knew that he had to wait a couple of seconds, turn in John's direction, make eye contact, and basically paraphrase what John had said. He didn't understand how so few people saw the trap.

After this, he was pleased that there were wine bottles placed out. As it was the last night, he felt a need to celebrate, but probably not for the same reasons as the others. He knew the wine would stop the feelings of terror which were always with him to some degree. He was right; the wine did relax him. Dotty, a 50-year-old woman, asked him to dance, and he accepted.

Later, Paul said to him, "John was so pleased with your response and said, 'Wasn't that great?'"

Andre didn't answer Paul or feel all that proud of himself.

He merely let his statement pass.

The next morning at breakfast, John took his attention to Andre one step further. He stood behind him while Andre was eating and placed his hands on Andre's shoulders while talking to him and others at the table. Andre felt some fear, in that others might have strange ideas about this action, and he couldn't look at anyone. He did feel a sense of warmth from this connection with John, and he found himself wishing that it hadn't ended so soon. He wanted a deeper connection with John from that point on.

iii

For the rest of the month when Andre got home, he was able to suppress his many concerns about the upcoming school year by telling himself that he would never have met John if he hadn't taken that short course at the college. This allowed Andre to read and use his computer even more avidly.

When the day came for him to spend the night at the college for orientation, the feelings of dread returned. They seemed even worse than the ones he'd had during the one-week course. This is so stupid! he thought. What is there to be so afraid of? I should be at least a little happy. But he was unable to suppress his negative feelings.

It would have helped if everything hadn't been so routine. There were a few meetings concerning what he thought of as common-sense issues. He couldn't sit far away from anyone, since there were so many people around: a much larger group, hundreds of people, compared to the dozen or so in the computer class he had taken on the island.

So he bit the proverbial bullet and somehow managed to get through the one night and two days. When he had the opportunity to do so, he spent as much time alone in his room as possible, brushing up on the college manual. He didn't learn too much from it, but preferred it over being with people he didn't know. One other reason he felt so alone and scared was that many of the people there obviously knew each other from the past.

Chapter 13

The Tangle Continues

i

A week later, Dr. Aguair met with John Kline again. "So, John," she asked him, "how was your week?"

"Not bad. I don't want to talk about the envelope with the materials concerning Andre. I have gotten all the information from my Schegnan contact."

"They can give you the information via the direct mind route?"

"Yes, Doctor. May I tell you more about the Schegnans and Metans?"

"Yes, of course, John. You're my last patient today, and as we discussed by phone, you don't have to worry about the hour. Just don't keep me here until dawn."

John chuckled. "Of course. Okay, I want to put your mind at ease. The aliens I've spoken of had nothing to do with the pyramids. I don't want you to be under the illusion—or think that I am suffering the delusion—that these beings had any effect on ancient cultures or religions. I am not a UFO fanatic. You'll see how outlandish the theories on unidentified flying objects are when I have told you all about the Metans and

Schegnans. I now have all the information they want to share with you and Doctor D'Erable, and maybe in time with humankind. I left you off in Arizona."

"Arizona? I don't understand."

"Sorry, I am assuming you can read my mind. The first nuclear test! Some say it was under the Chicago stadium in 1942 and the government won't acknowledge it. Let me use my notes.

"Okay. The Metans and Schegnans began disagreeing when humanity began developing nuclear weapons. Oh, I also want to clarify that I don't want you to entertain any thoughts of Area 51! I mean, do you think these advanced races, Metans and Schegnans, would be caught in a flying saucer? No, they would not! They wouldn't dare interfere with our evolution by having us discover them flying around in space.

"So, we bring ourselves to the end of WW II. The Schegnans and Metans were at a crossroads. Was that the place we last left off?"

"Yes, John, you're right."

"Good. Now I can tell you the rest. The fact is that both races were able to view our history with all kinds of sensitive scientific equipment without ever having to land on Earth. They could sit out at the orbit of Jupiter and do it all. During WW II, they knew that we didn't have any equipment sensitive enough to detect them, so they landed on the moon to get a better look. Both races agreed that they should use their technology to avoid detection by our telescopes. They didn't want to take any chances.

"As I said, the Schegnans were interested in stopping us from doing our damage at Hiroshima and Nagasaki, but the Metans convinced them not to interfere. After these events, the Schegnans decided to act alone.

"Martim, now viewed unfavorably in Schegnan history, went to Earth. He did this by matter transfer rather than risking landing a ship. I'm sorry to say that even the advanced races aren't immune to legends. Some say he fathered a human child. Others say many strange things. The one certain fact is that the Metans got wind of it and were, to say the least, very unhappy. I will not confuse you with the legends and myths about alien interference with our development unless it is a fact. I don't think even Martim would have fathered a child of a different species.

"The Metans simply stated that they were very concerned that Martim acted as he did. I will now read you a brief transcript from the MetSche alliance. Gav is the Metan and Luri is the Schegnan.

"'Luri, I am sure that you, as director of your observatory, are aware that Martim has physically gone to Earth.'

"'Yes, Gav. We approve of his mingling with humans.'

"'I don't have to tell you that I have already told Metamo–Prime of this.'

"'Predictable. I have told Schegna–Base. They authorized the whole operation.'

"So it went on. The Schegnans broke the age–old agreement with Metamo. Both worlds asked for the missions to return until the planets Metamo and Schegna could decide on a consensus. Martim refused to return to his ship, and the Schegnan government, or what we'd call a government, declared its right to separate autonomous exploration with or without Metan cooperation. The officials (for lack of a better translation) of Metamo urged cooperation and consensus.

"A blue beam as thick as a human hair but as bright as a sun was aimed at the Schegnan ship. In less than one–tenth of a second, the Schegnan ship was no more. Nobody on the Metan ship would admit to this outrage. With 58 Schegnans killed in cold blood, now the Metans could not rely on them for help in finding out who had done this horrible deed.

"The Metans were ordered home and obliged the officials of their planet, but they'd be back in less than a week. It seems they could have saved themselves the trip. When they got home, the Metan people almost all agreed that they had the same rights as the Schegnans and further vowed they'd prove to the Schegnans that they could physically go to Earth and not interfere. They also asked that the Schegnans show good faith and prove they hadn't interfered with human development. The Schegnans were outraged and stated that they didn't have to do this, because they were on a mission separate from the alliance.

"Another Metan ship showed up a week after the first one came back to Earth, observing it invisibly from the moon. The Schegnans were also keeping their ships invisible. When the Metan ship neared Jupiter's moons, a hair–thin blue ray was aimed at it from the Schegnan ship, destroying it almost instantly. Some say that one of our largest planet's moons is now going backwards in its orbit as a result of the Metan ship being destroyed. In any case, 5,113 of them died. Metans often reduce their size so they can have more scientists on their ships, something Schegnans cannot do.

"Both planets were horrified by this action. They grudgingly agreed to cease hostilities, which hadn't been seen on either world in 125,000 years. 'Even for science's sake, this behavior is abominable and reminiscent of a dreary past, one which was unintelligent and uncivilized,' said a prominent Metan. An equally high Schegnan answered, 'Indeed, the Metans are correct. We may have differing views in our science, but we must remain intelligent.' I must also state that the Schegnan who pushed the button was never discovered.

"Perhaps these actions were perpetrated by individuals who had a rogue ancient gene for violence. At least that was some comfort for the two worlds. They realized that nature itself is a cycle of creation and destruction. What made beings superior was their ability to control the emotions of yore. No, they should not deny their existence, but, yes, control was the only proof of civility. The two races quickly agreed and lived up to the Great New Alliance. There were no more incidents of hostility. The only change was that they could visit in physical form, as they had been doing on a few hundred worlds already, so long as they took great care not to influence the world they were visiting.

"The Schegnans made a powerful argument for aiding species, but they concluded that it was only a mental exercise and sided with The Great Laws of Nature. 'After all,' pointed out a Metan scientist, 'mercy is indeed a great trait, but nobody can argue that we should have saved the dinosaurs on our world. That very act of kindness would have made our evolution impossible. This is also the case on your world, Schegna, and we see this on Earth, as well.' The Schegnan scientist in the group answered, 'Yes, we all know that even bacteria have a right to live, but we must realize that neither of our races is intelligent or powerful enough to be making these planetary–scale decisions.'

"It is true that the two races both believed in a higher being. There wasn't a formal religion of any kind on either world anymore, but nearly all the individuals thought it would be arrogant, if not ridiculous, to think that the planets, stars, and all kinds of life forms were merely formed at random. They didn't believe in a Big Bang, either. I won't go into all the details, but basically, this theory, according to the Schegnans, and especially the Metans, leaves something coming from nothing as almost a religious belief, like that of God creating the Universe from nothing. Oh, we say that God created himself or herself, but God would have no sex—or gender, if you prefer.

"Metamo and Schegna might be described as being much like our Renaissance, or rather our ideal one. They don't have to fight a Church or anyone else. Patience usually brings consensus. We humans fight over things we can't prove, anyway. We can't prove a Big Bang, God, Christ, or almost anything else. Even when our scientists proved that Earth went around our sun, most common people probably didn't have the basic mathematical skills to understand the proof. The MetSche wants me to tell you that they are worried about our system. Most beings on their worlds don't have to argue about science because they understand it. Many on Earth are either afraid of scientists or take them at their word rather too easily at times, allowing power plays and politics to enter the picture. If more of us had a better understanding of science, we wouldn't have to rely on our media to interpret so much for us. Well, let me continue my story and not get into how bad the education system is on Earth."

ii

"So we would be amused and amazed if a Metan showed up in a bar and asked for gasoline on the rocks. Maybe they don't bathe on the sun anymore because some bright young astronomer might see them and get religion. For them, it is no matter and an afterthought. Turning oneself into a cat or other animal is of no consequence. Occasionally they have contests, not to show off their abilities, but more to beat time records. It takes a lot to consciously change one's DNA and change form. There would be instincts which would allow a Metan to put asbestos into the cell membrane if they were threatened by a flame from a lighter.

"The Schegnans, on the other hand, have brought up the prospect of what would have happened if they hadn't found each other's planets. Their ability to sense subtleties in each other and beings from other worlds is a definite advantage. They have developed a great linguistic tradition and see the ability to read someone's mind as an extension of language.

"It really wasn't necessary to transport themselves physically to our Earth, as they both had remarkable means to see and hear all kinds of things on our planet. However, it became seen as an additional benefit to interact directly with the plants and animals of a planet. They could tell all kinds of things from far away, but there was nothing like experiencing a planet's weather, smells, and other nuances by being there.

"The old rules regarding directly engaging beings on a planet were becoming blurred. It was agreed, for example, that saving a baby from a fire or preventing someone from being hit by a car wasn't going to change the fabric of a culture. Even if they had killed Adolph Hitler, both Schegnans and Metans agreed that Stalin probably would have filled in the void for him. They could have stopped Robespierre and saved many lives, but then the French Revolution might not have happened, and maybe another monarch would have been worse. If they had killed all the dictators and sadists, things might have been better for a great number of people, but then they would have had to govern, as well. In short, there were no easy solutions. They knew that anarchy could be just as bad as dictatorship. Democracy was a tricky issue. The aliens wouldn't breach this barrier because there were too many other inequalities to deal with, such as the distribution of food and medicine.

"The Metans and Schegnans could have saved themselves all the unnecessary death. Neither of them sent more than a few dozen scientists to Earth from the end of World War II until the present. When they got here, they merely enjoyed the climate and culture of our world. There were a few exceptions in which certain individuals were communicated with or helped for a specific purpose.

"I am one of about half a dozen people that the Metans and Schegnans are now actively engaged with. There are five people for whom a specific plan of action is anticipated. My knowledge about this activity of theirs is very limited. It is clear that even their miniscule presence and interference with our world would cause great distress and concern for many people. Not only would it disturb many government leaders, but the religious ramifications would no doubt lead to great suffering for humanity—greater than we might imagine.

"Considering all this, you might ask, dear Dr. Aguair, why this information should be imparted to you. Well, there is a plan whose details are known by me but can't yet be revealed. Suffice it to say that you and Dr. D'Erable are a part of it, as you might suspect. We must also wait for Andre to arrive, and before that happens, I'd like your permission to read more about him to you."

Dr. Aguair was puzzled. She was glad to listen to John, but a diagnosis and what to do about it were still mysteries.

"Well, that would be good," she said. "I wonder, however, if we might not want to speed this process up by meeting together with Dr. D'Erable, so that you can tell both of us the story. You have asked me, or told me, that you didn't object to him being filled in on the details. Would it not be easier to meet both of us rather than having me write to him?"

"Indeed it would! I'd welcome meeting the good doctor again. I see what you mean. Let me know what a good time would be, and I'll get back to you."

"How about next week at your regular appointment time?"

"Good. I'll be glad to oblige."

"Oh, by the way, John, can you fill me in on something?"

"What would that be?"

"Can you tell me why we've been getting Andre's story from overseas all this time, and now you want to finish the story?"

"I can't finish the story, but you'll be close to the end when we meet next week."

"All right, but as to the overseas letters we've been—"

"Doctor, I trust you implicitly. Please let me fill you in in my own way and time."

"Certainly. I'm just curious."

"Of course you are. I promise you, all will be revealed."

"Until next week, then?"

"Goodbye, and I'll see you next week."

iii

The doctors met and went to Ruby's Restaurant to wait for John.

D'Erable said, "John isn't due for another half–hour."

"I just wanted to show you the notes on my session from last week."

They both sipped their coffee, and after about 20 minutes of reading and rereading the transcript, D'Erable put the notes down and summoned the waitress. "More coffee please, Miss." He then turned to Dr. Aguair and said, "I appreciate your thoroughness, Marilyn. I don't want to diminish your work or John's story, but your call last week was a good summary of what I read."

"Well, Stephen, I appreciate that. I'm rather stumped as to our course of action, or even if there should be one."

"Yes, it's surprising that John has agreed to take various medications and that what we considered his delusions have not changed or lessened. We're both stumped. I almost wish I'd not answered your first call for help." Stephen was smiling and it was clear that he was joking.

"Stephen," said Marilyn, "you were never one to pass up a good challenge. So, seriously, what are we to do?"

"Short of believing him, you mean? He hasn't responded to

any medication. Oh, there've been a few side effects, but I mean he's not delusional at all!"

"No. Remember that lady who was found a while back? You remember, she was found on the street and was unresponsive. Well, what more can be said? What do we have? Three supposedly unconnected people who related stories of Schegna and Metamo."

"Right. I would try to find out how they're related. It's hard to accept."

"Yes, Stephen. I agree. John is too clever, though. He'll never tell us anything, and the other patients aren't claiming to know him. I don't sense that anybody is lying."

"No, but I suppose we'll never be sure. We can only let it play itself out."

"That's about it. You know, if it is true, we're wasting our time."

"Ah, but if it's false, we have to at least convince John and his three unrelated friends that they're suffering a strange delusion. Why don't we force his hand? I mean, he's been your patient long enough. Don't you think it's time?"

"Yes, but he just says it's the truth and that it will come out in time. We have to give him some sort of deadline now, right?"

"I'll let you know after we meet him. Here he is now. Hello, John! We're over here."

"Hello, doctors. Marilyn, are we ready? Oh, before I start, there's something I've been thinking of. My Schegnan contact suspects that one or both of you probably have doubts about my story. This disbelief is certainly understandable, but you must recall that you have proof. Don't you recall that cell sample you sent to France? How much convincing do you need?

"I'm sure that if I were speaking in terms of my religious beliefs or God, you would accept the story with no hesitation. The fact that my bringing you a truth seems to be causing you distress must be addressed. It has been revealed to me that you will probably propose a deadline for me to prove myself, and that you suspect I am having delusions.

"There is no way you'll be able to show that your other patients know me. Besides, you never told me about them, and yet I know about them, so that should be proof enough. But I'm sure you'll merely excuse this fact and somehow conclude that there was some contact between them and me at one point. This is reasonable. I can only say that in less than a month, you'll both have no doubts about the veracity of my tale. There is no argument that can be put forth or words that can be said that will convince you. I understand that you are very meticulous in your pursuit of scientific facts. It is my contention that since you are both psychiatrists, you must certainly be concerned with the causes and treatments of distress in mankind, especially things having to do with the mind.

"It is understandably a very tough position to be in. I am grateful that you are concerned for my mental health. It is not yet fully clear how you will be convinced, yet I am assured by the aliens that this task is vital for me to complete. They have been very helpful to me, yet I grow impatient at times. I have decided to stop taking all medications. It is sensible, since there is nothing wrong with me, and I was only complying to prove a point, which neither one of you seemed to get. If I were not rational in my thinking, it would follow that one of your medicines would work, but since I am telling the truth, medicine won't erase it. If somebody said they were 76 years old and you thought they were suffering a delusion, medicine wouldn't cure them of that knowledge.

"There have been, unfortunately, many people, for one reason or another, who have believed themselves somehow involved with aliens. Most of the time, treatment was successful. In my case, you doctors don't know why I would make such claims, and you simply assume that you haven't found the right treatment, yet. It can only be pointed out that I suffer no psychological, physical, or psychiatric disorders. You have ruled out a medical problem and most likely have concluded that I am rational and sound, but there must be a part of you that is looking for a disorder caused by some imbalance of my brain to explain my words. Is this about the size of it?"

The two doctors exchanged a puzzled glance. They both decided that they could trap Kline with his own words. It was reasonable that they couldn't argue with or challenge a delusion on their terms, so they'd have to coax him, hopefully, by letting him trap himself, or rather, disprove his own story on his own terms.

"Okay, John," D'Erable said, "you make a great deal of sense. It's all reasonable, and I'm sure you are aware that we've been through all of this in one way or another. I'm all for you taking a month. I wouldn't want to impose a deadline for you to have to prove your claims. I can easily wait for a month. What do you think, Dr. Aguair?"

"I agree. John. What do you want to do?"

"Well, doctors, I am pleased that you are at least willing to cooperate. I suppose that the Metans and Schegnans are wiser than I. They informed me that both of you would be unlikely to walk away at this point and that I should be patient. It seems that they will have the chance after all to show that what I've said is true. It will be interesting to see how things unfold."

iv

John was then told to meet the doctors the following week, at his regular appointment time. D'Erable and Aguair had to discuss how they would proceed from this point forward. They agreed to wait awhile and determine if they could unravel the mystery that Kline was presenting to them.

The following week, John was in the office with the doctors. He began, "There is something more I must tell you about the aliens before I go on with Andre.

"These aliens I've told you about were once as fervent as we are about our ideological differences. They were more advanced than we are only in that when they had wars over their differences of approaches to problems or disparate theories, they justified their actions in the name of science, whereas we fight more over religious differences or due to nationalistic fervor.

"My mind has been well scanned by the Schegnans. They almost gave up on me as a subject when I opted to tell you about them. Now that I have realized that none of your treatments are necessary, the Metans and Schegnans agree that the experiment can continue.

"The conclusion of the test will be when I have told you all about Andre. You will also know a bit more about the aliens, as well. It was my belief that I could tell you all about Andre, but I may have forgotten some details. This envelope, still sealed, has been delivered to me. You will notice that the stamps aren't from this country. I ask that you read it, and we can meet again next week to talk more."

The doctors agreed, and John excused himself from the room.

Dr. D'Erable opened the envelope. "Marilyn, I'll copy this for you. We can discuss it at length before we see Mr. Kline next week."

"Yes, that sounds good."

Dr. Aguair went home with her copy of the mysterious writings from across the sea. She was curious and began to find herself very interested in how things would turn out. She began to read.

Chapter 14

"Andre's Story, Part 7—Sunrise Hopes in the Clouds"

i

It wasn't that Andre wasn't excited about starting college, but rather that his feelings of fear and dread, quite upsetting to him, overshadowed any of the more positive emotions he had. His only desire was to turn off these bad feelings, but there seemed to be no way to do so.

When he met his roommate, Jeff, Andre was hopeful that things would be all right, but he really wanted his private space. Almost at once, all the people in the suite were getting along fine, making Andre feel alienated. He made a conscious effort to make himself visible and make small talk with just about everyone. Somehow, this effort didn't seem to make him feel any better.

Andre knew that it would take time, probably even four years, to make friends anywhere near as close to those he'd had in his earlier school days. He did welcome the quiet times he had eating alone, when he could think about how his college life was going. By the second week, a group of three or four young ladies had invited Andre to eat with them. This gathering became a regular suppertime ritual. At other times, they would also eat lunch together.

Andre was glad that Allison, one of the girls, was interested in talking with him about the weather, classes, and all the usual chit–chat. These short intervals were something to look forward to each day. He couldn't feel a part of the people in the dorm. By the time the first month of classes was up, Andre had arranged to move into a hall where he'd have his own room. He got along well enough with his roommate, but they really didn't talk too much. Andre found it hard to start conversations, but he also felt that people weren't very interested in talking to him.

On Thursday nights, most of the students went to the mixer to hear local bands and amateur startup bands, as well as to consume large amounts of alcohol. Andre looked forward to this, but the music was always too loud, and there wasn't too much opportunity to really socialize. One week, his dorm mates decided to all go together. One guy named John was unable to attend, as he claimed to have a lot of studying to do. Andre was kind of surprised that John asked the others to look out for him. In any case, the crowd all went together, but as soon as they arrived, everyone broke up into cliques, leaving Andre alone, as usual. This situation bothered him, but he soon forgot about it and enjoyed the music.

ii

The new dorm room was a blessing for Andre. It was private, and even the area where everyone gathered seemed much more conducive to privacy. At least the people were quieter than in his other dorm, and at first, they seemed a bit friendlier.

Andre was annoyed by the loud music that was sometimes played across from his room. He wouldn't have even thought of race as an issue had the noisy people not brought it up. He was saddened to hear them talk about all whites being racists. It seemed futile to try to become chummy with people who were already prejudiced against him. They were cordial enough, saying the usual "Hello, how are you?" and the like, but from behind closed doors, more immature remarks could be heard. Everyone was the butt of jokes and an object of laughter, and most disturbing of all, a bigot.

Even Mark, whom Andre had come to admire, could be heard making fun of blacks and of people of other nationalities. Andre had thought, however naively, that college would bring people above this sort of thing. He was sadly disappointed. Maybe it was that the old memories of childhood were resurfacing in him. He had become used to feeling like a victim; he had come to expect people to be intolerant—maybe not outright cruel, but certainly lacking in common civility. He grudgingly accepted this fact and carried on.

After he'd been in his new room for about three weeks, he was very hurt and disappointed by the behavior of those in his suite. One person had complained, in a bitter and annoyed tone, that he never ate with them. Andre felt unable to defend himself. By now, he couldn't go through explaining his vision impairment: that he couldn't see them from far away, and that they'd have to make themselves known to him if they wanted him to sit with them. He had observed that the people with normal vision were not shy about yelling out to each other in the dining hall, to get the attention of their friends when they wanted to eat together. Only Allison and her friends made an effort to sit with him and to talk with him, and he wouldn't fight for the privilege of being amiable with others. Andre knew who his allies were, even though he had only a small handful of them.

Sara was an advisor for the disabled in the student life office. She was very supportive and understanding of what Andre was going through. She didn't belittle his plight, but recalled how much tougher it was for her with polio when she was younger, also how many people had feared catching cancer through the air. It was clear that she understood his problems, but she always reminded Andre that "things were slowly getting better" and that "we have to stick together."

Andre was very happy to be with the small disabled community at the college for their meetings and to discuss their problems. The older students inspired him to stick to it, and besides that, John, the professor who had been so attentive to Andre the previous summer, was often there to talk to him and inspire the group. Andre viewed these weekly gatherings as the height of his social life.

John and Sara had nudged Andre to pursue some of his interests, so he had decided to try out for the chess club.

The Christmas season was approaching, and Andre was looking forward to a long winter break. Perhaps he'd be up to all these activities after a rest. The holidays passed with amazing speed. The only effect the month's rest had on him was to allow him to suppress his feelings and forget about things for a while.

Before he knew it, school was back in session. The cold and dreary days quickly reminded him of all the things he had put on the back burner.

He had a strong desire to go back to his old school. Ralph, whom Andre had known since childhood, would graduate that spring. Andre had wanted to keep his promise to Ralph. It seemed that they had never had enough time to spend together, and Andre felt that they could make up for some of this loss. Unfortunately, the staff at his old school didn't cater to Andre's college winter break schedule, and Ralph was kept busy with school or cottage chores. Nonetheless, Andre had decided to spend five days at his old school and recapture some of his past memories.

He knew a few other students who were still going to the boarding school. Roger, a much younger student, had always looked up to him. Not wanting to have the whole week be a bust, Andre went up to Roger's room, where they listened to music. Andre had brought a bottle, and they were both enjoying the music and conversation. Andre wanted Roger to remember a good time. It was natural that a boy of 16 was looking up to a young man of 20. Andre was afraid that the staff would break in at any moment and have him thrown off campus, especially when Roger got sick on the booze. Andre sensed that even so, Roger was having a great time, even though he couldn't keep up with Andre's drinking pace. Roger asked Andre if drinking increased his sexual desire, but Andre sensed that he'd better leave before he got the boy into trouble, and he answered that it didn't affect him that way.

It was not what Andre had expected, going back to the school, but he was glad he had gone back to see it in a new light. Now he could go back to college and look forward to the chess club.

It was certainly fun to go and play, even though most of the people in the chess club were older. He had never thought of himself as a chess master, but not being able to win a game took a lot of the fun out of things. The president of the club had convinced Andre to join them for the tournament. Andre said he didn't feel he was good enough for that, but the president reminded him that improvement would only come from practice, and besides, he should just go and enjoy himself.

By the time he arrived at the hotel, Andre didn't feel very enthusiastic anymore. He hated himself for not being assertive, but he couldn't visualize himself as engaging in any serious conversations with people. While it was mildly stimulating to talk about one's chess rating, even here, Andre felt cheated. He had the lowest rating, as he'd never played in a tournament before. All the people had their own cars, and as Andre was in a strange city, he wasn't keen on wandering about or exploring the city. He felt hurt that nobody invited him to go along with them. He hated himself for not being more imposing and making a pest of himself. He began to wonder whether the problem was his thick glasses or something else. He remembered being stared at as a child, and a few cases where a child would say, "Oh, look at his eyes!"

Once again, though, he resolved to make the best of things. He felt good that all he needed was in the hotel. Eating alone wasn't as bad as feeling alone in a group of people. There were a few instances when some of the people watched his chess game, but he had lost the last four games. He was glad that they were clinical about where he was making his mistakes. Andre filled in the low self-esteem comments by himself. There would be an early last game in the morning. Andre won the game, but only because the other player was a no-show, due to having slept in.

His desire for independence had become a sort of stubbornness. It had started with the entry writing test even before he had started college. If he had told the test-takers that he needed extra lighting or more time for the exam, he probably would have passed and not been required to take the literature class the first year. Andre enjoyed the class well enough, though. Some of the characters, like Madam Bovary and Don Quixote, expressed some of the mixture of hopelessness and optimism that he was feeling.

He was unaware that he could ask for more help. Doing so would have helped him do better in his classes. Unfortunately, he was too depressed to realize this. He knew rationally that some of his trouble in his classes was due to his lack of communication with his professors, but he desired to be as normal as he could and thus made things harder on himself. He had done the minimum in obtaining accommodations. He knew that he had to sit as close to the front of the class as possible, ask for extra time on exams, and record lectures, but he didn't realize that he could make his life a little easier by discussing some of his issues in more detail.

He tried hard to socialize with people. He made it a point to sit out in the common area of the dorm and go to the various activities such as debates, movies, plays, and musical events put on by the college. It was good to engage in small talk with others. Allison had invited him to a play in the city. He felt honored that someone was interested in him, even though he didn't particularly enjoy the venue. Afterwards, Mark, one of his dorm mates, asked him about the outing, and Andre said, "The music was okay, but the company was fine."

Mark seemed very smart and was always giggling. Andre wanted to include Mark as one of his friends, especially because Mark seemed to possess what Andre thought he didn't have. Mark was a top student, on the honor roll, and more important, he was able to have a lot of fun. Andre was glad that Mark took some interest in him, but he knew that this situation could only go so far. Mark was more interested in his other friends, and the fact that he never invited Andre to eat with him or go out to town with his clique let him know his limits.

By the three–quarter mark of the freshman year, Andre had come to look forward to solitary time in his own room. At least there he could listen to music, dream about positive futures, and leave his worries behind him. Earlier that year, his refuge had been disturbed when a student upstairs was very vocal in protesting the smell of Andre's pipe tobacco. Rather than putting up a fight for what seemed to be his rights, Andre accepted this man's complaint and took his smoking outdoors. There, he found himself enjoying the scenes of nature in all its variations. He was able to find shelter from the elements in the doorway of some empty building and began to look forward to the evenings, when he could find some peace outdoors.

iii

The summer went by quickly. He was glad to reflect on the previous year and was able to enjoy his movies and reading. He also applied some of the skills he had learned in computer classes to his own machine at home. Even though he dreaded going back to some of the feelings at school in the fall, he was also looking forward to advancing his knowledge.

Two events made his return in the fall difficult. First, Allison had gone to another school, so there would be a lot of time spent eating alone. The second thing, which was much more difficult to accept, was that John, the professor Andre had looked up to so much for inspiration, had gone to Alaska that summer and had died while riding his motorcycle. Apparently he had fallen off a cliff. It wasn't merely that Andre felt the loss of a close ally; it was the senseless way in which death had taken one of them. He was shocked that John would do something so foolish as to go riding in the wilderness alone, with no one to assist him in case of trouble.

Andre resolved to delve into his studies and improve himself as much as possible. At least Sara was still there to talk to. In addition, he was now becoming an advocate to others. He now felt that he was a little more experienced, and he was proud to be able to tell new students how to assert themselves when it came to obtaining assistance, even though he hadn't yet gotten the formula entirely right for himself. He was able to find strength in lifting others up to independence, and subsequently, he gained more freedom for himself.

This newfound zeal helped Andre talk to his professors more as equals. It was refreshing to see them as human as he was. Naturally, he had always known this to be the case, but he was learning that college was more about the experiencing of a fact than the simple knowledge of its existence. He was happy to discuss philosophy and literature, but in his computer classes, he was able to see the results of the lectures and books right in front of him.

However, he was doing a bit lower than average in his computer classes. He realized that he had to buckle down and do whatever it took to meet and exceed the requirements to get the degree. His advisor didn't share Andre's enthusiasm. He expressed to Andre that he should consider another major, perhaps literature, and give up his hopes of a computer science degree. By this time, Andre was having some difficulties with some of the math requirements. He was confident that he could work through the problems, as most of them were due to his not having realized in time that his disability was a factor.

He was hurt by his advisor's lack of support. He later became very angry and thought things out. Yes, he would not only show his advisor up by finishing his degree, but he would also consider pursuing a second major in English literature, with a focus on creative writing. The rest of that year would see a lot of doubts, but his resolve would pay off. Now, the second year was soon to end. Andre felt exhilarated by his improvement in computer classes. His grades were higher, and he found new enthusiasm for going on with his studies.

Mark had not become any friendlier, but Andre was hopeful that things would improve. He strained to make himself visible in the suite, especially in the evenings. This was a difficult exercise for him, as he didn't really see any results, and he felt nervous and out of place, but he felt that he had to put some effort into it. By the time spring came, he had given up hope. He had very low expectations that he'd make any real friends at college.

It was now May, and classes had ended for the summer. Andre's second semester had ended with a new sense of hope, yet a new sense of isolation had also cropped up. Andre's older sister had invited him to go out to a night club with her, and he had stated that he didn't feel up to it. His sister had become impatient and frustrated with him, and had insisted on a reason for his not going. He just told her that he was tired. His sister was always acting as though her ideas and life were more important than those of others. Being the oldest, she took it upon herself to be a kind of dictatorial mother. Andre didn't really think that she was deliberately being mean; it was simply that she couldn't see beyond her own world.

He would find himself severely tested when she invited him to go to the amusement park with the college disability group.

iv

That Saturday morning in May came swiftly. Andre didn't want to fight with his sister and make up excuses about why he didn't want to go to the amusement park, nor did he want to tell her the truth—that he felt very uneasy and would have preferred to stay home. He didn't know how she had found out about the trip, as she wasn't a student at the college.

Andre resolved not to fight it. He convinced himself that he might even have a good time there. When he was younger, he had enjoyed the rollercoaster and many other rides and the food, especially the chowder and clam cakes. How terrible could this outing really be?

However, his usual sense of dread crept in when he boarded the bus with the others. He was more aware of these feelings because he felt that his sister was evaluating his performance, even though he knew this notion was illogical.

The usually immature Joe was busy giggling and making fun of anyone in sight. At least he jeered those outside the window rather than the people on the bus trip. Andre sensed that Joe was actually a big coward and wouldn't dare tussle with anyone in direct earshot or in his view. Joe's actions didn't strike Andre as merely childish; they were also tiresome and annoying.

There were alumni from the college, as well. Most of these people, only about half a dozen, sat together and were calm in comparison to the others. One man seemed to be sitting alone. His name was John, and he called out to Andre. He asked Andre to sit with him and asked him if he recollected him from years ago at his old school, when Andre was a child and used to buy candy at John's store.

Andre was polite and enthusiastic. He vaguely recalled these events, but not as vividly as John. It was not necessary to feign his excitement concerning other interests that they shared. John and Andre both liked science and science fiction, and they discussed common memories of their old school. They even preferred many of the same rides at the park, and both were looking forward to the upcoming meal.

Andre thought it odd that John wanted to go on rides that most would consider childish, such as the Ferris wheel and carousel, but Andre didn't concern himself with these preferences and told himself that at least John was a kid at heart. The horses were a bit of a struggle for Andre, as he was very tall, but he elected to surrender to the spirit of enjoyment. This acceptance of John's likes and dislikes was no chore for him until they decided to go on the airplane ride.

Andre felt that the seat on the ride was much too small for him, never mind anyone sharing it with him. The attendant asked him if he minded if John squeezed himself between Andre's legs. Andre was quite cramped and couldn't wait until the ride was over even before it started. He wouldn't have minded, but his legs were in pain and John seemed quite comfortable to sit back even more. John enjoyed telling Andre to control the plane's flight by having Andre move the joystick up and down.

All in all, Andre was very happy to have met John. They exchanged phone numbers and some private information. Unfortunately, John didn't call him for nearly a month afterwards. Andre didn't really know what to make of this situation and knew he would see John at the old school's annual reunion.

V

After a month, when John had still not called him, Andre went to him and asked him why he hadn't phoned. John stated that he didn't really know what to talk about.

The situation was easily rectified as they both started where they had left off a month ago at the amusement park. Andre decided to take John to the local Italian restaurant. From that point onward, they became much closer.

They spent the entire reunion weekend together. Before Andre realized it, Sunday morning had arrived. The previous night, John had asked him to go home with him, and Andre had said that he'd think about it. He decided to take John up on his offer and figured the fear he had would go away in time. Besides, having so much in common with John was a good reinforcer.

They spent that Sunday afternoon listening to records and talking. Andre was sure he'd found a great friend and companion. Was this reprieve from his prior feelings of isolation possible? Time seemed to fly by, and things seemed to be going so well that Andre felt as though he was dreaming. He was able to express his many feelings without having to be afraid of reprisals.

The entire summer was one of great liberation for Andre. He experimented with all the typical youthful adventures that he'd heard went on in college, from group sex to night clubs. All of John's friends seemed nice, and they were all party people. The strange thing was, in Andre's summer of love and sense of great liberation, he always looked forward to the quiet times alone with John, during which they watched TV. They both loved *Star Trek* and *The Twilight Zone*, which Andre had not seen much of before that time. He was very happy to enhance his social education, which he hadn't had a chance to do in school. Both he and John were much more interested in ideals like equality, justice, and humanity's future than they were in the partying of their friends. Andre realized that to be truly knowledgeable, one had to live life as well as read about it.

In midsummer, Andre went with his family to visit his cousins and uncle. This was always enjoyable. He felt good that he could have a few drinks with his uncle, and even though his mother expressed some concern, Andre was truly an adult, now; he wasn't an alcoholic, like his uncle, and he didn't understand his mother's concerns.

One day he was swimming in the pool. His cousin always seemed unduly fascinated with Andre's normal abilities. His other cousin was a nurse and married to a very well-off salesman. She seemed more realistic about Andre and asked him what kind of people he was meeting in college. Andre replied, "All kinds," to which the cousin who was always amazed at Andre's normality just laughed, as though this answer was somehow out of the ordinary. Yet Andre knew that as a legitimate adult, he could make himself look more so by putting an air of mystery into his life, as everyone else did.

In Canada, the grandparents and cousins were more genuinely interested in Andre's lofty goals. They treated him much more as an adult, although his grandmother was concerned with his smoking a pipe, in part because her husband had been a smoker and had emphysema. Apart from this, Andre felt a bit more respected, now. This was a refreshing change from his treatment as a child, when they had seemed overprotective and strict, although very nice and lovable. His grandfather and aunt both worked in jewelry and watch repair, and Andre felt honored and proud to buy a simple watch from their establishment. He'd cherish this timepiece for as long as he had it, which would turn out to be a very long time.

He returned home to spend the last month of his liberating summer before he went back to college. He felt accustomed to his life the way it was, but he also knew that serious study was ahead. He felt that John would always be his friend, but when the start of his classes was only a few days away, Andre dreaded having to go back to the former isolation, loneliness, and fear that had plagued him before. It all made him quite depressed.

Once he started his classes, however, he learned that he was not entirely correct about his fears. It was true that many of the same feelings and situations in the dorms, dining center, and other aspects of his life were still there to plague him, but now he could call John as often as he wanted to. Having someone to converse with made the burden much lighter, or at least tolerable for a while. Andre used the weekends with John as an incentive to get through the rough spots.

One thing that Andre found somewhat odd was that even though he had met many of John's friends and had done a lot of social activities over the summer, he didn't feel much more confident than before with being the first one to initiate conversation—that is, saying anything beyond a simple "Hello" or "Nice day!" Perhaps something that had occurred at the start of school was partly responsible for his timidity. When a young lady had said, "How are you?" Andre had answered, "Fine." She was quite upset and made a point of letting him know that she wasn't addressing him. This situation hadn't helped, of course, but Andre knew his shyness was inbred. He couldn't force himself to be more outgoing than he was by nature. This unfortunate condition even prevented him from feeling comfortable enough to have John over at the school. At first, John didn't think much about it, but it would become an issue later on.

The academic challenges were mounting. Now Andre was much more active in the disability group and with Sara. She kept him very interested in issues, and he became the treasurer of the group. He successfully obtained a reading machine for the library. His gift of eloquence proved valuable in convincing the college of the need for it.

Computer science was tough, but he was determined, worked hard, and was doing better. The improvements encouraged him to keep on applying himself. He sought to prove—if not to others, then to himself—that he could succeed. John was also instrumental, as Andre could now seek solace in being with him. Andre determined, if possible, to not have any studies for the weekend. This plan usually worked out, and he could usually totally forget the stresses of college for a couple of days each week.

By springtime, he had decided on a second major. Yes, he would go into literature. He knew that the added workload would mean an extra year of school, but he was determined to press forward. Now another summer was upon him.

By the time school began again in the fall, Andre felt much more linked to John. The only person in the dorm that he had felt at all close to was Mark, but it was not a real closeness, and Andre still yearned for a campus friend. This fall, Mark had not returned to school, and nobody knew why or where he was. Also, Allison had gone out west somewhere to finish her nursing education. Now Andre had nobody to talk to after classes. Also, the sense of fear that had been with him since the start of college was becoming more severe. Besides Mark, some of the other regulars in the dorm had also left. It was harder for Andre to sit out in the suite, and he felt more edgy with the new people. Their loud music, laughing, and carrying on were also a source of uneasiness for him. He felt solace in his room with his music and privacy.

It was early in the fall, and Andre was eating supper alone at a table. The day had been gray, cool, and dreary. In the middle of the meal, a sense of dread nearly overpowered him. He had felt a general sense of fear before, but this bordered on terror. He didn't really know what he was afraid of, but his instinct was to bolt out of the dining hall. Somehow, with the greatest mental control he had ever had to muster, he got through the meal. He went back to his room, feeling sick to his stomach, weak, and tired. He decided to try the counseling center for help.

The first counselor seemed to make light of it all, saying that it wasn't sensible to not eat a meal, and that the desire for hunger should override everything. In another week, Andre found a counselor he liked very much. Just the idea that he had some avenue for help made things a bit more tolerable for him. Still, every day was a struggle. There were times when he paused at his bedroom door in terror, and he struggled to find the strength to go to classes and meals. Lectures were somewhat better, as he knew he had to attend them. Eating, although necessary for life, was much more difficult, and there were a lot more people there in the dining hall, as well.

John had been very understanding about this, but there was nothing he could do to change Andre's feelings. Andre's knowledge that John supported him helped some, but only slightly.

After six weeks or so, Andre confided in his counselor that he very much appreciated the help, but he felt that he might need medication and psychiatric care. The counselor understood this, and John was also supportive.

Soon, the combination of medication and counseling helped

Andre feel some relief, and it actually gave him hope that he could overcome the problem. At this particular time, early in January, that was about all he had. He didn't blame John for his inability to help him. Andre knew that the strength would have to come from within, and he didn't think that anybody else could truly understand the depths of his terror without having experienced it themselves.

One night when Andre returned to the dorm after visiting with John, he felt so nervous that he didn't know how he got to his room at all. He felt so exhausted that he nearly collapsed. These setbacks filled him with doubt, but giving up would mean his whole college endeavor and future career would be in jeopardy. Somehow, he always found the strength to go on. Without John and his counselor, he felt sure that he wouldn't be able to.

By springtime, there had been enough victories for him that he felt a bit more hopeful. Techniques from counseling and the fact that he liked and respected the counselor, coupled with the mild medication, helped him even more. Andre couldn't imagine a day when he wouldn't need to take the medicine, but he was assured by the counselor and psychiatrist that this was indeed a good possibility.

Classes had been more enjoyable this year, especially the literature lectures. They were actually fun. The computer science lessons were a challenge, but fun in a different way. It was a joy for Andre to write and execute computer programs to prove to his professors that he had a mastery of the subject matter. Early on, he had done poorly in computer science, but in the advanced level courses, he was able to show marked development. This impressed his favorite computer professor very much. The instructor was always supportive of him and expressed how he admired Andre's willingness to persevere and achieve his goals. Andre had taken classes with this professor almost exclusively. He was lucky that it was a fairly small college and that he had such a luxury.

The statistics requirement had been rather troublesome. Andre had dropped the course once, but now his nose was to the grindstone. Coincidentally, the instructor was also his academic advisor. He had been more than a little dubious regarding Andre's chances of success in the class, but with his usual persistence and determination, Andre managed to pull out a C+ in the class. Certainly this wasn't an honor roll performance, but he had passed with a bit better than the required C. After this small but significant victory, Andre felt more prepared to move forward.

vi

His last two years of college went more smoothly, even though he was much busier than before. He was now in the groove. His dreams of the future were grandiose and probably gave him the extra push he needed.

It was true that he was lonely compared to those he observed around him, but his involvement with his classes and the disability group on campus made him feel more a part of things than before. His involvement with Sara, one of the major advocates of the group, gave him a further sense of belonging. He knew deep down that there was no real friendship there, not in the usual sense, but there was understanding for his situation. At times, others even looked to him for advice.

The difficulties he had had were certainly not to be taken lightly, but he was improving each semester in all aspects of his life. Getting on the Dean's List in the last semester was a confirmation that his hard work had paid off. He did wish that he could have done better earlier, but at least he had improved. And after all, many people had enough trouble with a standard college course load, let alone having a double major.

vii

Graduation day arrived at last. This ceremony was very different than what he'd gone through in high school. Back then, he had felt a sense of great loss, as though he was leaving a close family. Now he felt relief that the hardships of college were over, but he also knew that he faced an uncertain future.

A school official was droning on about various trivialities, as had many of the other speakers that day, when the speaker's subject matter and tone suddenly changed greatly, grabbing Andre's attention.

He was speaking of a young lady who had attended the college as a student, and he began to describe the extreme hardships of her life. This student and her parents had trekked for many miles and days to escape the killing fields of Cambodia. Perhaps others who were listening felt that there was nothing particularly new in what the orator was saying, but Andre found it all fascinating and shocking. Most of all, he was curious as to the identity of the young lady.

It was certainly not a trivial matter that the scholar had reached the top of her class. This would be a feat for anyone, and of course the word "commendable," given her life's story, with all its physical and mental trials, wasn't enough to describe her great accomplishment. When at last the speaker gave the identity of the person, Andre was taken aback. Vana had been in all his computer classes. She certainly didn't seem the happiest soul, but one would never have guessed her hidden past. Andre had never been shy about speaking out and asking questions in his classes, but Vana's inquisitiveness had seemed particularly intense. Looking back, he could see that it certainly helped explain her accomplishments.

Now it came time to line up and receive the so-called sheepskin. It was comical, really, as the students all knew they would be handed empty diploma cases; they would pick up their actual diplomas later. The names were called one by one, and the usual applause and cheers accompanied the ritual. When Andre's name was called, there was little fanfare. He heard John, and also Sherry, a friend Andre had made through John, and of course his parents. John was the most vocal, shouting, "Yaaaay!" There were probably a dozen others who clapped. It didn't surprise or bother Andre at all, for he didn't feel the rush of emotions that he had experienced in high school.

John and Sherry were invited to the home of Andre's parents to celebrate the occasion. Billy was also accompanying John and Sherry. It was amusing to Andre that Billy was dressed as a woman and preferred to go by the name of Christine. What made this situation more comical was that Andre's father apparently found Christine quite attractive, and was not shy in flirting with "her." This secret would remain humorous only as long as Billy kept his true identity a secret, which he managed to do.

Andre often wondered why he didn't have what was known as common sense. John had given him a graduation card which was very open in its expression of how he felt about him. Andre foolishly showed the card to his parents. This action was almost in direct contrast to his usual reserved behavior. It was just that he felt so proud to graduate and wanted to share it.

Andre's father immediately threw John's heartfelt words into the trash. His mother was speechless, which was completely contrary to the norm for her. At any rate, by sheer luck, Andre's father must have been so shocked, disgusted, or whatever, that he didn't tear the card into pieces. Andre was later able to retrieve it and lock it up for safekeeping.

He knew then that he couldn't share any more of the truth of his and John's close relationship with his parents. It was clear that they would rather bury the truth by not speaking about it. This pattern was upsetting, but Andre also knew that it was normal as far as his family was concerned, and so shouldn't have been surprising.

Chapter 15

"Andre's Story, Part 8—Abyssmal Growth"

i

Within a month after Andre's graduation, he obtained his first computer programming work. It wasn't anything like what he'd expected. His boss didn't share Andre's enthusiasm for computers. It certainly wasn't necessary to be close friends with one's employer, but this relationship was rocky at best.

The man was stubborn beyond reason. He didn't really want input or anything else from Andre or anyone else working there. Andre tried to adjust to this, reminding himself that he was being paid to do his work, even if it wasn't appreciated. So long as he went through the motions, nothing else mattered. It was drudgery to force himself to work every day, but he simply pulled himself through.

By the second month at work, nothing had changed. In fact, it had grown worse. A job was given to the team, but the boss didn't really clarify what the point of this assignment was, nor was anyone sure what the exact reasoning or end point of the project was. After a couple of weeks, Andre realized that his misgivings had been correct. The boss informed everyone that they had been given the wrong job. At least the employer didn't punish his workers for his own errors.

By the time the third month came along, Andre's gloomiest premonitions had proven correct. He was to be laid off. What tipped him off was that the boss had called another programmer in for about a week to help out. Andre didn't feel slighted by this fact, but only that the man in charge of this small company had no real insight into what he was ordering his underlings to do. Andre knew he could have handled whatever concerns the employer had, but of course he was in no position to quarrel.

When he learned that this extra person was receiving more than four times his own wage to consult on this project, Andre knew he had little time left with the company. A week before, he had finished a job under pressure at the last minute and had run downstairs to inform the people who had wanted the company to do the work that yes, indeed, he had completed the task. The boss didn't have any words of praise for him, but rather was keen on focusing on his employees' shortcomings rather than face his own errors in judgment.

The day Andre was laid off, he felt more than just relief in knowing that this was the last day he would have to put up with all the problems on the job. The future was looking brighter. Now he could make his own path, hopefully with fewer obstacles. It didn't seem to matter that the day of his layoff coincided with the time his health insurance would have begun. Andre had told his boss that he didn't need such an excessive plan, but of course the superior was unmoved. Now it no longer mattered to Andre that his disability might have made his employer nervous about health care expenses and insurance issues.

However, his new job search was to prove less cheery than Andre had expected. It seemed that a lot of employers were looking for people with much more experience than he had—or was likely to ever get, if things continued this way.

ii

For nearly a year, Andre diligently searched for a job. He went to job fairs, the unemployment office, and so on. There was always the dream of having his own business, but he was realistic enough to hold off on that dream.

Even after over 200 rejection letters and the inability of the counselor at the Commission for the Blind to explain why he couldn't land a job, Andre still persisted, for that was the right thing to do. He would soon entertain, once again, the dream of his own business.

He went to one interview and felt that all was going well until the woman asked him how he was getting to and from the job. He told her, truthfully, that he was taking the bus. The woman was sure he was deceiving her. Andre stated that he had intended to emphasize his abilities rather than focus on his disability. He also told her that public transportation was actually more reliable than someone in a car. She remained unconvinced that he could actually do such a thing as use the public bus system. This attitude, this inability to accept his everyday competencies, was the biggest obstacle he would face in getting employment. Most others would not be quite so blatant about it, but in any case, he would have no recourse, no way of proving discrimination based on his disability, as it was one person's word against the other's.

So he started his own business. The work was all very exciting, whether he was actually writing the computer programs or learning about advertising and marketing. The financial rewards were never very large, but the knowledge that he was getting orders and inquiries was more than enough to keep him going. It never occurred to him that he could fail.

Naturally, the dream of making it big was always in the back of his mind, but he was making products to help the blind, which in itself was a noble goal. He was sure he could undercut the competition when it came to prices. Things seemed to be going almost too well until his own eye health came into question.

He had never considered himself sick or even blind. Oh, he had to keep up with his eye drops, but he assumed that all the surgeries he'd had as a child protected him against any trouble in the future. It was true that his particular eye condition, by the account of most experts, would not lead to total blindness if he kept up with it, as he did. More surgery was the last thing he'd thought of.

Even undergoing two simple laser procedures, which were supposed to be painless, was taxing on his nerves, but he went through them, as he trusted his doctor's judgment. Even when he'd been unable to keep his eye completely still, and the doctor had made some misses with the laser, Andre went through the second procedure a year and a half later, as the doctor had now figured out that he could use drops to keep Andre's eye completely still. In the end, though, the laser treatments were ineffective. Now, Andre had to face his deepest fears and contemplate more eye surgery.

The fear that he'd have to go under the knife was bad in and of itself, but the fact that he would not be knocked out, as he was when he was younger, bothered him the most. He remembered being a teen and looking forward to a surgery, as he couldn't remember the ones from his near–infancy. What really terrified him, although he wasn't aware of it consciously, was his memory of the time when he was six years old and the dentist had pulled his tooth. He'd been reassured by the dentist, his parents, and his friends that it would be nearly painless; besides, he wasn't too fearful of dentists. But the Novocain didn't take, so his tooth was pulled with great struggle and agonizing pain. Since that ordeal, he had had a few other teeth pulled, so he knew that one could indeed have painless and effective dental procedures, but he could not conquer his fear.

Contributing even more to his present terror was the bad experience he'd had in the hospital when he was five years old. When he had slipped and fallen, injuring his tongue so badly, they had brought him to the hospital emergency room to have the portion of his tongue that was hanging stitched back on. The shot they had given him to numb it had been ineffective, but at least they hadn't lied to him and told him there would be no pain.

His fear drove Andre to constantly talk about his upcoming eye surgery, the hardships he'd endured with his eyes, how unfair this whole situation was, and the like. He craved sympathy and understanding, but in fact, there was nothing that anyone could have done. Even his closest friends could not console him. When he had his pre–surgical physical, Andre said that he was terrified and should probably see a psychiatrist to calm down, to which the doctor replied, "You don't need a psychiatrist to tell you why you're afraid of an operation!" This rang true, dulled the fear for a day or two, and then faded into Andre's subconscious. So things went on as they had until the Christmas season.

Probably another reason Andre hated the idea of surgery so much was that his doctor had told him that it would take time to get his full sight back. He cherished the little sight he had, and he was very frightened of losing it, even if he only wanted to enjoy the holiday trappings.

The day of the surgery dawned soon enough. Andre thought he'd nearly bolt off the cart moments before his time came up to be wheeled into the operating room. A nurse noticed this and was very reassuring to him, telling him that he'd be on the I.V. unit soon enough and thus calmed down. Even the anesthesiologist told him that he should not hesitate to ask for more anesthesia during surgery if he felt the need for it.

Andre was pleasantly surprised when they put the drugs into the bottle which had fed him his sugar and salt breakfast. He had never felt so calm. The doctor had injected his eye nerve with a shot from behind and said, "That is probably the worst of the operation." Now, to Andre's surprise, the surgery progressed painlessly. He didn't feel even a twinge of fear when the doctor had to reprimand someone, probably a student in training, that if he didn't get the suction working, they'd have to abort the procedure. He mentioned something with a bit of urgency, that the eye was aphakic. Andre made a mental note to ask the doctor what that meant.

His recovery went as well as could be expected. Luckily his roommate was nice, offering him cookies and putting whatever Andre wanted to watch on the TV. The nurses were also very nice. One of them insisted that Andre take the pain medicine offered, telling him that he would need it later and wouldn't be given any if he didn't accept the first dose.

He was a very cooperative patient. His appetite, to the amazement of the staff, was excellent. The nurse had also given him TV privileges for free, even though Andre had directed her to go into his overnight pack and take the change out so he could have his television. Only after Andre went home did he realize that she had not bothered to do so.

In the hospital, by 11:00 p.m., he couldn't resist the urge for a cigarette, but he was so drugged and groggy that when he got up to sneak into the bathroom, he found standing nearly impossible; amazingly, he gave up the idea of smoking. He didn't sleep at all that night. When a nurse came in late to give him more pain medication, Andre expressed his wish to sleep instead of taking the medicine, but she insisted, saying, "It's only one pill." He figured it would help with the pain, even though he knew it would disturb his sleep for the remaining few hours of the night.

Things went smoothly enough after he went home the next day. Andre felt proud that he'd invented a computer program that could read the screen for him, as he would not be able to check his email or use the computer otherwise. He'd also gotten five orders in the mail. It seemed somehow a reward from God, even though Andre didn't go to church or really believe whole-heartedly.

As if this God had read his mind, a minor complication arose from his eye surgery. The doctor had told him he'd be nearly blind for about a week. He kept saying, "Well, give it another week or so." By the eighth week, the doctor said his vision would slowly improve over a period of up to six months. He applied some very painful glycerin drops, which seemed to start the process of bringing Andre's sight back to its old level of legal blindness.

Andre understood how devastating it must have been, many years before, for his neighbor friend to lose an eye while playing with an air gun. He felt that nobody could really appreciate their eyes unless they had only one that was working. Andre's older sister had her one good eye, and their father had often stated, "You should always take care of it, for it's all you have." Luckily for her, his sister's good eye worked at full capacity, so she was able to drive a car. Andre didn't feel bitter about this fact, but he felt that others didn't understand that he had a real disability. Of course he cherished his good eye. He was more than thankful that he could appreciate things like flowers, the leaves changing, and so forth. He assumed that he would never be able to drive, though. He knew that he would tremendously appreciate mobility and independence if, by some miracle, he ever got his one good eye to work perfectly, never mind the dud.

Andre went on with his business venture as normal. Time brought his sight back almost to its normal self. He had sworn that the laser surgeries had taken their toll on his sight, and his research had proven him correct. If he'd really been aware of the laser's overall ineffectiveness for his type of eye disease, he would have had this last operation first. He did count his blessings in the end, but at times, he would kick himself for "having allowed that doctor to do this" to him.

At last, as time passed, Andre got his emotional balance back, along with his sight, and he put away any of the thoughts of litigation that he had entertained for a while. After all, he had signed off on all the surgeries, and with no surgery is there ever a 100 percent guarantee of success.

iii

Andre kept delving into his business ventures. His lack of financial resources didn't deter his efforts. He was able to get the largest software company in the country to give him all the upgrades for his computer's operating system, since he was willing to be a tester for them. The world of big business and the blossoming online world that Andre was used to was about to change very rapidly.

He had adapted to the things that were predictable and remained the same in his business, but he also thought he was sufficiently versatile and could change as quickly as the world around him. He refused to accept the idea that one person could not buck the system or affect the larger picture. After all, he thought, I got myself in magazines, on TV, and published my own website without the big budgets of the large corporations.

It's just a matter of persistence and thinking of inventive ways to reach out on a shoestring.

This attitude had indeed been true in the pioneering days of his business. It cost him time and some bitterness to realize that his beloved field was afflicted by the same fever as all the other startups: greed, bulkiness, and—the worst of all for him—mediocrity.

Maturity would help him cope with the changes, but the days of the pioneering Bill Gates and Steve Jobs were truly over. Andre realized that there could be some good in all this, especially when it came to standardization. Although he had loved programming his computer in a jungle, he'd also yearned for some sense of normalcy and stability. Even though half of his wish came true, the fulfillment of it came at a high price, literally. Now, specialists abounded. It took Andre a while to realize that now his beloved field of computer science was going toward group thinking, consensus, and yes, mediocrity.

In time, he had to reduce his business activities due to all the changes. If his childish wishes and utopian ideas of how the computer field *should* be didn't carry him through the complexities, the fact that there were no more inquiries or sales was what really made reality sink in. He would never give up on his business, but he knew that it was at best a sideline. Perhaps the forlorn dreams of the past were what kept him from giving up the website. But he had lost the zeal he had had in the beginning. He said to himself, Well, the big guys won! It would be foolish for me to think that my meager budget and original ideas could overcome the resources of the major players. The day of the lone wolf is finished, at least on this turf.

Time would reinforce Andre's last quotation to himself and his closest friends. Reality has a way of dulling even one's fondest imaginings. In all this, Andre would never admit to bitterness or negative thinking. He'd concede that, "Yes, I feel bad, but there's certainly no point in dwelling on it." Indeed, this was true enough, but his real state of mind, driven by an unseen master, was more akin to hopelessness than fervor.

iv

It would be easy to sum up Andre's life before he turned 45. Others could judge it by merely looking. He didn't have many of the status symbols that most people his age did. Naturally, he did desire some material things, such as the fastest and most powerful computer available. Things like clothes, motorcycles, and automobiles, which he realized helped to bond other people and were favorite topics of conversation, were considerably less important to him. Unfortunately, many others obviously felt that status and superiority were very important.

Andre had never hated his uncle from Maine, but he had been envious that his uncle had started his own business, had plenty of money to live on, always bought the classiest cars, and lived in luxurious houses. Andre's other uncle, also well-to-do but not as rich as the first, had also done a lot to become self-sufficient. However, to Andre's surprise, his father had always insisted that the second uncle must have stolen to get where he was. Eventually, it became apparent to Andre that his father was not the only one with such an attitude. It seemed that almost everyone had the same materialistic American dream, but once someone had attained it, the attitude of many around that person was usually not one of congratulations, but jealousy and outright hatred. All too frequently, in their eyes, there was no way a person could achieve such goals honestly.

It would have been easy to fall into this same trap, this same mode of thinking, but Andre was bent on not being prejudiced, and he felt that these negative thoughts were wasteful. It was certainly true that there were a lot of crooks and cheats out there, and such people had even been rewarded. Yet he felt that there were, even if few in number, people who really had good ethics and shouldn't be condemned for their honest successes. However, it did seem that success was easier to attain if one had monetary assets to bolster one's projects.

Such considerations were trivial now. The 21st century, which had been seen as so full of promise when Andre was a child, had started out as anything but ideal. It wasn't the fact that there still wasn't a base on the moon or a robot in every home that bothered him; it was all the age–old problems: wars, brutalities, and torture, with all of this so often motivated and justified by religion. It was both irksome and disheartening. Andre appreciated science and reasoning, but he was certainly not against emotionalism, as long as one didn't hurt anyone else. He would have preferred watching a sunset or enjoying the autumn leaves to punishing someone on an ideological basis. And besides, the cruelty of it was enough to invalidate the whole reason for the fighting.

So now his country was at war, and the world was supposedly more vulnerable than it had ever been in history. Politicians eagerly stoked this perception. Perhaps the leaders weren't exactly lying, but they couldn't get good media coverage for saying something like, "Well, we aren't in as much danger as I said in my last speech, nor are we truly as safe as we were before. The truth is somewhere in the middle." Andre was all too well aware that the most sensationalistic presentation was the one that people were the most eager to believe.

He didn't want to become bitter or hopeless about the state of the world. There was progress to be observed, too. In both him and many others, there was still a lot of hope for a better future. One couldn't give up, yet it was necessary that one not waste energy in the wrong places. Even with all the natural disasters, the terrorist attacks, the chaos of confrontations, and humans' seemingly boundless ability to inflict terrible suffering on their own, Andre wouldn't allow hopelessness to overcome him. Yet the subtleties of his emotions, those deep within him, would keep him unable to fully control his own actions. The force was very subtle. If it had truly engulfed him, he would have been aware of it. Instead, from time to time, it merely misdirected him, therefore making him think that he was in full control at all times.

V

The time was a week before Thanksgiving. Andre and John usually enjoyed the holidays, but to John, this one was more about eating than anything else. Andre felt much the same. The luster of the Mayflower and Pilgrims had long since worn off.

In all the years Andre had been partnered with John, it wasn't unusual for Andre to hear John's concerns about other people. John was always very sensitive, and that was one of the main reasons Andre had been attracted to him.

For the past couple of months, John had expressed more concern with his neighbors and what they were doing. He'd been concerned about them snooping around in the hallways and spying on him. Andre was aware that some people in the building were indeed very nosey, started a lot of rumors, gossiped endlessly, and basically made life miserable for others simply because they could do so. Or maybe that tactic was a way to make themselves feel powerful and important. In any case, Andre felt that John was making more out of the situation than he should have.

Their close friend Ray had had a run of bad luck, and John had decided to let him stay at his apartment on and off for a while until Ray could get his life back on track. Ray had noticed that John seemed worried about things with the other tenants and told Andre that he felt John was overreacting. Andre agreed, but they couldn't convince John not to worry.

The Saturday before Thanksgiving, John, Ray, and Andre were all sitting together in the early afternoon. John had become very agitated, even yelling out the window, reprimanding the neighbors, telling them not to bother him. No pleading from either Andre or Ray could calm him. The situation persisted all night, with John slamming doors and yelling. Andre and Ray were convinced that John should be committed to the hospital for observation, as this was far from normal behavior.

Andre felt abandoned by Ray when Ray panicked and left mid-morning on Sunday to make other living arrangements. Ray was very emphatic with Andre about calling an ambulance for John. Andre feared that Ray was right, but he thought he could solve the problem, or maybe even that John would snap out of it on his own.

Shortly after midnight on Monday, Andre's decision was made for him. John's paranoia had advanced to the point where he thought that certain individuals had placed listening devices and cameras in his apartment. He had even warned Andre that the laptop Andre was using had surveillance software in it.

All of these worries came to a head when John decided to call the police. Andre begged John not to make this call. He believed that this phone call would certainly lead to having John hospitalized for observation, but he decided that it would be better if he let John make the call and let things take their own course.

Andre was shocked that the police didn't consign John to the sanatorium or even suggest to him that he might need help. The officers were quite patient, and also tried their best to convince John that he was safe. But there was no reasoning with him. John argued with certainty with Andre as to why he wasn't mentally ill. He said he was shocked and dismayed that Andre didn't support him and believe him after all the years they had known each other.

At mid-morning on Monday, John went downstairs to check his mail. This created an opportunity for Andre to call various psychiatric facilities for advice and help. The basic message was the same from all the people he contacted. They couldn't forcibly have John hospitalized unless he was clearly endangering himself or others. They suggested that Andre have John go for counseling, to which Andre replied that John didn't think he had a problem. Andre felt that John was harming himself with the stress caused by all his worrying. Unfortunately, this reasoning was not sufficient grounds for the hospitals or ambulance drivers to come to Andre's aid.

The day before Thanksgiving arrived. John had called law enforcement three or four times to report his false concerns about his neighbors. Each time, the police were calm, tried to reason with him, asked him how he was so certain of all this, took their report, and left, never hinting to John or even to Andre that they thought John should get medical help.

From time to time in years past, Andre's family had been kind enough to offer a ride to John to eat a meal with them for the holidays. It wasn't a thing that could be counted on, but his family had lately grown more accepting of John in Andre's life. This year was no different. Andre's mother had called to ask if they'd be eating Thanksgiving dinner with them and told him what time to be ready. Andre was very hesitant to explain why they wouldn't be there. He had hoped that his mother would accept "John is very sick" as an explanation. But in the end, he felt able to tell his mother everything.

Naturally, as a good mother, she was worried for Andre's safety. He emphatically told her that John wasn't violent, but his mother feared that such a situation could develop. With Andre's permission, she also had his sister call, as she was nearly finished with her social work degree and might have some insight. Andre was relieved that his sister called promptly.

His sister was a bit surprised that this type of situation could arise, especially since John was relatively old and didn't have any prior history of mental illness. She allayed Andre's immediate fears and told him what signs to look for in regard to calling an ambulance. His sister also confirmed what the other professionals had stated, that there was no way, save going to court, to force John to go for treatment.

Andre had been very close with John's family. He even considered John's foster parents closer to him than his own. He'd emailed and sought their help. John had practically agreed to commit himself to the hospital, but this was, for Andre, a passing relief. Things did not resolve themselves until six days after Thanksgiving. Andre, and of course John, had not slept very much. When Andre did fall asleep, John would awaken, frightened out of his wits about the neighbors. He was engaged in conversations and confrontations with them, as he was convinced that they could see and hear everything he did. He was certain that some of them had even spied on his sex life.

Andre decided to go see Gerry, an old acquaintance of theirs. Gerry's now–deceased girlfriend, Marilyn, had dealt with similar demons for years. Gerry had, for the most part, been able to control her outbursts for some years, and Andre thought he might be able to help. There was also an instinct in Andre that John was holding onto him as a thread to sanity, and that if Andre left him, his fears and delusions might crash in on him. Nonetheless, Andre felt that he must leave John alone to go talk to Gerry.

Gerry had no real advice to offer. He said that Marilyn had had paranoid episodes, but none had ever compared to what John was going through.

About 45 minutes after Andre had arrived, and many cigarettes later, Gerry noticed a fire truck in the front of the building. There were always various types of emergencies in the building, and one could count on the rescue truck being there twice a week or more. At this point, Andre was beyond any hope of John calling for help, and jokingly said, "Wouldn't it be something if they were here to pick up John?"

When they went to check the back parking lot from the hall window, Andre was shocked and relieved to see John, with an ambulance attendant, walking under his own power toward the ambulance. Gerry urged him to run down and see John off, as they were so close, but Andre, exhausted from lack of sleep and frazzled nerves, declined. Now there could be time for him to have a little peace of mind and rest, to think about what to do next.

vi

Time and circumstances left Andre and John in a state of limbo. Andre had not been as lucky, or perhaps as ambitious, as others in his job search. He'd been fortunate enough to land some part-time work over the years and was getting a very good hourly rate, one which was normally associated with a computer consultant, but with no health insurance or other benefits. However, boredom took its expected toll, as idleness often does. There was only so much reading, studying, creative programming, and other intellectual pursuits that could be done. Even entertainment could become repetitious. More than ever before, Andre felt that he needed to break out into something different, into another mode of life. His feelings went beyond the usual wanting a vacation or other common ways of escaping. It was more that he felt disillusioned with the ways of the world and humanity in general. His sense of futility kept on building.

The emptiness in Andre's soul went deeper than the usual disgust at mankind's ability to wage wars, commit unspeakably senseless and cruel crimes, or remain apathetic in the face of horrible famine and natural disasters. There was still in his mind a glimmer of hope, less than in his youth, but still unshakable at its base. The core of the problem was that he felt incapable of effecting any changes.

But wasn't this quandary one that had gone on throughout all of history? Wasn't it a rare person, perhaps one individual per century, who could shake the consciousness or knowledge of civilization? Andre didn't really expect or desire to be a prophet, to obtain great fame, or to be a revered orator. Such fantasies were indeed sweet, but he realized that despite all the gifted persons over the centuries, grand though they were, and even though they may have changed things for an instant and left great ideas and feelings of hope behind, in the end, most things remained unchanged. Oppression, abject poverty, seemingly unshakeable superstition, and ignorance never seemed to go away.

One would have thought that the technological and social advances of the 20th century would have remedied all those ills, even wiped them out. Granted, those in the developed countries, as long as they had jobs, had it far better than so many others in the rest of the world. Yet most of those who were fortunate enough to be blessed with the benefits of science seemed unaware of, or at least indifferent to, the grinding poverty of the majority of the Earth's population. Sometimes even Andre looked back at the ideals of his childhood, at the overblown expectations that 21st century science and technology would be able to solve all our earthly problems, and think that perhaps his mother had been right when she had criticized his fascination with reports of space technology and so forth. "We have enough people starving and hungry here at home," she would say. "We're just wasting money on space exploration!"

Andre hated to think that his mother was ignorant. Indeed, she had more common sense than many who appeared to be more intelligent. Nor was it simply that she was religious, for religious belief, in and of itself, does not have to be a bad thing. But he felt that she was too willing to wait for her God to produce a miracle, rather than put her trust in the ability of humanity to pull itself out of its quagmire.

So, in the end, he was no different from his mother. She expected either a biblical apocalypse or the Rapture. He, on the other hand, still expected that science, technology, and higher reasoning could really make the world a better place. They both had to accept and live with gritty reality. But to give up hope would be to say that there was nothing worth living for, and Andre wasn't inclined toward such dark thoughts. Perhaps in a passing moment such thoughts had gripped his soul, but he still held onto a thread of hope, even if that thread was frayed. Maybe God could cast down a safety net, since it didn't look like the scientists were going to come up with one in his lifetime.

Chapter 16

From Orpheus's Desk

i

This is the night of hopes. There comes to all an awakening in which one may understand. It is not enough to have dreamt, only to awaken thereafter and lose the meaning. There are always those who would be the prophets, but they are false, not because the messages they claim to reveal are not valid.

There had been a search for many millennia regarding the one who could really understand. It wasn't the intention of the Schegnans or Metans to cause an uproar; however, the writers of the Bible and even Nostradamus didn't have it right.

The aliens never denied the existence of a God or so-called supreme being. This concept was in no way contrary to their science. Indeed, a circular universe could probably best be explained by some higher power. For any mortal, including these alien observers and in some cases interceders, having a beginning and end-point along with infinity was hard to explain.

The MetSche were astonished to discover that there were such battles of so-called religiosity taking place on Earth. They had based a lot of their original objections to interference on this very notion, that any type of meddling could inflame a culture. However, the problems weren't due to the aliens. The races discovered that the wars and disagreements over such things as scripture, practice, or application of any system weren't based on any misreading of sent psychic messages or dreams. Rather, all the turmoil was due, almost exclusively, to an idea that the alliance called a sense of hypercorrectness. This meant that most humans couldn't or wouldn't accept the notion of their ideas standing up to any scrutiny whatsoever. Even more horrifying to them was the concept that their ideas might be incorrect.

The whole collage of wars, witch–hunts, executions, gang violence, and general outright killing of one another from the time of Copernicus to Galileo and beyond was such a disappointment to the MetSche. Yet, on rare occasions, they did observe the caring side of humanity. They saw the bravery required to stand up to injustices of this type. Even when it was clear that death would come, still a message had to be delivered, and this action made the aliens more hopeful for the future.

By the beginning of the 21st century, it seemed again that the hopes of the aliens were to be dashed. It was refreshing that the 50 years of nuclear cold war had been survived, and even new alliances hardly predictable to the aliens, let alone humanity, were being forged.

Yet even with these glimmers of hope, there remained the age–old problems of mass murder due to ethnicity or religion— or, in this day and age, economic status, an idea which was repulsive to the Schegnans and Metans alike. All these injustices seemed to be based on different varieties of hypercorrectness. The observers of Earth could see that it didn't take a human of exceptional intelligence to realize that many of their kind, for one reason or another, would rather strike out in anger and violence than reach out to another of their kind. How interesting it was to see that they all felt similarly alone and hopeless, and yet so wanted to connect to one another. The age–old crises continued. Every age brought its villains, heroes, and saviors, as well as new awareness of the inhumanity, yet every new age seemed to repeat the mistakes of the past in endless hopelessness.

This reason alone was enough to propel the dual race that had an eye on Earth to do something to assist. Oh, they could have come down and exercised some form of control, but humanity resisted being oppressed as it was, and the main idea was liberation. No freedom could be imposed, or it would lose its meaning. Sadly, the people of Earth had seen many futile attempts at this before.

Psychic linking was a delicate process, as well. It was bad enough to be labeled unbalanced or insane, even in the more or less enlightened 21st century. To find someone receptive to the alien message was not so difficult. It was finding the one being who could really understand them that was difficult. Then this whole search was complicated by humanity's own systems of control. It wasn't enough to find someone to deliver the message. That individual had to be considered credible by enough people to have the exercise be worthwhile.

ii

So there comes a message. There, one can see a large city with the most unusual colors of buildings. It is not merely that they are immensely tall, but one can also see that they are very numerous. Yet in this horde of edifices, one doesn't find the expected smog, nor does there seem to be the kind of traffic congestion normally associated with metropolises.

Indeed, one seems to feel a sense of barrenness here. That

sense is short–lived, however, when one spends some time here. In fact, there are all kinds of activity going on, especially inside the structures. Even outside, one sees a number of individuals walking about, but sparse evidence of any type of motor vehicle.

There is certainly no sense of urgency in the activities that one witnesses here, yet it is clear that important work is going on. As an alien to this land, an individual from Earth would not be sure what, exactly, was being done. Yet even the most uneducated human could sense things of great scientific importance taking place. This fact would be evidenced by the unusual gadgets and devices.

The outsider is inexplicably aware of the great altruistic purpose of the scientific experiments and discussions going on around this megatropolis. Yet, upon further observation, one can also observe these great beings enjoying music, literature, drama, and all sorts of diversions similar to but much richer and diverse than those of humankind. One can almost never express these images in words. Certainly the poets of Earth have tried, and at times, they were quite successful. Some languages captured subtle nuances better than others, but no language yet written or spoken could really capture dreams or emotions.

The dreamer sees all, but again, lost for explanations, may try fitfully to convey it to others. The usual result is simple ridicule, as most think the speaker is "insane." The other reaction is similar, but kinder. The response is simply to brush off the images and eccentricities of the person as an unusual, yet harmless, childlike game. The former reaction is often hostility and ridicule; the latter is usually a grudging acceptance and then dismissal of the orator's message.

If the aliens are satisfied that the receiver of the message can comprehend, the process continues. The person must be intelligent enough to wait to send out the MetSche codes. These are difficult but not impossible to figure out. Many well–educated persons have failed the test, while so–called imbeciles were able to pass it. Success or lack thereof was not seen by the superior beings as something to reward or punish. The life forms from the two observing worlds wanted to communicate, to offer advice and assistance, but they had no desire to use any negative reinforcements. Even rewards, it was decided, could be distracting. The one who obtained the prize was satisfied that gaining this new knowledge was the reward, as opposed to physical or mental enhancements, gifts, cures, or other such nonsense spewed by the false fanatics who put aliens on a warped pedestal.

iii

It was only when the aliens showed the viewer the Schegnan scenes that any knowledge could be gleaned at all. The great cities of Metamo were not superior to the vast pastoral scenes of Schegna. One would be mistaken to think that Metans were more scientific than the Schegnans, or that the Schegnans had a corner on the arts and humanities. These ideas had had some validity before the MetSche alliance, but that had now been in existence for scores of millennia.

The human observer's knowledge would be closer to complete when he or she realized that languages were the real defining difference, at least in terms of planetary nature. The allies had used several common written and spoken languages, but this was for convenience. At base, the two worlds had two very different ways of communicating. Neither world was arrogant regarding which way was better, but they agreed that the two forms of advanced contact were preferable to the ancient spoken and written tongues. Even their common communiqués, written and spoken forms for inter-world use, were much more concise than any developed on earth. It was thought that it would be a rare human, using all his or her brain capacity, plus adding 10 percent more to their cortexes, that could even begin to fathom the diverse symbols utilized, of which there were over 250,000. At first glance, one would call this inefficient, but the symbols were always being updated. Additions were carefully reviewed, and there were no duplications or the possibility of confusing one symbol for another, as is common in terrestrial languages. Words, symbols, letters—it was all semantics, but the MetSche had solved this dilemma long ago.

The case of the Schegnans would be easy for humans to understand. They had various sophisticated written and spoken constructs, as there were not complete mind reading and communication on the planet. The other ability transcended words and, paradoxically, emotional labeling. It was simply what it was: common understanding of two or more beings in synchrony with each other. They could, via the telelinking approach, almost instantly understand one another, thus avoiding great conflicts.

The Metans had written and spoken tongues as well, but they had few if any minds that could meld with one another. Yet it was they who were able to develop the MetSche language, due to the fact that the common Metan language was unique. As a simple example, anything tagged as Metan specifically dealt with the culture of the Metans, describing the inhabitants. Anything said to be Metamic dealt with the physical aspects of the planet, like weather, geology, etc.

The original and most natively used language of Metamo, the universal Metan language, could best be described, in simple terms, as Metan color language. It would rival any Schegnan arts or music. It was the use of elaborate small crystals that existed on the planet that allowed the language to be used and the scientific knowledge of the inhabitants to be communicated.

At first, each Metan carried a small crystal, which would emit anything from a hair–thin line of light to a shaft of light as thick as a silver dollar. The length was irrelevant. Being seen by another Metan was what mattered. The way the colors swirled and changed, the durations of change, the thickness of the heptagonal beam, the timings, delays, and minute shades of color all blended together in various combinations to express ideas, not merely words. The human eye, it is said, can see 50 shades of one color, and that is when attention is being paid. The Metan ocular organ evolved to be able to distinguish 500 shades, and beyond this fact, they could detect light in the darkness at one hundredth the brightness that humans could detect. Even Schegnans, whose eyeballs were much like those of people on Earth, still had eyesight superior to that of humans.

These factors made it necessary for the Metans to adopt a metalanguage, as they correctly thought that most aliens wouldn't be as advanced as they were, and at any rate, the other forms of language were probably more common. Even Schegna, a rare example of dual separate evolution in one solar system, had a simpler form of communication, but they had the great advantage of directly tapping the mind of the one with whom they were communicating. This greatly enhanced the Metans' conversion of the color language to an accepted symbolic form. There were some 300 or so concepts specific to Schegna and Schegnans that were put on the list. These were related to the experience of telelinking.

An odd thing seemed to be occurring on planet Earth. Both planets of the MetSche alliance noticed it and discoursed on it for almost a century. At the end of this time period, it was decided that, for whatever reason, certain disabilities in human beings enhanced certain areas of the brain. A great many Earthlings believed that some "handicapped" people had heightened senses, but they couldn't be aware, as the Schegnans were, that it was a change in the way the brain of the afflicted individual worked and rewired itself that allowed greater receptiveness to the contact from the aliens.

The Metans saw this, as well, and they could prove it scientifically. It was agreed, however, for reasons of evolution and genetic diversity, that the search for people who would be able to understand and receive the messages should be within a statistical sample of the entire populace. For the most part, the agreement was followed. But both sides realized that they weren't doing anything having to do with mating or the cloning of humankind. So, in the interest of saving time and for good scientific efficiency, they sought out those disabilities in the people of Earth that lent themselves to advancing the altruistic goals of the MetSche.

The initial reaction of the overseers, the ones who never went to the worlds but concerned themselves with ethical and philosophical issues, was disappointment that the "fielders" were breaking the agreement. It was easy enough for the scientific teams who regularly visited the Earth to show that what they were doing was getting the results that the MetSche had always wanted, and that, above all, they weren't harming anybody involved. There was also the fact that the receptive humans—the shunned, the disabled, those seen by their own as inferior—could actually be emotionally fulfilled by this type of contact. It was agreed, at any rate, that no harm would come from the new policy. At the same time, some very alienated humans would feel better about themselves and would feel a sense of importance—and, it was hoped, could enlighten the important humans concerning the magnitude of all of this hard work that was being done to assist civilization.

iv

"This is a report of the MetSche regarding the search for 'the chosen one' or, if we could be so fortunate, 'the chosen ones.' I have, upon insistence of the council, translated the finding into standard American English for the sake of posterity. In any case, I cannot imagine a situation where anyone on Earth would read, let alone believe, this report, but there are some on this board who have a logic that escapes me.

"The search has recently been abandoned, because we found an individual who is receptive enough and possesses the necessary intelligence to know what to do with our communications. The male Earthling predictably fit our profile. He possesses the visual disability and brain enhancement that we had so often discussed. It is thought that one of his eye medications, along with other dietary, metabolic, and chemical factors, have allowed the being's brain to be very open to us.

"By his own planet's standards, he is not exceptionally accomplished, but he is proficient enough in the primitive computer science of the planet, has an appreciation for many types of musical genres and literature, especially their sometimes very well constructed science fiction, and in general, there are no indications that he is bitter or prone to illogical emotional outbursts. He is not violent. He is compassionate and cares very much for the greater truths.

"The most troubling aspect, once we found the individual that met our goals, was how to get other people on the planet to be interested in him, let alone listen to him and our message. I, however, along with the council, am very confident that this minor setback will be overcome, and our seeds have been planted where our work can now begin in earnest.

"His intelligence, by the standards of the planet, had at one time put him above average, yet not overly so. In terms of our objectives, this is actually an advantage. One who had been considered a genius would often not be able to communicate with the common man. His somewhat higher than average intelligence, along with his training in letters and computers, which enhance his logical ability, definitely make this human our prime choice. There are many other reasons, which it is not necessary to go into at this time. Suffice it to say that this man is ready and willing to do our work, but he is not as yet consciously aware of this fact.

"Our greatest asset has been the ability of Maurine, our most prized Schegnan psychic and empath, to communicate clearly in the rapid eye movement phase of the human sleep cycle—or more directly, to use the dream state. We regret that we first attempted to contact someone very close to the chosen one—his lover, in fact. This was a failure. The Schegnan did not do her homework—an unforgivable crime of science. Not only was conscious direct contact with the awake mind strongly discouraged, if not forbidden. There was also the gross oversight that was made early in the experiment. This sloppy Schegnan assumed that the man's hallucinations were due to her trying to contact him—which, normally, would be a good hint to discontinue the experiment. But she assumed that things could be corrected. It is not really important now that the man's breakdown was precipitated by a physical head injury, and that it would have occurred at some point in the future, anyway. But it is inescapable that the inept worker had a great responsibility for the collapse of his reason, along with voices in his head and much confusion and anxiety among his close friends and family.

"Fortunately, the psychiatrics on Earth, though imperfect, are admirable, and treatment of this person is rather effective. You are all aware that there are some rare cases when the Schegnans, for whatever reason, usually slipping through the screening process, have caused the mental breakdown of humans due to mental stress and trauma. This was always a result of breaking the 'forbidden waking contact' rule. Only when the person has reconciled a conscious understanding of the dream messages can he or she choose to have first contact with us.

"So, this is the situation with our prized human male. He is, unfortunately, by habit and training, a very high-strung individual. Normally, being subject to panic attacks or other nervous illnesses would be a disqualification. This man's situation is different. Most of the stresses arise out of the primitive brain due to his being disabled, and besides, he has undergone a lot of counseling, or rather training, to control his fears. He has adjusted quite well to his emotions and is generally in good control of his mind–body relationship.

"It was naturally decided, however, in light of the rare, grave errors made in the past, to use a numbing field on the man. This is the only form of mind control accepted by the council. The only way we could really control the humans would be through tampering with the emotions, especially in the brainstem, or possibly using hallucinogenic electromagnetic waves, but that would be in great contrast to our goals of peace and co–advancement. The field, more technically, will use EMR to dampen his brain to the possibility of panic or outright horror, which he might not be able to control. His training is good, but he hasn't achieved 100 percent control at the time of this writing. This numbing field is very safe, since it will be specific to his brain and emotional reactions, along with Maurine's commendable interactions and study of his dreamscapes.

"It is necessary to point out the current status and progress of the Terrans' scientific knowledge. They have a very optimistic view of their abilities and futures. This bright outlook is laudable. We see this potential as well. If it weren't for the fact that they have not yet tamed their violent predilections, their race might have already achieved many of its aspirations.

"As I stated, they have come a long way scientifically compared to other races we've encountered since discovering Earth, especially when one considers where they are on the evolutionary scale. Given their negligible field experience in outer space, it is amazing that they have come up with their theory of relativity and the idea of warped spacetime. We are naturally inclined to belittle these ideas, but when one considers how they can make things work out mathematically, another field where we find they have excelled, it is astonishing that they have such a grand view of the cosmos and interest in it.

"It is true that they have made a start in computers, but they have really only just begun to reap the rewards in any practical sense in the last half century or so. I have often pondered how I could explain to a human a trip that takes only a few hours from our world to Earth without warping spacetime. It stirs my heart. I am not quite sure if their brains are even yet capable of the immense new languages and symbols, maybe 250,000 or so, that would be required for them to comprehend the real nature of the speed of light, the size of the universe, and such matters.

"It is interesting to watch how the people of Earth marvel at their savants and geniuses. Again, as with the computer, medicine, and much of their technology, they have just begun to comprehend the vistas that are before them, let alone grapple with the ethical and religious aspects, which have sadly slowed their progress. We may consider ourselves fortunate that we broke from our primitive cycles of violence and passions. Indeed, it is only relatively recently that they discovered that other animals, even the monkeys, are capable of using tools. The biggest hitch with humanity is that they tend to become arrogant and think themselves the masters of their world, rather than being a part of the entire universe. Any Earth individual would certainly argue with us here, seeing how we control and maintain our own planetary environment, but we must recall that they aren't yet versed in the universal rules. They have indeed thought in terms of this concept, especially in their religion of Hinduism, but they must still discover so much more.

"Recall how they react to geniuses and savants. Such people are seen by them as having either great gifts or disabilities. Thus, either their brain cortexes must evolve, or they must find a way to utilize their not yet used capacity to move forward. It might be that a "brain-man" or such could do well on our worlds when it comes to intellectual function, but as you know, the humans wrongly put emphasis on super memory or calculating abilities. As an example, I could not recall pi to the 25,000th digit, or even calculate two-digit number division or multiplication in my head, but the fact that I can speak our MetSche language is proof enough that my abilities are beyond that of the Earthlings. I wonder if we will find any that could manage this feat, but the point is, of course, that we want to find people with other abilities, not those who are like us. Besides, we want to intervene so they can improve their own lot, not to amuse ourselves.

"Alas, the humans are still utilizing the age-old method of resolving conflicts, and most of all, they cling to these misguided ideals in an age when reason, technology, knowledge, and individuality are supposed to be so important. The people and countries supposedly with the most liberties are often the fiercest aggressors against their neighbors.

"Of course, not everyone on Earth is bombastic or violent. Indeed, I would say that the majority of the Earthlings are peace-loving and merely want to survive, work, and raise families—and, if possible, improve the miserable lot of their fellows who are suffering.

"The fact is, even in the places on Terra with the most freedom, the oligarchy rules. This situation is further compounded by the arcane economic system. Still, many may share a view in opposition to the governing body, and in the so-called democracies, this method of opposing and questioning authority is actually encouraged. Yet the old school prevails, and those who want change and who have logical reasons for their views are still shut out of the mechanism for transforming their societies.

"We've seen occasions when citizens are invited to make and change their own rules by majority rule, making concessions to the minority at the same time, but the systems are set up in a very cumbersome manner, making real change very slow, almost impossible. Too many self-appointed experts are involved in the process. While the desire to protect citizenries against themselves by legislating health and social protocols is understandable, often the unwieldy tools are illogical and prevent change.

"Now, recently, nearly the whole planet has, almost by the rule of one strong male leader, involved itself in a new type of warfare. Rhetoric has become a replacement for reason and common sense. The truth is that humans have been using the same tactics in their conflicts for millennia. Stating that something is revolutionary or novel naturally doesn't make it so.

"So, most of the so-called democracies are in a fervor over a heightened vigil against what they call terrorism. This causes them to try to organize major operations on amorphous battlefields with largely unseen enemies. As a result, they have inflicted great suffering on the inhabitants of countries that aren't really linked with the roots of the problem. Some aggressors are given blanket powers, and no matter what kind of operations they undertake, the bodies assume that these acts of violence are justified and should not be questioned. Those who object are called unpatriotic and are even accused of being allied with the enemy.

"It is true that there are two very strong factions at work in the latest strife plaguing the planet at this time, but that isn't a new phenomenon. As outsiders, it would be easy for members of our esteemed MetSche alliance to think that the antagonism is religious in nature or has to do with radically opposing views about who rules and how they do so. This observation is valid enough, but it doesn't get to the heart of Earth's troubles.

"Hypercorrectness isn't really a good description, either, and members of our group are working to find a symbol to add to our plethora of symbols to precisely explain what the root troubles are with humans and their propensities toward violence. We may look at our respective histories for parallels, but this isn't really fair, as we evolved in similar, yet very different circumstances. I wonder what would have happened if Mars were similar to Metamo and Sol had had a dual race, as we do. I sadly recall that even our races recently had an incident with two ships and lasers. This reminds us that even we are still ruled by our ancient animal instincts. That explanation would no doubt soothe many humans' minds, but it is obvious that many in both high and not so lofty places are subject to selfish passions and megalomania.

"We know that some writers on Earth, in their science-fiction genre and even back to ancient times, have been aware of these issues and have grappled with these very things. Awareness of a problem is a good thing, and we are confident that the human race is very aware of its problems, but the powers that be cause resignation to the sad facts, and it sometimes seems that no effort is being made toward solving the problems.

"Even some individuals of great wealth and power are very altruistic, and the Earth media systems speak in awe of the billions of monetary units being thrown at the problem. These selfless acts give the council great hope for the future of the planet.

"One is aware that optimism isn't enough to solve problems, but it is seen as a great motivating force for many on

Earth and should be applauded. It isn't my intention to paint such a bleak picture of events, yet I wasn't interested in laying out the great visions or dreams that their poets, musicians, artists, and regular folk often share. We can only judge by what we've observed. It is true that I haven't taken the time to note exceptions to these obviously general traits of human society. They seem to be trapped in an endless black–and–white sort of struggle. True, they are aware that their reality isn't of a binary nature, yet somehow a vast majority of them fall into this trap, perhaps because it is so easy to do.

"We may look at how they grapple with their ideals of family, life partnerships, alternative lifestyles, freedom of speech and expression, and so many of the fundamentals that are at the foundation of their societies. The biggest issue, as far as our observers are concerned, is that they all want to be brothers and sisters sharing a common goal, bettering their lots, yet they haven't found, as we have, a method to have all cultures, ethnicities, and races coexist.

"I suppose that Earth is so strong in our minds and emotions because we've been observing it the longest of all the worlds we've found that have intelligent or self–aware life. Since then, we've found many orbs with races on a lower scale of development, and a mere handful with abilities approaching ours. It is true that we've acknowledged that the planet LugGahro has had a civilization for one million years longer than Metamo or Schegna. We are pleased that the LugGahrolites are willing to be patient with us, yet we are also aware that such a long period of superior development can't be understood or absorbed by us in such a quick time. In one million years, most likely, we'll have come up to the level of LugGahro's great culture and technology, but by that time, they'll have evolved beyond us by that amount of time.

"This seems to be a rule of survival, or nature. We can't be impatient with humanity, for if they evolve and survive for

250,000 years more, it is a safe assumption that they will have knowledge and awareness similar to what we now possess. We are amused at their fanciful concept of time travel, but the fact—which may take 250,000 years for them to realize—is that one can learn from the past, but the future will always arrive in its fixed fashion, and being prepared for it is the best way to deal with the problem.

"So, nature has cycles and seasons, and the universe breathes out stars, solar systems, galaxies, and all its wonders. One star dies, and a new, fledgling civilization is born. This observed and indisputable fact is very hard for a race like Earth's to grapple with. Even a Metan, who lives for an average of 10,000 years, is struck by grief when even a mayfly or bacterium expires. We aren't concerned with an afterlife or reincarnation, yet we also entertained these simplistic ideas at one point in our evolution. The reality of what happens to one's soul is so incredible and marvelous that we, with our language of 250,000 symbols, are only beginning to describe it. Earthlings would be happy to learn that death is only a beginning, but no words, pictures, emotional states, or any other methods we could employ would be sufficient to soothe their limited minds.

"A human could not, for example, expect a mosquito to understand a symphony, but the truth is that all life forms, from microbes to super–beings, are players in the universe's symphony. The LugGahrolites have informed us that this is still the case for beings which have evolved a billion years ahead of them. That is the only thing they could understand from such a superb, non-corporeal type of life. Even on LugGahro, the evidence is that life, in all places, evolves from a nearly molecular level, up to beings with complex systems, hearts, brains, and limbs, then to rarer beings that are able to modify their own genetic codes and gain great psychic ability. Then, finally, they evolve to a non–corporeal being that is only one step below the most superb, all–knowing being(s), which we would all call, loosely, God. This food for thought should be followed by relaxed contemplation and the realization that no one sub–being can ever have all the knowledge that the greatest being—that is, the universe—possesses. The hand or foot of a human can't possibly be aware of the whole being, but a being like the universe can be aware of its individual atoms, dust particles, stars and planets, and all gradations, civilizations, and forms of life that make it up.

"I always find closing statement etiquette rather strange, but considering the recent mishaps of one Schegnan, I will close here with the usual customary words. May all those who will take the path in joining be afforded all the good luck they will require. May the forces in the universe that are yet to be understood and may never be guide the journey with good fortune and to a successful outcome.

"Inscriber & Translator of MetSche, Mewl–Lee–Um"

Chapter 17

Illuminations

i

It was a clear, bright morning. Dr. Aguair was indeed fascinated by the "ramblings" of John Kline. She was certainly not a convert to his religion, as she now believed it to be, nor could she resist learning more of his and Andre's stories. When John walked in, she noticed that he looked much more serious about the session than usual.

"John," said Dr. Aguair, "you look very serious this morning."

"I am, Doctor, and I have never been more so. It is obvious that you don't believe a word I have said!"

"I have been honest with you. I suspect that this is a very valid and comforting religion. It wasn't that Dr. D'Erable or I questioned your sanity. You've been very cooperative. All the tests have confirmed that you are more intelligent than most people, but more important, you don't possess any kind of mental illness. I can't pretend or patronize you, John."

"Very well, Doctor. I am at least grateful that you are willing to listen. I am right, aren't I?"

"Yes, John. Please continue."

"Okay, Doctor. I suppose I should be glad that you aren't just agreeing with me. It is my hope that you will understand in time. The Schegnans have told me that both of you would understand and believe my story in time. I don't care anymore, but at least you are listening. I should be thankful for this token.

"I have been directed to clear things up for the two of you. Perhaps you don't understand science, but I dismissed this idea when I realized that as psychiatrists, you and Dr. D'Erable employ the same scientific methods that I do. Andre is also well versed in this method, but the Metans and Schegnans are the true masters of science.

"I feel that you doctors consider my story a religion because you have come to the correct conclusion that everything I have told you is very well organized. It is my confident hope that you will understand this oration and Andre's chronicle as an undisputed fact. Until then, I can only bring you the words. I do urge you to keep an open mind. If you can accept a patient's views as a religion, then you are, in a sense, validating his or her ideas. I ask you to accept my religion, not as a follower, but that it may be the truth.

"I must warn you though, that your use of the word 'religion' isn't quite accurate. I see most religions as attempts at controlling one's life. There are a few that try to self–actualize a person. The Metans and Schegnans could not be happier if we Earthlings could each excel to our fullest potential, but more important, have true empathy for one another. Shouldn't any religion's goal be the same?

"So it is logical to ask why. What would not one, but two, races care about our Earth? The answer is that they have a universal sense of empathy. Any advanced civilization can only become so by eliminating warfare and violence, but beyond this lofty ambition, the hope cannot be kept to oneself. It is only fitting that a race that achieved this ideal would desire to continue and propagate it beyond its own solar system.

"This doesn't quite describe the Metans and Schegnans, unfortunately, because they had some serious disagreements about how to interact with our race. There were a select few, throwbacks, who actually resorted to violence to achieve this end. The very realization that they were not quite gods gave the Schegnans and Metans cause to rethink their place in the universe. They knew that they had not achieved perfection, and that from time to time, even such advanced beings as they must reassess their wielding of power over others.

"I have told you that both these races, far more advanced than we are, do believe in a higher power. The most important thing is that they admit they don't know everything. They value religion and science for what they are worth, and they accept the possibility of being incorrect. I ask both you and Dr. D'Erable to do the same thing in this case. You would have the right to call me a zealot if I insisted that you accept my words without question. The Schegnans, Metans, and I are quite stimulated by this challenge.

"After the terrifying incident of the Metans' and Schegnans' disagreement over how to interact with humanity was over, the two alien races almost decided to abandon the mission altogether. It was more than an embarrassment. By this time, it was seen on other worlds how inhumane human beings could be to one another. Where we were the first race they had observed, to settle a disagreement with violence showed them that we were more related than they would like to admit. No, I am not advocating the old myth of an alien seeding program. As I stated, they discovered us in our ancient times, and had nothing to do with our evolution until...

"So, the Metan and Schegnan ships were about to leave, yet the fact that we were reaching outward, toward the moon and beyond, became irresistible to them. They met and decided to observe some more. They decided to agree to disagree. But now there was a new idea.

"The aliens decided to question some of their own sacred cows. It was unthinkable to interfere with evolution or in any way change the natural course of things. One great Schegnan, considered so because he was thought to have the highest mental ability on his planet and had achieved much in both the arts and sciences, began to speak to his own people and the Metans in a most convincing manner.

"The 'Great Schegnan' went by an affectionate name. He was known as Eguichual. He stood six feet, eight inches tall and weighed 275 pounds. This was a result of his great athleticism. The Schegnans' averages are just about where humans' are, so his achievements and good genes were well appreciated. The Metans, on average, are about 10 percent smaller than we are, so it is understandable that they appreciated Eguichual as well.

"He said, 'Now, Schegnans and Metans all, let us consider all of this.'

"I must clarify that normally, Eguichual would have communicated with his mind, but since he was addressing both planets and not all beings possessed equal ability, he decided to use the spoken word to deliver his message. Besides, it would be easier to have the words transcribed for historical purposes.

"He continued. 'We are now at a point of great decisions. We must question some long-held beliefs, and I will help clarify this for you all. That is my hope.

"'It is indisputable that our races have advanced far beyond Earth's by nearly 260,000 years. We don't propose a show of force or major uprooting of their society. I commend you all for the discretion shown in observing the race in question undetected. That was not really much of a feat, considering that we are far beyond them technologically, but I bring this point up because the humans are becoming very active with the so-called UFO frenzy. We certainly don't want to give them a false sense of self-importance by showing ourselves so blatantly. I think we can all agree on that!

"'Yet I propose that we do intervene. It is clear that they are on the verge of many breakthroughs. The saddest fact is that they have developed the means to destroy themselves without the wisdom to coexist peacefully. It is in this area that we must concentrate our mission.

"'It goes without saying that we can step in and put a stop to all of this, but this isn't my proposal. I think we all feel that if they decide to destroy themselves, then we shouldn't think of them as so advanced and should let the universe go on with its recycling act. I would subscribe to this notion if I hadn't read the minds of some of them. I must tell you of these experiences.

"'I was present in the streets of a large city on the northeast coast of America when their leader was assassinated. Excuse my choice of words, but that is the mentality we are dealing with. These creatures may generally not accept violence, but a leader's murder is seen as more horrific than the killing of one of their lower citizens. They preach equality, yet use the arcane system of money to subvert each other. I feel they are aware of this, yet their greed hasn't allowed them to overcome the problem. The failure of the experiments with Communism and Socialism has further dissuaded them from finding an answer. Yet, I have also seen devoted individuals with great altruism selflessly aiding the less fortunate amongst them.

"'As I said, their President Kennedy had been murdered. This stirred the country up, as they were just beginning to grapple with issues of equality. They had abolished slavery and replaced it with financial oppression, the ages-old sorrow of their race, and they were still dealing with other issues that should have been seen as trivial, such as skin color. Humankind, especially in the country seen by many as the freest on the planet, was still struggling with racism, criminal indifference, and mob violence.

"'There were many who did try to deal with the issues, both publicly and privately. Unfortunately, disagreement was often met with brutal murders and tortures of all kinds. It certainly looks on the surface that they are on the path of self-destruction.

"'If the ones in power, those with the money, aren't being listened to and are being brutalized, then how indeed can they be helped? We don't advocate intervention and full planetary takeover, no matter how tempting those are emotionally. It would be a very easy move strategically, but I want to remind you that they would rebel against us eventually, even if we placated them by giving them a utopian world. They have much literature devoted to subversion. Their George Orwell captured the sense of this very well, and I base my resistance to overthrowing them largely on this writing. Yet their whole history is rife with examples of power and oppression.

"'It seems, then, that the best way would be to empower some of the weakest members of their societies with some sorts of gifts. I'll discuss this idea in more detail later. There are a great many humans who are very intelligent, but for one reason or another, regardless of their inborn talents, they are overlooked. Given the general structure of their societies, I can't say I am optimistic. But please note that I don't think they are beyond help. If I did, I would not entertain the thought at all.

"'Their media for communications, arts, and so forth often demonstrate that many humans are aware of their plight. The children are most affected by these fancies. Unfortunately, many of them, as they get older, lose hope and become very pessimistic. This situation often leads to apathy and sometimes self-destructive behavior.

"'It occurred to me that we could pick and choose the ones with the highest mental potential or those who are the most altruistic. You can all read how we'd choose. The bottom line is that there would only be the need to interact with as few of them as possible to achieve the goal of having humanity reach its highest potential.

"'The concept of farmers and hybrids is not the best argument, but most understandable to argue for helping Earth. Developing larger fruits and vegetables, breeding animals with more protein, and so on, have been examples of how we use our science to improve our lives. Read my papers and you'll see how I've outlined a case for the betterment of humankind.

"'We Schegnans use only about 95 percent of our total brains. We'd be very grateful to find ways to bring that to 97 or 98 percent. I understand that the Earthlings are less advanced, but their use of only about 10 percent of their brains is pathetic, especially since some of them have used 12 percent of their brains and have come up with technologies that could be misused for the subversion of others. It is refreshing that they are experimenting with democracy, yet they often fail to choose as their leaders the individuals with the greatest intelligence and understanding. They are much like the so-called lower animals, in the sense that they have cultural standards of physical beauty which are often substituted for and placed above the other values.

"'Standards of natural beauty are good for mating purposes only; they don't have anything to do with empathy or intelligence. There are exceptional human beings whose intellectual and emotional capacities far exceed their physical attractiveness. These are the ones we would start with, the people who have a greater understanding of and hopes for the race.'

"Eguichual went on to give dozens of case studies. He compared different cultures, geographical differences, nutrition, and other factors to demonstrate his understanding of the planet. Ultimately, he convinced them to meddle, but with dignity. He outlined very specifically how to intervene and how not to. For example, it was clear that any subject would be carefully observed. Nobody with any mental instability would be contacted, nor would anyone who was interested in great fame for its own sake. After a subject was picked, mental contact would be made. There might be physical meetings to illustrate to the person that all that was being communicated was true. Plans for mating to enhance the species were almost overwhelmingly rejected. There was some understanding that this would be left to the Schegnans' discretion, but a direct mating, which would yield a sibling of superior quality, would be a very rare option. It was also because Schegnan anatomy, especially relating to the male sex organs, would no doubt be a dominant trait, and might alarm some humans. Females would be a better choice. Again, there was no outright prohibition on any of this, and it was clear that all cases having to do with Earth were to be shared with the MetSche. Nobody would act alone on the planet. It was agreed that the two alien races would discuss and decide together how they would proceed in the intervention. Great caution was the accepted strategy.

"By the summer of 1962, they had begun their intervention.

"It was not the intention of these aliens to make genii or any such superhumans. They were looking for those with the best traits of humanity to foster and nourish us. They were also very interested in not having it known by too many people that they were among us. They would not and did not abduct people. It was easy enough for the Metans to use sophisticated scanning machines without having to actually take human tissue. They could easily scrape a person in the street by accident and get DNA profiles that way, where they wouldn't be noticed. To actually bring a subject onto a ship was seen as not only taboo, but highly crude and unnecessary.

"By the time man had landed on the moon, the Schegnans had observed tens of millions of humans and were in direct contact with six Earthlings. The Metans were also involved in the studies and contacts. It was decided that four of the six would be physically met. The other two were deemed not capable of absorbing such an emotional event, so they cut off contact with one and communicated with the other via her dreams.

ii

"This brings up the time before there was real agreement between the MetSche. The aliens roamed about with humans. They were very careful not to be detected. As they looked human, this was generally very simple.

"The one case that signaled the need for more caution among the extraterrestrials was very alarming. It was clear that neither Schegnan nor Metan could afford to make such a mistake again.

"There were two lady friends who were professional models. Anne, the first one, had been contacted by the MetSche. She was a good candidate for research. She willingly hosted a Metan, yet her psychic powers weren't developed to the point where she could share the thoughts of her friend with her alien guest.

"On this particular day, Anne was watching Debbie modeling. The Metan communicated to Anne that to read Debbie's thoughts would be no problem. The alien could easily leave Anne and go into Debbie unnoticed. Anne agreed to this, as she believed that Debbie would not be aware of the Metan in her.

"When the small, worm–sized creature entered Debbie, she was modeling. One would not assume that anyone was aware of the alien, but a few people saw a small creature crawling on Debbie's breast. It moved quickly, but the damage had been done.

"Many people assumed that Debbie had been playing some kind of practical joke, and needless to say, her career didn't look too good thereafter. Everyone assumed, to the surprise and confusion of Debbie, that she was some kind of sick prankster. As if this weren't enough, the Metan communicated to Anne that Debbie had an as yet undetected cancer and had months to live.

"Now it seemed that Anne's power to reach Debbie's mind had increased, as Debbie sensed this knowledge and became very worried and concerned. Debbie was naturally resistant to the idea of her death, but she was more depressed that she would now know the day of her demise.

"Through Anne, the Metan was able to communicate that Debbie could be made to forget this information and eliminate the premonitions she had. This was achieved via Anne's strong friendship and a quasi–hypnotic state being imposed on her best friend. Each day, Debbie's mind was preoccupied as she went into a trance. Anne sensed a counting of Debbie's heartbeats through the Metan communication. This exercise was done every day, and as the day of Debbie's death approached, the counting seemed more urgent, and the numbers didn't really make sense to Anne.

"The moments before Debbie's death were quite intense for Anne. Debbie, even though under control, could sense the oncoming moment of death and said to the Metan, 'Let me die, Jack!' She passed in seconds, leaving Anne feeling empty.

"The next moment, Anne's mind was filled with visions of flying over the city buildings, through the deep blue sky, on that spring morning. She sensed that someone else was with her, and she seemed not to recall, perhaps due to the shock, that an alien was with her. She asked if the creature was an alien, to which the being said, 'No.' Anne then asked, 'What about your parents?' The Metan gave the strange answer, 'When they died, I was born in this form.' Now Anne's mind had been so confused that she would never be believed, and she could no longer understand that she'd been chosen for study.

"This incident was of no great consequence for humanity. Anne couldn't and wouldn't be able to put all these experiences into words. Although the Metans weren't as proficient as the Schegnans in mind matters, they were correct in believing that they could handle the human mind and not be detected. Although Anne and Debbie's story didn't reveal any alien presence to humankind, the MetSche decided that stricter polices were needed in the future, and Eguichual was the main factor in the future changes.

"I must point out that when they decided on their new policy, I was only six years old, and Andre would not be born for about seven months. Of course, as a six-year-old child, I had no conscious knowledge of any of this. Yet I must make it clear that the alien races scope out a prospect for many years. It is generally true that these observations have no side effects, but I suppose looking back into my childhood, I can sense at least some Schegnan influences with my friendships.

"I think I must clarify something. The Schegnans are superior in their psychic abilities. The Metans are masters in shapeshifting. Some Metans have developed some mindreading and communication abilities. It is not possible for a Schegnan to change into a cat or some other animal like a Metan. The main point is that these beings aren't to be feared. They don't want to invade our planet or our thoughts. They used their power to make Anne forget her experiences for her own good. They can't really force us to act against our wills. Oh, I suppose they could, but since the beings are more interested in being covert, this tactic would be very risky. They have the best intentions for humanity, yet they also respect our freedom of choice, even though we may not choose the wisest path. Those they pick are the people they feel can speak for and achieve the most for our planet's future."

iii

"So, John," said Dr. Aguair, "excuse me for still holding out the notion that this is a religious belief, but you only want mankind to live in harmony and achieve its highest goals?"

"Yes, Doctor. I know. You suspect that this religion is like all the others, in that it seeks to have people get along, not do violence toward one another, and basically find methods to advance our race. I must ask you about all those mysteries. What about the lady in California and the sample I gave you?"

"John, this doesn't prove anything. As you claim to be for the scientific method, not knowing what something is doesn't constitute proof, as you should know."

"Yes, I know! You are not really employing the scientific method, either. I feel you are afraid to admit that I am telling you the truth, and that is why you hide behind science. You don't want to admit that the sample I gave you is Metamic, nor that the lady you found is more than a missionary of my religion."

"John," said Aguair, "you should know that using debating tactics isn't the way to prove things scientifically. We can't get anywhere via arguing, no matter how eloquently."

"What would you have as proof?"

"Oh, perhaps if you could have me meet one of your friends."

"You don't demand that the Christians, Muslims, or Jews produce their God."

"True, but you are stating that these beings physically exist, have planets, and so forth."

"All right, fine. I guess all I can do is continue, if you'll allow that!"

"I think we should do this next week, John. You seem a bit upset."

"It is only because we are going around in circles. It is more than insulting my faith! Many people of religion, I suspect, get used to people doubting them, even if they can't produce their gods or prove their stories. This condition goes back in the Church to Bernadette of Lourdes, Fatima and all that."

"John, I think we can do better than belief being enough for you, yet having no proof that is sufficient for me. You're creative. Come back next week with something. I think you are capable of doing that."

"You're on! I'll give you indisputable proof. I think you and D'Erable are simply stubborn to the point of not seeing what is right in front of you. You are both so sure that you are the best scientists and arrogant to the point that you can't admit that you are in error, and you're sure that my accounts just have to be an elaborate religion, coping mechanism, or some such thing. You only let me go home after none of your medicines affected my story in any way, and you could tell that I wasn't mentally disturbed or suffered phobias, neuroses, psychoses, or anything else. I cooperated with you, even against the objections of the Metans and Schegnans, and took your medicines. I had hoped that this would be enough, but, alas, the aliens were right. You two doctors may need a demonstration of their power."

"We'll both see you next week, John, if you don't mind Stephen sitting in."

"No," said John, "I would rather welcome that. Until next week, then."

iv

Dr. Aguair had been recording her sessions with John almost from the onset of the meetings. She felt justified in doing so, as Dr. D'Erable had suggested that this would be of immense help to both of them. Two days after John had seen her, she sent the tapes, as she always had, via an overnight mailing service.

The faithful doctor returned her calls as he'd done so often before.

"Marilyn," said Dr. D'Erable, "I got your last tape and found it fascinating."

"Oh, I suppose, but my suspicion is that we won't get any more out of John except more details about the aliens, Andre, and perhaps some of his childhood!"

"Well, Marilyn, I suspect that John feels the same way. Let us, for the sake of argument, say he was telling us the truth. His frustration must be far in excess of ours."

"I suppose so, Stephen. I'm merely wondering what more can be done. We can't just accept his story, for then John would know we were placating him. What more does he want from us? And I must ask you, Stephen, what do you make of the sample and the woman that we picked up?"

"To tell you the truth, Marilyn, I can't explain the cell sample. It would be easy to explain the woman, though. She could easily have met John at some point in the past, and he coached her."

"I hate to admit this, but a small part of me almost believes that John is telling us the truth, that there really are Metans and Schegnans. I'll be curious to see what he comes up with next week."

"Do you have any feelings about what he'll spring on us?"

"No, I can't imagine what he'll say or do! I wish I could dismiss these inklings that he's telling us the truth as easily as you, Stephen."

"Marilyn, that is the only reason my skills are slightly superior to yours; you get too emotionally involved with your patients. That isn't meant as a criticism, and in some cases, such empathy can make you a superior doctor."

"Yes, yes! Let's give it a rest and wait until we see John in five days. Or maybe he'll make his move sooner."

"I'd bet on it."

Chapter 18

Changes from the Dreamscape

i

Dr. D'Erable had always considered himself rational and not subject to flights of fancy. He was sure that he'd dreamt, but was quick to dismiss any nocturnal visions as trivial. Perhaps the good doctor was a bit fearful of facing his own shortcomings and weaknesses, but he'd never admit to it. No, there weren't any significant neuroses, phobias, or other unresolved emotional issues in D'Erable's life that would explain his recent vivid dreams. Surely John Kline's story and the life of Andre could not be influencing his subconscious!

The week leading up to the next meeting with Kline did bring many oddities in the night. At first, the doctor was only aware that his dreams seemed more numerous and clear than usual. Surely he'd dreamt like this before, but each night brought more striking images and sensory panoramas than D'Erable had been accustomed to. It was likely that Stephen had not wanted to look too closely at what the reveries suggested, but the last night before meeting with John Kline brought forth such a strong experience that it could not be ignored.

D'Erable had followed his normal routine while preparing

for bed. He had, however, felt the need to go to bed a bit earlier than usual, feeling both relaxed and tired. It was normal for him to read something not too stimulating before bed, perhaps something almost boring, so as to leave his mind essentially empty. This night, he'd watched an old movie that he'd seen many times before on his DVD player. The movie was interesting enough that he had expected to watch it to the end. He expected it to end at 10:30 or so. He had started playing it at about 9:00, but by 9:45, he was quite tired. The strong sense of calm and the desire for sleep took him by surprise. He was in bed, fast asleep, by 10:00, nearly two hours ahead of schedule. He would awaken at 6:00 very refreshed, but with a mind full of dream experiences.

The dream started innocently enough. He was walking through a sunlit field, and the sun was directly overhead. The weather seemed a bit chilly to him. He couldn't get over the feeling that the sun wasn't as bright as it should be at noontime, even though there were no clouds obscuring it. It also seemed odd and delightful all at the same time that the sky looked very dark, like a winter's afternoon going toward sunset, yet that dimmer–than–normal sun was overhead.

He felt relaxed and sat down in the grass, which was also different from any he'd seen before. It looked as though it was tinted a dark blue, and it was fluffy all over. The stalks were about a quarter-inch thick, and they branched outward on top into three tufts. The vegetation stood only four inches or so high, but he was somehow sure it was never mowed. Indeed, it was somewhat similar to unmowed grass in a meadow, yet unfamiliar to him.

He noticed that there was a sea a few miles away on either side of him. The air had never smelled so fresh. Although he considered himself quite the connoisseur of herbal and plant fragrances, he couldn't recognize any of these perfumes.

Suddenly, a cow strolled up alongside the sitting doctor.

This wasn't surprising to him, but upon looking at it, he realized it was full grown, even though it was about half the size of cows he'd previously seen. It also had a calf with it, which began drinking milk from its mother. The cow's hide was the usual brown and white patchwork he'd often seen as a child, but he noticed that the calf's white patches had a turquoise tint to them.

He then found himself in a forest, but the color of the trees was unusual. The leaves were much like ones he'd seen, but they were tinted a dark blue. He was walking without direction, but sensed that he was being guided.

The next scene found D'Erable walking down a large city street. He couldn't place the city, but sensed that it was a major metropolis, maybe even a capital. The most striking aspect of the city was that the sky was dark, as it had been in the forest and field, and the sun looked darker than usual. The smells were those of a lush, wild area rather than the usual dirty odors of most large population centers. The buildings seemed equidistant from one another and extended into infinity. They were all very tall, but he couldn't see the tops of them, even though there was no smog or haze. They were all shiny, and they varied greatly in color; they were silver, yellow, blue, green, and numerous other hues. Many of them were cylindrical or square, but the majority of the buildings were shaped like hexagons.

It was strange that the streets were so wide. He never saw an automobile, truck, or bus going along the streets. He was walking along the wide sidewalks, which were covered with reflective aqua bricks with many other people, but he didn't feel that he was in a crowd, as he would have expected if he were walking in any other city with the sun nearly at its zenith.

Suddenly, as if time had compressed itself, it was night. The windows of the buildings shone with as many different colors of light as their reflections had shone during the day, although he couldn't remember if the greenish–yellow glow from some of the windows had been the color of the exteriors of those particular buildings. He looked for the moon in the starry sky, but his guide communicated to him that this was a silly habit, as there was never a moon to be seen from here.

The doctor was then given the power of flight. He swiftly rose above the darkened city, still not seeing the tops of the buildings. Finally, he could see the earth below him; he looked down to find the land and water spiraling about each other. He felt no panic in reaction to either this strange sight or the unknown force that was driving him onward. He then heard words being spoken to him as he felt the sensation of flying increase. All he had seen was replaced by a fascinating collage of spiraling colors, which merged and separated. There were also geometric shapes of various sizes floating about in the colorful burst. He heard words spoken to him in a voice of authority, but also of great gentleness. It was deep and echoing, and it made the doctor sense great peace.

"I can't give you the words, and the images you've seen are not sufficient. We only wish that you understood our language of colors. It is much more than pictures, but we know these strange flashes and swirls can't convey our message to you. Is it not true that your own language, replete with many words and styles of prose and poetry, does not even begin to express your hearts and minds? No, do not answer!

"I will bring you to see my friend. It is possible that then you will better understand what I am trying to convey to you. It is sad that your kind has suffered and still is suffering greatly. It seems that your words, no matter how you order them, no matter what art forms you develop, can't ease your plight."

After the doctor had heard this oration, he felt overwhelmed. It was similar to the sense of relaxed surrender that had brought him to bed, but the myriad shapes, swirls, and simple brilliance of the color show in his mind and body were overwhelming him.

Dr. D'Erable seemed to sleep for an unknown length of time, but when he awoke, he was elsewhere, and his journey continued.

ii

It was a great relief to D'Erable that where he was walking now seemed more like home. The grass and trees looked much as he would have expected. The sun was of normal brightness for the height it was in the sky. He was aware that he was being given a tour, and as before, it was from a source that defied any explanation. He sensed that it was telling him to take a closer look at his surroundings.

Yes, the sky was a pinkish-purple! How he had missed this observation the first time around was inexplicable to him. He observed many calderas and other signs of extinct volcanoes in the distance, but sensed that everything here was now safe. He saw, as he soared about, many forests, meadows, streams, lakes, and seas.

He sensed that a lot of people lived throughout the various landscapes. It never seemed that there was squalor or overcrowding, but there were large cities, much like the ones he was familiar with. Yet there was no sign of pollution or congestion. The buildings weren't as numerous as those he'd seen previously. Some of them did seem to reach into infinity, but those were much rarer. He could also see that this place had a lot more trees in its cities. It wasn't that any growth was encroaching upon the cities; rather, the inhabitants appeared to be seeking more of an aesthetic quality than the people of the other place.

The structures were strange to him, but he could sense that they were possibly museums, universities, and churches. In the other place, the shiny, geometric grandeur of the buildings didn't indicate their purpose or function. At least here, even though there were no recognizable landmarks, the doctor knew that he could probably adapt to living in a place like this, even though the sky was a strange color. At night, the moon seemed familiar, even though it looked a bit bigger than the moon as viewed from Earth, and slightly more purple than he'd imagined a moon could be.

As he soared above this world, he instinctively looked down. The land and water ratio looked more or less right, although the oceans, sky, and clouds had that distinctive magenta hue. He knew that all the continents, islands, and so forth would be a challenge to him. That is, he knew that he'd see something unexpected when he looked down. It was probably the unfamiliarity that made Stephen feel uncomfortable. Again, a voice spoke to the doctor. He knew he was hearing a different person, even though this one addressed him similarly to the last one, and the voice sounded almost identical.

"My good friend asked me to talk to you. I can understand you and hopefully relay the message better than last time. It is obvious that words, music, colors, and so forth aren't sufficient. Only by direct thoughts and feelings could your kind ever understand anything.

"It is very disconcerting that you aren't yet masters of your feelings, either. The complexity of language makes that understandable, especially when it comes to finding common ground. With my words, I tell you that you claim to share some common thoughts and feelings. Sadly, I have observed that somehow each of you finds himself or herself to be an island in a sea of others."

After the words stopped, D'Erable half expected to see the colors again, but this time, all was totally dark. He did feel a rush of emotions. It was hard to pick out one from another in the flood of depression, desire, fear, and joy. He sensed a great loneliness overshadowing the swirl of feelings. He also sensed a desire for understanding and oneness. It seemed to overwhelm him and suddenly stopped. Now he seemed to be in a void for an eternity.

iii

The good doctor awoke to the usual sound of his alarm. He couldn't shake off the dreams of the night before. He tried to dismiss the experience of the night before as he'd always done, but there was no way to accomplish this feat.

As he sipped his coffee, D'Erable mused that it was naturally difficult to avoid thinking about a thing when you were consciously trying not to do so. Despite all his knowledge, he found himself trying to divert his attention from the dreams by trying to force his mind to focus on how wonderful his eggs and bacon tasted, how good the Danish pastry was, and how he loved his coffee.

He was certain that he would look weak if he brought this dream up to anyone, especially Marilyn, since he was the one who had taught her most of what she knew. It could have been male ego or simple arrogance, but to ask for her help in determining what meaning, if any, his dream had was out of the question.

When Marilyn met Stephen in the office, she spoke first.

"Steve, I had the most unusual dreams last night! I think I'm letting John's story get to me."

"It could be." He paused. "You know, he's usually early, but today he's late."

"Yes, that's odd. But as I was saying, I dreamt about all kinds of landscapes and structures on Metamo and Schegna. It's strange how all the details of the sky color and sun came through so vividly, and how I dreamt of the dark sky on one world and the purplish sky on the other. There were also two strange messages I got from the aliens. Of course, it was only a dream."

D'Erable listened intently. He hadn't dared think about the planets, but now he had to admit, as Marilyn's account of her dream was almost identical to his, that John's story was rubbing off on both of them. Yet he somehow felt that this explanation was missing something.

The phone rang. Marilyn answered, listened intently for a minute, then turned to Stephen.

"It's John. He says that he'll have to come in next week. He wants to say something to you."

Stephen took the phone and spoke. "Yes, John, so you can't make it this week? Is everything okay?"

"Of course it is. As I told Marilyn, I feel you two should have a lot to talk about, now, as you have been contacted by the aliens. Try to tell me that it is purely a coincidence that you both had the same dream! Then, Doctor, try to explain to me how I even know about this fact. Until next week." John abruptly hung up the phone.

Stephen faced Marilyn and couldn't disguise his emotions of surprise and shock. Marilyn looked back with an expression of sympathy. Both doctors realized that there was little they could say to one another. What possible explanation could there be? How could they have had nearly the same subconscious nighttime experience, and how could their patient be aware of that fact?

As they left the office and went their separate ways, they were both thinking along very similar lines. It was certainly tempting, on the emotional level, to accept John's story, or at least the main parts of it, but as scientists, the doctors couldn't accept this possibility at face value. To give in to emotionalism so easily would not help John at all. Then again, it was unclear how either one of them could assist him. If he chose to believe in these benign aliens, then, as they had told him, his belief could be seen as a religion. Yet why did John insist on the need for such elaborateness? Perhaps it was better to let things alone for a week.

Besides, it might have been too frightening for the doctors to actually admit that they believed him.

iv

Later that day, Marilyn copied a report to Dr. D'Erable via email. It read as follows:

"This is an addendum to the intake report of our mystery patient admitted to the LA hospital last August 11th. It is only regrettable that she, the patient, wasn't more cooperative with us. She did not pose any imminent danger to herself or others, and was insistent that she was unwilling to accept any chemical medication that would to dull her reality, as she put it.

"The patient became responsive after several hours in the hospital. She was finally able to satisfactorily identify herself. She said it was urgent that she leave the facility to continue her important research work in astronomy, as her work with SETI was essential. No arguments of any kind would keep her in the facility. We expressed that we were concerned that she might have another episode, but she only insisted that we couldn't keep her.

"One assistant psychiatrist was reprimanded later for not giving his observations of the patient, but in hindsight, this information would not have been enough for us to forcibly hold her. The woman had evidently told him that she had psychic abilities that allowed her to receive communications from aliens she called something like 'shennans.' She said they were observing humanity with another advanced extraterrestrial race she called 'mettans.'

"It was brought to the attention of the assistant that such behavior, as he should certainly have known, could be indicative of some kind of mental anomaly or condition. He was most apologetic regarding his oversight, but insisted that this information was given to him in confidence, and she had said that she would deny it to the doctors if he dared bring it up. 'Besides,' she had told him, 'I will not be held prisoner for my so-called beliefs in things you can't prove or disprove. There are many religious fanatics whom you probably should lock up, but don't! This is the truth, and not just mine. All of mankind's future depends on it.'

"It was certainly a compelling argument, but admittedly, even those with severe delusions can come up with convincing systems of logic. In retrospect, this information would have certainly compelled us to try more earnestly to keep her under observation for a longer time, but it is doubtful we'd have come up with a different result.

"I would be interested in having any other of your colleagues who attend these conferences share any similar cases with me. I find such phenomena very interesting. Naturally, I will respect any and all patient confidences."

Drs. Aguair and D'Erable had actually phoned this co-worker a few times with details about John. This doctor was, in their opinion, a bit overzealous. He had wanted to meet and interview John to try to decipher what was going on.

Aguair and D'Erable knew that John was at the end of his

rope and not interested in trusting a new person with his story and Andre's. The amount of time John had spent with the two psychiatrists was very much appreciated. The rapport the three had developed could almost be considered a friendship, and by now, it was much more than a patient–doctor relationship. That in and of itself was one of the main reasons that the analysts felt the need to break their affiliation with John.

V

The next six days were uneventful. Stephen had wondered when Marilyn would call him. He admired her ability to think things through and not rely so much on his judgment. However, he knew that she would want to talk things over with him before their next meeting with John, and she did.

"Well, Marilyn," he said when they next met, "I'm glad you decided to call me and that we can spend the evening looking over our notes on John."

She smiled. "I had to find an excuse to have you spend the night."

"Okay, so where do you think we should start?"

They mulled over all the papers, and they agreed that the following day would be the last time they met with John. There was no question that Kline was intelligent, and that neither one of them could do much more to help him.

It seemed important to John that the doctors believe his story, but neither Marilyn nor Stephen could agree outright to take him at his word. They also knew that he would be smart enough to know if they simply paid him lip service. They decided that they would play some of their plan by ear and not decide on anything definite until they met with John the next morning.

They suspected that he would try some trick to make sure they continued to meet with him. This challenge usually had something to do with John pointing out that neither doctor could outright disprove any of what he was saying.

Marilyn then spoke to Stephen. "I think we should challenge him. I know you've been resistant, but let him produce an alien. After all, isn't that the crux of the whole problem? How do you suspect he'll react to that request?"

"Hmm, it's worth a shot. It's certain that he'll come up with some reasonable out, as he so often does, quite skillfully. We might not have our last meeting with him in the morning. I suppose we should get some sleep."

"That's a good idea, Stephen, but I suspect that we won't have to wait until morning. It strikes me that you haven't figured out his next move."

"Ah, Marilyn, you're mistaken. I'm sure he'll have figured out what our intentions are. I'm inclined to disbelieve you only because it's already well past midnight. I suppose he could call us at any time, except that he doesn't have your home number."

Marilyn and Stephen both checked their office voice mails, but John had not tried to get in touch with them. Doctor D'Erable now felt stumped. He was sure that John must be aware of their intentions to abort the sessions, and he suspected that John might try to put a stop to that.

Maybe, thought Stephen, he accepts this situation and will wait until morning. Or maybe he really isn't all that intelligent after all.

What happened next came almost too rapidly for Stephen to absorb it.

Marilyn had been getting ready to go to bed. She had bid Stephen good night, and he had decided to watch TV for 15 minutes until the news headlines came around again.

The tone in her voice was a mixture of fear, pleading, shock, and excitement.

"Stephen! I can't believe this. Come to my computer room! John is calling us!"

"I'll be right up," he answered, not giving thought to how John could have called.

He rushed upstairs to Marilyn's office. It struck him as strange that the door was closed. Marilyn had sounded so concerned. I'm making too much of it, he thought. He knocked on the door. He heard a voice, the deep one from his dream, talk to him. It sounded as though it was coming from every direction, and at the same time, it seemed to emanate from inside his head.

"Stephen, you need only open the door. All will be explained soon."

Doctor D'Erable opened the door, trying to ignore the voice. He stepped into the office and was about halfway to Marilyn's desk when he realized she was standing off to one side. He was about to ask her why she hadn't put the lights on, but things happened so quickly that there was no time or need to speak. The doctors were now standing in the room lit up by a plant-green, glowing haze. What they saw and heard next occurred in what seemed to be an eternity. Later, they would both recall that they had somehow been beckoned to observe the sights and sounds there.

Chapter 19

The Rapture of Andre

i

A late, sleepless night had turned into an early dawn for Andre. It was certainly not the first time this restlessness had plagued him, yet there was a new sense to the insomnia this time. He hadn't felt like this since childhood. He found himself taking a walk outside in the early morning; this was certainly a new thing for him.

He felt that he was looking for something new and wonderful, even though there was also a sense of dread deep within him, as though it were in his bones. Never before had he felt so beckoned and yet helpless at the same time. He was not yet aware of his destination.

Again, he found himself walking deep in the woods. He knew now that he was totally lost and would never be able to find his way back home. Yet he felt that he was trying to find the path he was meant to travel. What was awaiting him? He knew that even if he was losing his mind, he must let this walk reach its elusive end.

Now, in the hot, humid air of late summer, the sun was surely rising outside the deep woods. He knew this by the brightening color of the sky that could be glimpsed occasionally through the canopy of the trees. Somehow he was aware of something being said to him. Could it be that he was hearing something beyond just the chirping of the birds and various other forest sounds?

Oh, was this a dream? He would gladly have traded the comfort of his bed and the air conditioning for a real excursion into the maze of tall trees about him. Even if he had wanted to find his way back to the start of his journey, he could not muster any of his senses to accomplish the task. The most fearful aspect was that he didn't *want* to return, even though he thought himself insane for wanting to continue forging onward.

He came to a clearing where there was a beautiful field with a large pond in the center. It must have been a couple of acres of prime real estate, but Andre couldn't see any dwellings, and he knew that none were needed. He went over to the pond and sat down on the soft bank, where he removed his sneakers and socks and bathed his feet. It was odd that the water was not cold at all. Nor was it warm, but it seemed to calm him immensely. A thirst which had been building up since his trek had begun several hours before was quenched when he used his hands to scoop up a great quantity of the water. He also spied some nearby bushes, from which he ate some large blue berries. They tasted divine.

Andre overlooked his own foolish disregard for caution when drinking the water from an unknown pond and eating a berry that he could not identify. Though the berries looked much like strawberries, their blue hue was much like a dark sky of a deep winter's dusk. The water, too, seemed very special. It was clear as glass, and Andre thought it was the best water he had ever had. It seemed that this banquet had been prepared especially for him.

After he had gorged himself on berries and water, a sense of delightful sleepiness came over him. He went back into the woods to get out of the hot sun and lay down in some soft pine needles to enjoy a short nap.

ii

A sleep—one filled with an abundance of awareness and knowledge, filled with what one would call dreams, but which were more akin to messages, yet not quite prophecies— overtook Andre in the few moments after he had begun his rest.

The reveries came in rapid succession. Even in this state, he knew that there would be no way to recollect them or to decipher their symbolic or psychological meaning. Nor would he be able to use any other method that he normally employed to try to make sense of his dreams. As the maze of colors, images, sounds, words, odors, and flashes of grand insight continued, along with a sense of euphoria which could only have come from Paradise, Andre realized that when he awoke, he'd have all the answers he needed to finish his journey.

It was also refreshing to be able to control the negative aspects of his dreams, like the paralyzing fear and sense of overwhelming sadness. He knew that these two emotions, the terror and sadness, were easily overpowered by the mission which lay ahead of him. Although the bad feelings threatened to tear at his very sanity, as they were the worst he'd ever experienced, the greatest sense of joy he'd ever known was more than enough to balance things out in his mind.

Some of these sights and sounds could have been described as similar to others that he had witnessed all of his former life while dreaming. There were the usual landscapes, where he re-experienced aspects of his childhood, convoluted incidents in his current life, or maybe a mishmash of both youth and middle age. But there were other worlds that were totally inexplicable. It would have been the greatest injustice or understatement to even try to describe with words what he had seen and felt. These so-called dreams were somehow a new kind of awareness. It was clear to him that he was living a new part of his life, experiencing things that few others ever would. His fabled 10 percent of brain tissue that he used to think and live his life was being pre-empted by its full potential. And then there was the effect of other brains in touch with his own inferior organ of reason.

iii

It was now clear, through the rapidly passing, myriad sights and sounds, that Andre was to pay particular attention to what was to commence. Without words, or even conventional human awareness, he found himself paying close attention to the group of otherworldly events which now presented themselves to him.

There, suspended in space, Andre sensed himself coming closer to a solar system—which, on first impression, was humanity's. Suddenly, a subconscious awareness made him realize that this wasn't the case at all, and that two of the orbs here were the homes of the Metans and Schegnans.

As Andre's body came closer to the sun, his acceleration slowed, and he clearly saw the planets Metamo and Schegna filling his field of vision. His awareness now shifted from the view in the cosmos to what he knew to be very important events concerning the beings who inhabited these faraway worlds.

He found himself suspended over a large Schegnan city.

There were many trees artfully intermingled with large buildings, making it reminiscent of the campus of an old New England university, but the scope and size belied this illusion. Andre knew that there were at least five million inhabitants here, all busy, either with research or pleasure, and that none of them expected what was going to happen. He wanted to warn them, but then he was made aware that this experience was part of history, that it had occurred nearly 50,000 years prior.

From the magenta sky, Andre could see that it was nearly nightfall. He then saw razor–thin, light blue lines coming from the midpoint of the atmosphere and going downwards in all directions to the ground. He was nearly entranced by the lights coming out of one locus and beaming down in all directions when he became aware that he must follow these lights to the ground.

He observed the rays touching many buildings. When they did so, the edifices glowed a bright white for just a second, and then they were gone. After a structure had disappeared, the shaft of light would extinguish itself. Below where each building had formerly stood, light gray sand could be seen. This horror went on until all the lights had completed their awful task. Now, scattered around in the woods and where the structures had once stood, what looked like people were staggering about. He knew there weren't more than a hundred of them there. They appeared to be in shock, aimless, and horrified that such an attack had occurred.

Somehow, Andre now knew that the confrontation between these two worlds had been going on for some decades before the point at which he was made aware of it. Next, he was shown large cities on Metamo, the other planet involved in the war. Its cities were as impressive as the ones on Schegna, but they seemed to be more sanitized. There were hardly any trees to be seen, and there were large highways absent of automotive traffic, as well as various–shaped buildings of immense height.

They ranged from non-reflective gray, square shapes to shiny, eight-sided, yellow wonders. Andre was aware of many millions of highly intelligent beings, unaware of the history that was about to unfold.

In the same manner, except for the sky being dark blue instead of a purplish color, he observed the scourge of the blue rays. With a bright-white flash that lasted perhaps a tenth of a second, an edifice was gone, destroyed, leaving only grayish soil behind. Again, only a few score of horror-stricken, wounded, wobbly humanoids were left, directionless in their wanderings.

Andre was made aware of a few dozen of these attacks, each of which lasted less than a minute. It seemed that he was being brought from one planet to the other to witness the flurry of attack and counterattack, until he was aware of the sheer terror of all these battles, which had occurred millennia ago. There came a tremendous sense of raw emotions, indescribable and more intense than anything he had ever experienced or could ever put into words. These feelings, Andre now realized, were the total combined hatreds and reasoning of both of the adversaries.

Eventually, he became aware that the conflict had finally ended and that the two cultures were now very cooperative and friendly with one another. Together, they would forge an alliance that would be the envy of the conflicting factions on Earth—if only Earth could learn of this wondrous agreement. He knew that the conventional descriptions of such a war and final peace would hardly be applicable. The reasons for the past conflicts were quite foreign to him. He knew, however, that even wars on Earth were never explained in simple terms of hatred. Even with the current ideological terrorist attacks, there were always deeper explanations and reasoning.

Before the reveries ended, Andre was made aware of a very profound truth. He wasn't able to figure it out on his own, but was given the epiphany via a third party. He knew it was a

Schegnan who had communicated this to his awareness.

What had Andre learned from this lesson in extraterrestrial history? It was that intelligent beings, in advance of humanity by nearly a quarter–million years, had convictions, emotions, and points of view, as any sentient entity of that type might. But what was most important was that after this struggle had been resolved, the creatures had immensely advanced their civilizations in wisdom. Both of the worlds had succumbed to a great hubris, but he knew that this word merely scratched the surface of the truth. They had both been so blinded by their separate senses of certainty and correctness that they couldn't have conceived of the notion that any of what they desired could be fallible.

It was now a vivid reality in Andre's mind. The knowledge that these two worlds had waged a war that had annihilated nearly 80 percent of both planets, coupled with the complexity of emotions, both familiar and alien at once, made him aware of a variety of horrors and wonders. The ultimate realization was that no souls were truly wise if they believed that their ideas were unchallengeable and correct beyond question. The wonder of it was that two races, two worlds, had been able to forge an alliance, making compromises over differences, to the point that they could overlook them altogether.

Andre's mind and body were practically overwhelmed by all this information. He could sense that the aliens knew that they had brought him knowledge, but also that his mind was not fully able to absorb all the intricacies of that knowledge. It seemed sufficient that he had gleaned a principle from this experience. An idea was forming, cleanly and clearly. He realized that the notion of the survival of the fittest, in the more simplistic, popular sense that the strongest will prevail, explained a great many things in the natural world. This theory was correct as far as it went, but beings of so–called higher intelligence had a rule that superseded the previous rule. It was that only enduring cooperation could ensure that those who had evolved would continue to exist and thrive.

The two worlds of Metamo and Schegna, planetary neighbors, had nearly ruined each other's worlds, and they could have destroyed all life on both planets. This strategy was obviously not going to work if one wanted to reach out into outer space, seeking knowledge and kinship with other civilizations and star systems. Conquest of the other might ensure that one world would survive physically, but it was counterproductive for any advancement of intelligent beings.

Andre was now completely exhausted. The message and knowledge of the MetSche had been successfully transmitted to him. He knew that they couldn't be expressed very precisely with human language, or even felt adequately with his human emotions and primitive brain. It was clear, however, that these alien intelligences had enough faith in him to give him this information. Now he felt the need to rest, sleep, and dream, as he had always done after completing a project.

But just when he felt that he must soon drift off to sleep, there arose a new urgency, and he got a second wind.

iv

"Wake up, child!" was the last thing Andre heard in his so-called sleep. He quickly rose to his feet, barely realizing that the forest and clearing with the lake were gone. After all, this visual reference was only meant to soothe and bring him the new knowledge of the two races. The great sense of wonderment in his mind was now shaken by his former human weaknesses. Why had these beings put such an immense burden upon his very essence?

He walked down a darkened corridor. The only sense he had was akin to the one that had greeted him when he had begun preschool so long ago. It was dread and joy revisited, yet this description would not be sufficient. After all, when he had started boarding school, there had been no choice on his part. The difficulty that faced him now could never be envisioned or comprehended by a child. A small boy or girl can decide what kind of candy he or she prefers, but even all of Andre's previous adult choices, correct or erroneous, paled in comparison to the decision he had to make now.

It was very clear that there were no right or wrong answers, but somehow he knew that he was expected to possess enough knowledge to make a new path for himself. At the same time, he was obliged to realize that it wasn't a quest only for himself, but for all of those who had been in his life.

All the visual cues in Andre's view were now gone, except for the man standing about 10 feet in front of him. There seemed to be some sort of spotlight illuminating the man. He looked very much like Andre, tall and slender, except that he wasn't wearing the thick glasses that betrayed Andre's visual disability. He was facing Andre and was totally nude. Andre would have sworn it was his double, except that the well-endowed man, fully erect, had two penises joined at the base. Andre could also make out the alien's three testicles. He immediately knew that this was the being who had given him his knowledge when he was napping in the forest.

Andre knew that he needed to speak no words, but his old habits of speech would not easily pass. The sexual feeling, if it could be called that, went much deeper, beyond anyone's words of description. He began to address the man. He had never known what name to call the Schegnan, but at the same time, he was aware that names were meaningless in this context.

"I am more than honored," he began, "to have been chosen

by both the Metans and your race to be given such a choice." At this moment, Andre could sense an image of Dr. D'Erable to the left and of Dr. Aguair to the right of the alien. Besides the fact that the two doctors were fully clothed, he was given the knowledge that they were not physically present, although the psychiatrists were being made aware of this meeting. It was also clear, as communicated by the naked Schegnan, that regardless of Andre's choice, the two doctors would be totally convinced that John had been completely honest. It was not merely because John was convinced of the veracity of his delusion, but because this truth was universal to all of sane humanity.

Andre then began to speak, almost pleading. "I know you are already aware of my feelings and arguments, as you have a very clear and sharp mind, but I know you'll indulge me and let me finish. It is difficult for me to choose either of your worlds to inhabit, especially since you are close neighbors. This exercise is obviously some kind of test I am to pass or fail, even though you have made it clear to me that there is no correct outcome.

"There is no way I will be convinced that if I go to live on Schegna or Metamo, anything will be gained or lost, except perhaps in my regretting my decision. Surely you don't expect me to believe that any choice I make is final! Tomorrow could bring a change of mind, and your races could oblige me in any case. Why is this of such importance? I know you have the ability to divulge all, but for some reason, you have left me in the dark, so to speak.

"Nearly any Metan could appear and look as you do, so that is not the issue. You both live in peace, now, and fully share knowledge with one another. Your cultures' unity would be enviable and a great example of coexistence to all of humanity! Diversity is embraced by all your members, and you and the Metans are rightfully proud of this great accomplishment. I could have the benefits of your knowledge regardless of which one of your worlds I decided to inhabit. Why could I not share both worlds? I mean, couldn't I go to one and then the other for a short time? Please! Please! I am so filled with joy and words and even thoughts that are beyond description! Let me know what to do! Guide me! Surely you are aware, even after you have entered my mind and soul, that I am limited even still!"

The naked being, still erect, spoke to Andre. It wasn't the speech itself that took him by surprise; it was that the Schegnan with no name had a voice that was so similar to Andre's. Unprepared for this by anything that he had been experiencing, Andre would have sworn he was hearing voices and losing his mind. After his surprise had passed and he had recovered, the alien spoke again to him in the same way.

"Oh, poor Andre, we had expected so much more from you! It is not the intention of either of our races to emotionally tax you. You are aware that every few centuries, we offered this gift to one human whom we considered worthy. Realize that it is our respect for your intelligence and your ability to make decisions that has led us to choose you. You possess analytical skill as a computer programmer. Your love of science and your emotional sensitivity are what we are most drawn to. I understand the burden, especially on the emotional level, that this offer has placed upon you.

"We were so sure that you could meet the challenge. It is not entirely surprising, nor is it any fault of yours, that we may have been premature in asking you to make such a decision. The fact is that the path is obvious—or so we thought. Some of my friends on both Schegna and Metamo warned me that perhaps your race was still not ready to meet the challenge. Andre, do not feel sad or fearful. It is perhaps not to be in your lifetime that any human can make the choice we offer. I am still optimistic that you are capable of making the correct decision. True, one choice is not superior or inferior to the other, but I think you are aware that there is a preferable outcome. It may be too much for your race to deal with at this time. Yet I feel you must speak, and it is now time to see if you can represent your race properly or not."

Andre felt a bit weak, but he knew it wasn't time to sit down or give up. In a quick moment, a great sense of understanding came over his body. He felt a renewed sense of physical and mental energy. He was also aware that this new sense of awareness was his alone, and that it couldn't have been given by an alien.

He approached the alien. He felt so many emotions, similar to those he had had before, but these were now much purer, and they seemed to have a meaning deeper than description could allow.

As he was now in the Schegnan's personal space, Andre couldn't help himself or contain his actions. He took the alien into his embrace and was briefly aware that the alien's body temperature was slightly higher than his own. He was also aware that the sense of physical attraction was practically meaningless, compared to all the other thoughts in his mind. For the first time, Andre realized that he was not clothed, either. This fact made Andre feel even more kinship with the being in his embrace. Now tears began to well up in his eyes as he began to speak.

"Oh, my God, I know that a name would not do anything for you, but I wish I knew what to call you!" His embrace was reciprocated by the Schegnan. This made Andre's sadness fade a bit.

The alien whispered to him, "It's all right. Awareness is in my mind, and that is why I know that speech is so valuable for humans. How often has your race nearly destroyed itself for a lack of appropriate spoken words. Oh, Andre, tell me now what is in your heart!"

The embrace became more affectionate, and Andre was now able to express what had come from his flash of insight.

"You know that it would be my privilege to inhabit either

world. I am thankful for your visit and genuine caring for our world. My Bithumn and I have often said that no advanced race would be interested in Earth. We are so hotheaded, so warlike, and seemingly beyond hope or help. My Morning Star has often said that we would be destroyed even before we got beyond this solar system, and that any such violent race could not and would not evolve.

"Bless you, and thank the Metans, too! But I have my love here on Earth. My father's health, my aging mother—an uncertain future is before me and the crazy human race. To have chosen me, a useless member of society, disabled, shunned for who I am and who I am not—God, my lover's fate is the same! Oh, the Earth needs to have more kindness and understanding. Leave it to an alien to make us see it!

"So, yes, I am sorry for having thought that you were giving me a hard time. Leave it to stupid humans to think so badly of others. We have become so used to hurt, anger, hate, and enmity! How will we ever overcome our sick, insane weaknesses, our jealousy, hate, suspicion, and simple distrust? Thank you, my dear Schegnan! I know now that I must stay on Earth. I can't understand why the choice seemed so confusing.

"Of course I would want my lover to join me, but that was not in the cards. I am comfortable with that. We certainly can't reach for the stars before we fix our own world. I used to be so entranced by our reach for the moon, Voyager probes, and all of that. Yes, these are great hopes for our world, but now I know the answer. I will not leave my lover alone for pursuit of a better life. I won't go missing on my parents and have them worry. Humanity is my future.

"If I could live a few hundred more years, I'd like to be here and take you up on your invitation then. Maybe then a person will go to your world to live amongst you, and that will be the right answer. But now, my lover, my terrestrial future, and my Earth are what I must chose. Now, perhaps more than at any other time in our history, I will try. Even if I fail, I will be honored to make some small mark and show humankind how to give up their irrational fears, hatreds, angers, and destructiveness. Oh, God help me, it will take until the day I die before those who know me realize I never wanted to hurt anyone. It has always been my hope for peace, love, and understanding. I fear that on my dying day, it will never be known except by me."

At the end of this, Andre began to cry again in the alien's arms. The Schegnan held him more tightly, conveying also with his superior mind that he understood Andre's pain. He spoke to him in a soft tone. "Oh, my poor dear, you have at last made the right choice. I commend you for realizing that all things must come from caring about one's own race and one's own Bithumn. Let us hope that in a few centuries your race will be truly ready. We are now more hopeful than ever before."

Andre then found himself back in his bed. Dr. D'Erable and Dr. Aguair had been talking together about John when the Schegnan took over their minds. They had both witnessed the episode with Andre and the choice he'd made.

D'Erable said, "Oh, my, even after all this time, I had never realized that Andre was John's lover!"

"I know," said Dr. Aguair, "that we were both stumped, but who would have believed in aliens? I guess we can tell John that we are done."

"Yes, of course," said D'Erable. "We all have to get busy! A few centuries aren't really a long time to rid the Earth of all the ills of humanity. Imagine if Andre had made the wrong choice!"

"What? You mean if he had opted to go to the other planet?"

"Yes. It would have been difficult for him to accept."

"No, I think the MetSche is intelligent enough to find someone who realizes that much work needs to be done here at home before one can reach for the future. I only wonder why they chose Andre."

"I think Andre can see the whole picture and is probably in a good position to explain things to the others."

"Yes, but Stephen, what makes them think things are different this time?"

"Oh, Marilyn, it could be some centuries before the aliens get it all right. We mustn't forget that great power of insight and intelligence don't signify infallibility. It would certainly be a tall order for any being to be perfect. I wonder if we could handle meeting such a being, God, or even alien?"

"I wonder too, Stephen. It seems we had to be shown the error of our ways, or we would have locked up Mr. Kline—and, God forbid, have had him on medication for who knows how long. And for what? We were supposed to be so superior to the average person, but we didn't believe him. Even with that genetic sample in France..."

"Oh, I'm sure that will disappear, Marilyn. You know how we humans respond to the truth. We bury it, destroy it, or warp it beyond all recognition. I suspect that if we are still at each other's throats in, say, three centuries, a forced freedom might not be so bad. At least then we'll all be equal in some way."

V

I have decided to write down my impressions of Dr. Aguair, John, Andre, and the recent contact with the aliens. Suffice it to say, I met Andre and John for a few sessions after Marilyn and I witnessed the strange happenings the night that Andre was— what would you call it?—tested.

If it were not for Dr. Aguair and me witnessing these strange events, how indeed could we understand? For a psychiatrist, it is often a good idea to have things proven, or dispelled, to show a delusional patient the way. In this particular case, Marilyn and I saw the same events. This fact makes it almost impossible to state that the ones involved—i.e., John and Andre—are mistaken. There is also the fact that the strange material in France is very compelling.

It would be very simple to chalk the whole thing up to mass hypnosis, group hysteria, or some other mechanism of group dynamics to explain all the events of the past year which led up to the visitation. Of course, as I recently told one of my patients, when the indisputable truth is right in front of you, and especially when more than one person attests to it, one must indeed take notice and give credence to the evidence. So, I have decided to take the more difficult route here. That is to say, it would be very prudent, or maybe desirable to some, for me and Dr. Aguair to find an explanation for all these phenomena. I have chosen to believe in the senses of my esteemed colleague, as well as my own, and of course the two men, John and Andre. Yes, there have been groups of people larger than this one who have led themselves into all sorts of delusions or believed in something that would be, to all outsiders, a fantasy, not factual.

What we are faced with here, beyond what Dr. Aguair and I witnessed, is the account of John and Andre. That might be dismissed, as they had known each other for many years, but we can't forget that the same words were used by the woman in California. She had no connection to any of us, yet knew more than was reasonable for her to know.

I find myself drifting back to John's argument about religion and how a psychiatrist wouldn't question such a belief system. That assertion isn't entirely true, however, as I'd draw the line at cults, or any system that didn't allow the participant to freely choose its tenets. Of course, I've had many patients, as has Marilyn, who have been brought up in a mainstream religion, many of which use fear of God's wrath to keep people from opting out. This line of discussion, however, is not valid in the case of the recent contact we all had with extraterrestrials.

Yes! The evidence is all there, and I submit, as does Marilyn, that it would be delusional, irrational, or just plain stubborn to ignore our senses—along with the sample in Paris, the connection between John and Andre, and even the mysterious patient on the coast. All of these events have led me to ask and answer some difficult questions.

First, I do agree that the Metans and Schegnans have an intellectual capacity far beyond humanity's grasp. Even with all our brain power brought to bear, we might still not comprehend these beings' language, concepts, and so forth. With this in mind, my question regarding their non-interference with Earth is easily understood. We can only grasp the concepts of aliens rescuing, enslaving, or destroying us. What is clear is that there are what they have called precepts in nature or the universe which go far beyond this simplistic viewpoint. We humans arrogantly meddle with animals and plants, but I believe that most of us do care for our environment. Often, either because we wish to or have to, we let nature take its course, as when we don't save an animal from natural predation. The extraterrestrials here are not oblivious to our condition. They have lent and they will continue to occasionally lend a hand, but we can't expect them to do the work to make us worthy.

The second issue I had was with Andre. Again, this is due to our limited knowledge of how these non-humans view things. I was stuck on the fact that Andre could have asked to go to either Metamo or Schegna, and I dare say that if I were he, I might have asked to go. I don't think the aliens knew with certainty how Andre would respond, but I do think the beings' intellectual capacity to understand us better than we do ourselves made choosing Andre a very reasonable act on their part.

The fact that John and Andre have physical disabilities, specifically blindness, was another concern for me. I asked myself, "Why would aliens choose to make the more imperfect person the one they'd prefer to contact?" I thought about this for some time and realized that the average person might not understand the darker side of human nature as well as those who've been subject to it, namely prejudice and so forth. I don't think the disability itself is the issue, nor do I feel that sexual orientation issues are, either. It is just that those types of individuals have a different and more acute awareness of the human condition than the average person does.

So, the MetSche assure us that sometime in the next two to three centuries, we'll be evaluated again. We needn't be fearful. Humanity will either have evolved or regressed, but hopefully, we will at least be on the right course. The extraterrestrials aren't to be feared. They have hope for our species. I hate to admit it, but I sometimes think that they are more hopeful than I have been. Potential is the key word here. If we were beyond hope, why would we even be observed and contacted? We know that they can't know the future, but they can make reasonable guesses based on observations.

When we have evolved and eliminated bigotry, bullying, and derision, and especially when we are able to resolve conflicts without wars—or, better yet, develop to where conflicts will be only a long–distant memory—only then will we be close to sharing the wealth of knowledge and great gifts the MetSche have to offer. Equality will have to be present on many fronts, both social and economic. The day when a child can be genuinely interested in understanding and celebrating the differences between individuals will only dawn when the teachers themselves can rejoice in the wonder of how we are all unique, and yet, at the same time, share a common goal and planet.

Yes, I have often thought that a few centuries are hardly enough time to even begin such a Quixotic mission, as we are so programmed toward violence that I sometimes fear we can't escape it. Yet, if the Schegnans and Metans could find peace after nearly obliterating one another, I suppose that we here on Earth will be able to do so as well. If we keep focused on our potentials rather than our faults, we might have a chance. It strikes me as odd that these two alien races, so advanced in comparison to us, have not given up on ideas of religion or a higher power. Of course, we must remember that they have had many millennia to improve themselves and were traveling in space while we were just beginning to become civilized.

Finally, what struck me about this entire ordeal was the concept that we humans are very stubborn at times, and we still believe that we have to be correct. We don't see that any other view can possibly be right. This is a great problem that we must overcome.

The other oddity is that so many of us feel so alone, alienated among our own kind. I have felt this myself, and Dr. Aguair has told me of her similar feelings. I was a bit arrogant when I started my practice, thinking that only maladjusted individuals had these sorts of thoughts and feelings. It seems to me now that this sense of isolation is one of the biggest hurdles humanity must overcome. If we can't connect to one another, or if we feel alone, isolated, like aliens in our own species when we do try to connect, then I fear we will lose all hope.

Yet, there is hope in me. Recently, my dreams at night have been glorious. Far beyond words are the sights, sounds, and experiences that fill them now. The word utopia is insufficient to describe the visions the aliens have sent all of us in this small group—John, Andre, Marilyn, and me. We all communicate and know a greater truth because we were privileged to have the aliens speak to us. We know that we are no more or less worthy than any other person on Earth.

So, if we can begin to look beyond our past, a new day can be ours. Oh, the dreadful cruelty and atrocities we have been capable of perpetrating upon one another! The mere fact that we can annihilate ourselves is most distressing. Yet, as we four have all had such vivid dreams of wonderment and hope, we have regained some of our own hope.

Eventually, when we find the words in our limited languages to describe this possible future, then we will have achieved this new vision of ours, and it will be shared equally with all the other glorious individuals who are peppered throughout this vast, endless, and ever–evolving universe of ours. Hope must never die, and of course neither can honest effort. For when we remain isolated, afraid, disconnected, mistrusting, and in such a desperate state, we will never grow, but rather we will languish.

So now we can dream of and also work toward a brilliant tomorrow. Many have tried in the past. Many have failed and lost their way. But the Metans, Schegnans, John, and Andre have awakened a new optimism in Dr. Aguair and me that we never thought would be possible.

About Stephen A. Theberge
in His Own Words

I was born in Lewiston, Maine in 1963. Shortly thereafter, I moved to Attleboro, Massachusetts with my parents and my siblings, Denyse and Remy.

In 1968, I began attending Perkins School for the Blind in Watertown, Massachusetts as a residential student, graduating in 1982. I enrolled at Rhode Island College in 1982. I graduated from there in 1987 with a BA in computer science and a second BA in English literature, with a focus on creative, technical, and analytical writing.

In the late 1980s through the early 2000s, I tried my hand at my own business, which focused on software for the blind and visually impaired. I have done various types of work in Web testing, computer programming, and usability studies.

I am currently living in Attleboro, Massachusetts. I work for the Massachusetts Bay Transit Authority as an ADA Compliance Tester. I also work for companies as a Usability Tester for the blind and visually impaired.

Contact Information
Email: Etienne@aaahawk.com
Home phone: 774–203–3159
Cell phone: 774–219–4433
Website:
http://www.dvorkin.com/stephentheberge/

Editing and Publishing Assistance

This book was proofread and edited by David and Leonore Dvorkin, of Denver, Colorado. David Dvorkin did the cover layout, the formatting and layout of the manuscript, and the publication of the book in e–book and print formats.

David and Leonore are both much–published authors, with more than 30 books (both fiction and nonfiction) and many articles and essays to their credit. Almost all of their books are available for purchase on Amazon, Apple, Barnes & Noble, and other online buying sites in e–book and print formats. A few are in audio format and available from Audible.com.

David's most recent nonfiction book is DUST NET: The Future of Surveillance, Privacy, and Communication: Why Drones are Just the Beginning (© 2013).

Leonore's memoir, *Another Chance at Life: A Breast Cancer Survivor's Journey,* is available in both English and Spanish. Both are © 2012. The English edition is also in audio format.

For details, please see their websites:
David Dvorkin: www.dvorkin.com
Leonore H. Dvorkin: www.leonoredvorkin.com

34752082R00178

Made in the USA
Middletown, DE
03 September 2016